In Florence Town, people appear to live life without a care in the world. When members of one of the leading families are suspected of building bombs, FBI Agent Nicolas Hayes is sent undercover to investigate. He learns a lot more than anticipated about the dark secrets behind the scenes of a placid rural life.

Chosen Brothers
Copyright © 2020 Ann Raina
ISBN: 978-1-4874-2851-8
Cover art by Martine Jardin

Published by eXtasy Books Inc or
Devine Destinies, an imprint of eXtasy Books Inc

Look for us online at:
www.eXtasybooks.com or www.devinedestinies.com

Chosen Brothers
Nicolas and Jacklyn Book 4

By

Ann Raina

DEDICATION

Muse, even at times when you've got your mind filled with real life problems, you stop by to help me with your wisdom, your jokes, and your ideas. Thank you.

PROLOGUE

Alexander leaned into Charlene's warm hand and closed his eyes. He relished the time they spent together and hoped that soon they could move to a small house, closer to his home and therefore far away from Florence Town. He imagined them sitting at a table to celebrate the birth of their first child, and that his wife would vow to be his for all time. His heart swelled with joy that was partly a trick of his mind. He wanted a woman at his side. The years of living single had been filled with missions, but success lacked the warmth of a friendly soul waiting for him.

His marriage to Deborah had been short. She had left him for a rich snob, acting as if their time together had been a nuisance. The pain following the separation had been life changing. He had felt substandard and unworthy, a man no woman would desire as a partner. Even four years later, he was still single, spending more time at work than ever to forget the void in his heart.

Charlene lifted her head from his shoulder and caressed the curve of his ear. "I knew you'd be a gentleman when I saw you enter the diner for the first time."

Alexander smiled in the darkness, remembering her statement that a man's ears told much about his character.

"I'm so happy we met." Her words were as soft as her body resting next to his. "You're so gentle. After everything I've come to know in this town, I want to be with you and only with you."

Alexander heard the yearning in her voice and winced.

1

Since the day he had met Charlene at the small diner where she worked, he had felt drawn to her and was astonished to learn that she felt the same for him. Since then, they had stolen away to meet secretly in her father's house whenever possible. However, he felt the sting of danger whenever he entered the old man's premises. If Carlton Loman were to see him walk into his daughter's private quarters, he'd most probably call the sheriff first and his vigilantes next.

"I don't see your father giving us his blessing."

"I don't care." Charlene traced his temple down to his jawbone with her fingertips. "You saved me from Milton. You saved me when I couldn't save myself. My hero."

Alexander had a vivid memory of that night in January. He had seen Charlene with her apron trailing to the floor, running from the diner's kitchen toward the yard, her face covered with tears. Milton, drunk as a skunk, had been behind her, screaming for her to come back. He'd been like a demon running after a soul, his face covered with sweat. Without hesitation, Alexander had intercepted him, knocked him out, and dragged his unconscious body out of the yard and into the alley.

The next day, when Milton had entered the diner for breakfast, he acted like nothing had happened the night before, even though the large bruise on his chin said otherwise. Charlene had stopped by Alexander's table to thank him, then fled with reddened cheeks when one of the regular customers took a seat at the counter. Alexander had been touched and intrigued by her actions and pleased to meet her again under better circumstances.

"Oh, and there's another wish on my list. Once we're far away from here, I want to start a family with you."

Glad she couldn't see him, Alexander thought of his own desire for a family. He wanted to have children to share love and life. He wanted to see them grow and learn, teach them what little wisdom he had gathered. He imagined how they'd look — a striking mix of Charlene's gentle features and his dark blond hair. He swallowed, not trusting his voice for a moment. The idea of having a wife and kids was scary, both from trepidation and honest yearning. "Yeah, that would be nice."

Charlene kissed his cheek. "I imagine every night that we'll leave together. That we find a home somewhere far away from here, and I will give you *all my loving.*" She hummed the *Beatles'* song as she nuzzled his cheek.

Alexander smiled though she couldn't see him. They shared a love for the *Beatles* and possessed a collection of their greatest hits. Charlene knew all the words by heart and would sing them at any given moment — much to the joy of the guests and the portly cook at the diner.

Alexander took a deep breath. His plan of keeping an inner distance was smashed by her warm lips on his and the sensuous kisses that followed. For the second time that night, they made love — gentle, caring, enjoying the intimacy.

Charlene was such a sweet woman, warm-hearted in every way. He was amazed at how quickly he had fallen in love with her, and at the same time, ashamed that they had met under pretense. He knew she wouldn't forgive him once she learned the truth. Twice, he had sought for words to explain his situation, and twice he had failed, for fear he would lose her. He wanted their relationship built on trust and love but didn't know how he could accomplish that mission. The inner conflict took his breath away. Deep down, he wanted them to drive out of town, to never return, but he knew he couldn't do it.

Charlene rested her head on his chest, sighing and obviously oblivious to his inner struggle. "I didn't know that I was alive until I met you." She lifted her chin. "Will you take care of me?"

Alexander choked on his words, then placed a light kiss on her brow. "I'll do whatever's in my power."

CHAPTER ONE

"Good morning, Nicolas." Jason handed Nicolas a cup of freshly brewed coffee and followed his gaze toward Senior Agent Gerald Sullivan's office. "Yep, he's been in there with this black guy for about an hour. I dunno what they're talking about, but he's been looking at me frequently, and I really don't like that."

"Thanks." Nicolas took off his thick jacket. It was March and freezing cold in Washington, DC. He hoped for a warm May to spend a pleasant vacation with his girlfriend in a wood cabin in Shenandoah National Park. The trip had been his Christmas present, and he couldn't wait for it to start. The more days passed, the higher his expectation of what Jacklyn would come up with. His thoughts centered around handcuffs, chains, and his lady in nothing but high heels, a crop in her hand, and a mischievous smile on her lips. In a good mood, he sat down, sipped his coffee, and switched on the computer. "Did a new case come in?"

"I don't know about your energy level, but in my opinion, the pile's high enough." Jason leaned back in his chair and scratched his beard. "I wrote the report for the last case. I wanted to send it to Sullivan, but I think you'd better have a look at it. I don't want to be browbeaten for any typos or missed details." He glanced over his shoulder toward Sullivan's open door. "What the fuck is he doing? I feel ants crawling up my spine."

"The ants again?"

"This looks like a really intense conversation. I didn't know he had it in him."

Sullivan turned and looked straight at Nicolas. A beckoning move of his hand followed, and Nicolas got up.

"Looks like he was waiting for me. So you're out of it. Lucky man."

"I've got a bad feeling about this." Jason grimaced. "Don't give in, no matter what he wants."

Nicolas smoothed out his tie and fastened the button of his jacket. "Well, maybe he's going to promote me, since Matthew and I solved that bank robber case."

"Nah, I don't believe that. The wicked sister's still on the run."

"Thank you for reminding me."

Jason laughed. "He'll do that for sure."

Nicolas braced himself for another round of questions concerning the last robber still on the loose and probably beyond the reach of the FBI. His attempts at finding and arresting the sister had been futile. Even though the FBI had initiated a nationwide search and broadcasted her image in the media, she was still missing. No matter what they did, the woman had managed to escape the police and the FBI. She was obviously clever, determined, and apparently a step ahead of the investigation. Knowing she had money in abundance didn't make it easier to find her. If she possessed a legal passport, she'd probably fled the country to never return, leaving behind her two brothers, who awaited trial in jail.

Nicolas knocked on the door.

Sullivan nodded and got up. "May I introduce Special Agent Nicolas Hayes. This is Special Agent Vernon Freeman from the Bureau of Alcohol, Tobacco, Firearms, and Explosives."

Freeman was an African American with a head as round and smooth as a marble, supported by his broad shoulders. He possessed an equally wide and thick chest, while his waist and legs were trim. Nicolas assumed he'd been a boxer in his younger years, given his large, fleshy hands and a handshake that was firm but not bone breaking.

They sat down. Sullivan pursed his lips. Nicolas felt Freeman's scrutiny in an intimate way, as if the man was comparing details from Nicolas's personal file to what he saw sitting next to him.

Nicolas looked straight at Freeman. "Would you mind telling me what this meeting is about?"

"Gladly." Freeman handed Nicolas a file with numerous photographs and twenty pages of text. "There's a settlement in Virginia—Florence Town. About two hundred and fifty people live there, cultivate their farms, breed cattle, and other livestock. Some have little shops for the daily necessities. They're living pretty reclusively, and as you can imagine— it's not a tourist attraction. Three families have been controlling the village for many generations—Turner, Steward, and Reese. They divide the important public offices between them—mayor, sheriff, public health officer, and so on. We assume that Jacob Turner is the most influential of them."

Nicolas looked at the photograph of a man in his seventies with long white hair and a white beard, the incarnation of Rafael's version of God. His eyes were a watery blue, his gaze benevolent. Also attached were several shots from his campaign and his slogans. He promised a clean, picturesque town in which all people could live in harmony and with exceptional health care.

"The Turner family is one of the oldest in Virginia with excellent connections to politicians, police, and jurisdiction outside Florence Town," Freeman continued. "No one knows exactly how far their influence reaches, or with whom they are connected. All three families are greatly esteemed because they've developed the lands for at least ten generations. Aside from shares of various companies, the Turners own about eight hundred acres of land used for growing corn, grapes, soybeans, and other commodities. They also keep goats, chicken, and cows for meat and milk. Instead of thinking big, they sell their goods to local markets, claiming they're helping the people live healthily. Breeding horses is Jacob's hobby, but an intensive one."

Nicolas looked through the photographs of buildings, granaries, and plantations, of people in working gear, and drawings of access ways and structures. All the photos appeared to be taken from a higher perspective, perhaps by drones.

"They aren't into guided tours, hmm?"

Freeman gave a quick half-smile and shook his head. "Nope. Any tourist stands out like a cockroach on a wedding cake, and I'd bet my salary that no one passes through without being noticed."

"I've heard of towns organized like this. No matter how friendly you are, the residents reject you simply because you come from another town." Nicolas twitched his lips. "Not home-grown, as my father would say. And in this case, the Turner premises looks like a village close to a town."

Freeman rubbed his clean-shaven chin, drank some water, then set the glass back down to continue. His deep voice grew intense. "The Turner family members consider themselves the chosen leaders. These days, Jacob Turner is sitting as the mayor." He shrugged and frowned. "If you want to know more about them, you run up against a wall. We tried to locate former residents for interrogation, but we couldn't find anyone willing to talk. And my boss didn't want a nationwide appeal."

Nicolas frowned. "What's the interest of the ATF? And what's the case?"

Freeman handed him another file with fifteen glossy photographs. "Six months ago, my agents took these photos of a known weapons dealer at the port of Baltimore. His name is Angel Roti, an Italian immigrant. He's been under surveillance for months. The other man in the picture is Samuel Turner, the youngest son of Jacob Turner. We assume but don't know that he's the son who runs the finances and makes the business decisions. Jacob appears to spend a lot of time with his horses and his grandchildren." He paused as Nicolas browsed through the file. "Young Turner wasn't on our radar screen until he bought small quantities of detonators, cable spools, and other material we couldn't determine, then took off. We haven't seen him since. We've watched the Turner premises, but nothing out of the ordinary has happened. Judge Field, who's responsible for the district, wanted more than a set of pictures to issue a search warrant. He argued that the equipment might be legally used even though illegally purchased." Freeman shrugged causally. "I think he's right. Also, if we had interrogated or even arrested Samuel Turner for buying detonators illegally, it would've been a minor offense, and the family would've learned they were under scrutiny. I assume they'd have bought whatever they need elsewhere but would've hidden it better." Freeman scrunched his face. "Since we didn't have an initial suspicion—and no support from the judge—we couldn't start an official investigation. We decided to have a look at the goods they transport to and from the premises."

"Did that deliver any results?"

"No. The Turners buy fertilizer and other goods they can't produce. Goods for daily life, you know—for the bathroom and kitchen. After all, they employ about eighty people. The next big warehouse is fifty miles away. We checked some of the deliveries under false pretenses but couldn't detect anything illegal. Of course, such spot checks outside of town can't be overdone, or they'll raise suspicion. Members of the local police ordered us to cease our activities. The Turners are quick when it comes to complaining to the governor about harassment. Like I said, they're well connected." He lowered his chin. "The sheriff of the town belongs to the Reese family and is friends with Jacob Turner, as you can imagine. Reese's daughter is married to one of Turner's sons." Freeman shrugged.

Nicolas studied the pictures and closed the file. "You assume the Turner family is done with peaceful living and about to build bombs? Why?"

Freeman nodded gravely. "We couldn't obtain any hard proof—no dealers, no transports with explosives, no other suspects who bought supplies and took them to Florence Town. There was no link to the Turners or the other families. Therefore, we selected an agent to move into town and investigate, unobtrusively, in case there was anything going on." He made a face. "And then . . ."

"You lost contact?"

Freeman lowered his voice. "In the beginning, Thomas reported in irregular intervals and claimed he needed more time to gain the family's trust. He reported that he was a groom on the Turner premises, and as soon as he wasn't being watched as closely, he'd search the compound. A month ago, his reports stopped. I don't know if his cover was blown. They might've killed him, but I . . ."

Nicolas frowned when Freeman hesitated. "Did you send someone to check?"

"As I pointed out, you can't go there undetected, and I couldn't risk raising suspicion by sending another agent to ask about him. If I'd done that, I would've had to pull him out immediately."

"Is it possible that your agent has made another decision and discovered the country life for himself?"

"Unfortunately—that's spot-on." Agent Freeman made a face like he had bitten into something sour. "You should know, Agent Thomas Zutarski became a soldier at the age of sixteen. He left the army at twenty-two to support his mother, who was raising his younger brother — alone at that time — and joined the ATF at the age of twenty-four. He's thirty now, divorced and single, and truly not a happy camper. He agreed to go and was certainly perfect for the assignment, but — "

"But he was also susceptible to a new life in a small town with all its benefits." He winked. "Maybe he found someone to love."

Sullivan cleared his throat, and gave Nicolas a disapproving glance. "At this time, the ATF wants to know whether the Turners are building a bomb or if they've already built one and are ready to place it. If so — what target did they choose?" Sullivan pointed at Freeman. "Additionally, Agent Freeman needs confirmation of Agent Zutarski's whereabouts. I want you to go undercover and come back with information about possible bombing targets and the agent . . . if he's still alive."

Freeman lifted his hand. "Wait a second, Gerald. Agent Hayes should know more details before he decides."

Sullivan gave Freeman a withering look. However, he didn't offer a more elaborate explanation of why Nicolas couldn't reject the order.

Nicolas looked at the photographs once more. "Call me curious, Agent Freeman, but it's highly unconventional that the ATF is coming to the FBI for support. Usually — "

"The cooperation is much better than you think, Agent Hayes," Sullivan interjected. "And concerning this case? Vernon and I have known each other for decades, so his request for help *will* be met, one way or the other."

Freeman curled his lips to a wry smile. "Well, Agent Hayes, as much as I appreciate Gerald's enthusiasm, the real reason for my request is simple. I don't know whether the Turners — or the other two families — have connections to the

ATF in DC. It's possible, and there are suspicious facts supporting that theory." He nodded when Nicolas gave him a doubtful glance. "Like I said, the Turners have lived in Virginia for a long time. Their wealth has supported governors and police chiefs, as well as senators. I believe in the autonomy of our agencies, but not at the cost of the life of one of my agents. So I didn't tell my superiors of my plan, and I deployed agents I trained to support the case. If you accept, it would be your task to find evidence and let me know how Agent Zutarski is faring."

Nicolas avoided Sullivan's impatient glare as he examined Zutarski's official picture in the ATFs personnel file and had to smile. The angular face, the dark blond stubble, and the crewcut made him look like a model for an advertisement of the agency. He had light brown eyes and a long scar on his chin. The file said Zutarski had suffered the deep cut in a severe fight but didn't go into detail. The years as a soldier had left Zutarski in good shape, so he had passed the physical exams with the best grades. He was an excellent shooter and known for his thorough investigations.

"Why do you want me?" Nicolas asked Freeman.

"Gerald told me about your accomplishments, your clever investigation in various cases of violent crime, and your ability to adapt to changing situations quickly. He also noticed you're a good shot, a criterion that might be useful. Not least, you're single."

"I'm in a relationship."

Sullivan rested his arms on the desk and looked at Nicolas with the same sternness a judge chose when he sentenced a criminal. "But you're neither married nor do you have children. That's what Vernon meant. Summing up—you're the agent for this assignment."

Nicolas wanted to decline the order, if only to contradict Sullivan's judgment. However, Freeman seemed concerned for his agent and not merely interested in results.

Once more, Nicolas ignored Sullivan for Freeman. "I won't have to pack and move to Virginia tomorrow, right?"

Freeman beamed at him. "You'll move to a safe house for a thorough briefing. I won't let you ride into town without proper knowledge of all necessary details and the families' genealogies."

Vincent McGuire loved being outdoors, and he loved dogs. Consequently, he had combined his fondness for both into a profession that was more satisfying than he'd ever hoped it would be. He trained search dogs that specialized in finding corpses. Several homicide divisions in Virginia bought dogs from him, and Vincent's chest always swelled with pride when a dog he had trained did a good job.

This morning, he had prepared a test for his young German Shepherd in the woods. It was the first big challenge for his trainee to find a severed hand among moss, grass, fallen leaves, and pine needles. Vincent had made it easy enough — he hoped — to grant the young dog a feeling of success. As it was his habit, Vincent had plenty of treats in the pockets of his overcoat, and he was always generous. He knew that every achievement, every move in the right direction, must be rewarded to keep the dog at it. A search dog was efficient when it loved its task and wanted to please its owner.

Vincent felt proud when the Shepherd, Handsome, put his nose to the wet soil and started sniffing his way along the small path. Soon, he swerved to the right. Vincent let the long leash slip through his fingers, eager to see how the dog would find his way to the prey. It didn't take long, and Handsome started digging. Intrigued and yet bewildered, Vincent watched the dog's paws claw through the leaves and soil until he finally barked — the sign for a discovery.

"Good dog." Vincent moved closer, and when the dog stepped back, tail wagging with excitement, he patted his furry head. "What did you find?" He crouched and swept away more leaves and soil. To his surprise, he glimpsed the nose and cheekbone of a man buried in the ground. "Oh, Lord in Heaven!" Trying to get away from the body, Vincent fell back on his butt. His stomach heaved, and before long, his breakfast reappeared.

Beside him, Handsome was still wagging his tail and lolling its tongue. Vincent found his dog much too cheerful for this gruesome find.

Jacklyn stared at Nicolas after he had recapped what the ATF wanted him to do.

He finished his summary with a small smile. "Obviously, there are no ATF agents matching the description."

"But you fit."

He squirmed at her incredulous tone. "You prefer blonds, too." He couldn't trigger a smile, and holding his breath, waited for her outburst.

"Don't tell me you volunteered."

Nicolas cast down his gaze. While at Agent Freeman's house earlier that day, his tasks had made perfect sense. Seeing Jacklyn's worry now, he wasn't sure anymore. "No. Not in the true sense of the meaning. But I've learned a lot about the ATF agent. He's only a few years older, and he went there by choice to solve the case. He's truly dedicated. Yes, my boss thinks I'm the right man for this job. And the senior agent of the ATF does, too." He shrugged. "I can't refuse such a request."

"Yes, you can, and you should've done it." She pushed away from him. "Going undercover isn't your usual task."

"But it might give me points for the next promotion."

She wiped the argument away. "Nicolas, this means living a totally different life! You're a big town boy. You haven't worked on a farm for a single hour. How will you pretend that you're a boorish guy without education who couldn't find another job?"

Nicolas remained quiet, unable to sum up what he had learned about Florence Town and its inhabitants. It was the proverbial back end of the world, a place for living in peaceful harmony with nature, but also under the heel of three families with enough power to keep everyone in line.

Besides what he'd been told about the Turners, he learned the Reese family had gained their wealth some eighty years ago with soaps and cleaning agents. Then, in recent years, they had expanded their business to include disposing of toxic waste.

The Stewards had once been big in coal mining and made a fortune that no one could exactly quantify. Their offshore accounts were a maze. The ATF had tried to determine the family members' positions in the business world, but they seemed to enjoy their lives without regular professions. The bar owned by the senior Steward couldn't be regarded as a source of income. It appeared to be more like a hobby.

As he learned from Agent Zutarski's few reports, the inhabitants of Florence Town appeared anxious not to talk about the *Big Three*. The agent had the impression that the inhabitants shared a secret they kept hidden from outsiders.

"Listen, Jacky, you'll furnish that beautiful new house in the meantime. You'll make this our home and keep it warm for me. I'll come back as soon as I've found the agent and eventually the bombs they might be constructing."

"You say that as if it's a piece of cake." She bit her lip, then pounded her fists against his chest with every word. "You'll be away for months."

"That's not yet clear."

She went on as if he hadn't spoken. "You'll be in danger every day. Your cover could be blown by anyone who saw you on the news last year."

Nicolas felt the impact but didn't defend himself. The pain was minor compared to her obvious frustration. "That's forgotten. I don't think anyone saw me standing in the background at a press conference." He tried to smile. "Who knows whether the townspeople have TV sets, after all? It could be a community that is completely dedicated to life in nature."

She stopped and looked up to him pleadingly. "But wouldn't it be better if they excluded you? Your life would be in danger if someone recognizes you."

Nicolas hadn't thought of that possibility, but it was too late to withdraw his agreement. "Don't make this too hard, Jacky. I'll be prepared, okay? I won't go in there blind, and I'll have backup from the ATF."

Jacklyn narrowed her eyes, the leniency and worry gone from the tone of her voice. "Yeah, right. They'll equip you with microphones and give you a cell phone to call someone who's miles away. Yep, total backup."

"It's not like that. I'll be careful, okay? I'll have a car and can drive to the next town if need be."

"Don't you see? This might be a large and well-organized criminal enterprise. I bet the families, and those depending on them, have their hands dirty, and that's why they'll watch you like a hawk. But, hey, you wanna go there and have fun with the danger. Fine." Jacklyn crossed her arms. "You play hero, while I sit at home and worry. What's the next step?"

"I'm officially off-duty—like a vacation—and will leave in a few days. The ATF will bring me up to speed and equip me with everything I need, then I'll drive to Virginia."

"I don't want you to do this job. I don't want you gone for an unknown time." She shook her head and retreated when he moved closer to embrace her. "No, that's not what I want.

That's not why I started this relationship. Really, Nicolas, you can't leave me like that."

He dropped his arms to his sides, at a loss for words. "I'm not leaving you, Jacky, I'm going to work. Only this time, I'll be away for more than a few days." He hesitated, seeing her anger turn to open rebellion. "Don't tell me you'd kick me out of your life because I'll be helping a fellow agent."

If anger was wind, it became a full-blown storm. "Right, make it sound as if you are a shining knight riding to the rescue! Bullshit, Nicolas! This isn't about solving a crime. This is about your fucking boss misusing you because he doesn't like you. He chose you over all the other agents because he wants you to fail. He wants you out of the bureau because he's jealous of your standing." She paused to take a breath. "No, don't shake your head, damn you. Quite obviously, you're too young to understand the dynamics in your office. Sullivan can only cement his position if men like you are suppressed. You've told me that Sullivan's decisions were wrong more than once. He relies on his agents' good work but tries to claim their successes as his own. Now, what's his next step? He sends you off on some obscure mission. While you think it's for the best for the agent, and in the greater context, for the lives of the American people, Sullivan hopes you won't find out anything or don't come back." She shook her head, pursing her lips. Tears trickled down her cheeks. "I don't want you to leave, Nicolas, because *no one* will have your back when you need it most."

"I will come back, my wonderful mistress." Nicolas hung his head and took her in his arms. "Don't give up on me so easily."

When Vincent's blood pressure recovered, he called the police. In the meantime, Handsome put his nose to the ground again and moved on, obviously eager to please his master. He went left and right, and Vincent got back to his feet, following the dog's path through the undergrowth. It wasn't long before Handsome started digging once more. Vincent made ready for another surprising discovery, and this time his shock at seeing another ill-buried body was less. He spoke a short prayer for the poor souls who'd found their last rest in such anonymity, but also praised the German Shepherd for his excellent nose and fervor.

Two policemen and two detectives from the homicide division arrived, and Vincent showed them the crime scenes. While the men got ready to mark the places of the bodies, and Vincent answered the detectives' questions, Handsome was either bored or agitated by his recent discoveries. He padded through the leaves, nose on the ground, motivated by treats and his master's warm words. He found his way further away from the path and stopped close to a mighty tree trunk. Once more, he clawed at the ground and barked.

Vincent looked at the detectives, who raised their brows. "I didn't put anything in the ground so far away from the path. Honestly, I don't know what he's found."

"Let's have a look." The portly detective with the small-brimmed hat, who had introduced himself as Banner, went first. His partner, Detective Burke, older and taciturn as a clam, followed. While Handsome dug up more soil, a foot surfaced. The detective sighed. "Oh, damn it." He put on gloves and helped the dog, who was eager to lend his paws to the job. The third body was as naked as the other two, and the worms and other inhabitants of the woods had already started to dissect him.

Vincent's stomach dropped to his knees again, and he turned away, retching quietly. He gathered his strength to praise the dog and take him away, so the policemen had room to work. Back on the path, he patted the dog's head, thinking about the promising start to the day and how it had gone downhill. Nevertheless, he was proud of Handsome, who shoved his muzzle under Vincent's hand. "You're a clever fella," Vincent said quietly. "Do you wanna go on? Search some more?"

"Two shot, one stabbed," Detective Banner said, grimacing at the findings. He looked left and right, then made eye contact with his partner. "I don't like the idea, but it looks like this could be the burial grounds of a serial killer. We'd better give the FBI a call." Banner shook his head, and while his partner pulled his cell phone, Banner followed the dog with his gaze. "Hey, what're you doing? This is a restricted area now."

Vincent waved a hand as Handsome moved on with the gait of a dog on a mission. He heard the detectives breathing heavily behind him as they tried to keep up with the dog's pace.

"You think there're more bodies?" Banner shouted, strained. "If so, don't let him dig again. I want at least one crime scene undisturbed."

"I'll do my best, but—" Vincent stumbled, fell on his knees, and let go of the leash.

Happy to bust free, Handsome gained speed. Banner helped Vincent get up, and together they followed the dog until he stopped and put his paws to work. He barked once.

"Damn it!" Banner growled. "I told you—"

"Don't worry." Vincent smiled, even though he was still sick to his stomach. "This time it's the bait I prepared for him."

As if making a point, Handsome brought the severed hand and dropped it in front of their feet. Tail wagging and smiling like only a dog could, he waited for appraisal.

"Good dog," Vincent said and fed him a small treat.

The detectives huffed and turned away. Vincent found his smile again. He knew Handsome would become one of the best search dogs he'd ever trained.

CHAPTER TWO

During his first week on the Turner property, Alexander had learned that the working schedules were tightly organized. The crew followed strict daily routines, supervised the entire time by the foreman, Sebastian Taffner. The man with the round bearded face, broad chest, and hands the size of plates was as severe as any drill sergeant Alexander had ever known as a soldier. The man would address the grooms every morning at six o'clock, even though their daily chores didn't change much. They had to check the horses for injures, take them to the corrals, and muck out the stables. Taffner turned into a roaring animal if a groom neglected his task or a horse was found going lame or even with a bleeding wound. Knowing that Jacob Turner loved his horses as much as he did his family, the employees did their best to please Taffner as well as the old patriarch.

Later each day, several grooms had to work the horses while the others took care of repairs or mucked out the stalls of pigs and goats. There wasn't a day that went by when a groom could twiddle his thumbs. Alexander had needed a week to get into the rhythm and manage the hard work and the time spent outdoors without collapsing on his bed after sunset.

After work, the crew went to their rooms in a building close to the stables to shower and eat dinner—provided by the Turner family. Because Florence Town was six miles away, the employees typically got their meals from the large kitchen, where they also sat to eat, played cards, and spent the evenings drinking booze if anyone could afford a bottle. The crew was split between Florence Town residents, who occasionally stayed for a game of cards, and men who had come to town for the work. The grooming crew had better accommodations than the other farmhands, who lived in barracks on the premises but were still separated from the Turner family's private mansion.

Alexander's attempts at befriending the townspeople were met with open scorn. The locals called him an outsider, and therefore barely talked to him and hardly answered his questions.

He got tired of being shunned by his fellow workers, so he'd taken a trip into town to go shopping and get some contact with the locals. Since he had skipped dinner, he decided to eat at the diner on Main Street. Upon entering the warm and cozy room, which smelled of bacon, steak, and freshly cut onions, it immediately got quiet, and all the guests turned and stared at him. After a moment of hesitation and unpleasant quietness, they continued their conversations and meals. Alexander sat at the polished counter and waited for the waitress, aware of the continued glares from the people behind him that seemed to spear his back.

That night he'd seen Charlene for the first time. She wore her curly blonde hair short, making her pretty face seem all the rounder. Her pink dress with a white apron fit her feminine figure perfectly. She was anything but a skinny young woman, yet appeared nimble in the way she scurried around the diner. It was her smile that caught his attention and warmed his heart. Though she must have been tired after a long workday, she'd beamed at him like he was the only guest she served. Alexander ordered bacon, scrambled eggs, toast, and strong coffee.

"You've got a pleasant voice," she whispered. Instantly, she blushed. "I'll get your order, sir. In a minute."

He kept an eye on the guests sitting in the red-upholstered seating areas, enjoying their dinner. Their conversations were muted, not the loud, enthusiastic chatter Alexander was used to from any diner, bar, or restaurant in Washington, DC. For a moment, he felt thrown into a science fiction movie, like *The Invaders*, and expected the crowd to turn against him at any moment. *The nightmare continues.*

The dark thought slipped away when Charlene served his dinner with a broad smile and warm wishes. He stared at the plate heaped with food and the neatly folded napkin she placed at the side. He noticed her hands trembled.

"Thank you, that looks tasty."

"I hope it'll suffice for a man of your size. By the way, I'm Charlene."

"Alex."

Once more, a shy smile accompanied her words, and Alexander couldn't help but smile back at her. She behaved as if she wanted to make up for the rejection he had suffered from the others in the diner. And it worked. He felt much better instantly.

After several stops and many meals at the diner, Alexander could no longer resist Charlene's sweet charm and invitation. Their first time together, they kissed in the alley behind the diner after hours. The second time, she asked him to walk her home. The third time, she invited him to her father's house but with the strict order that he come without anyone seeing him. When asked, she explained that her handicapped father didn't like strangers and that Alexander was a stranger with a capital S. From that night on, Alexander was a frequent guest — turned lover — in Charlene's abode.

The order to avoid being seen troubled Alexander. He didn't want to jeopardize his mission, and yet he was unable to defy his attraction to Charlene. He couldn't stop thinking how much better and more rewarding his life would've been if he'd met Charlene years earlier. As he passed the back entrance through the kitchen and climbed the stairs, avoiding the creaking second step, Alexander smiled into the darkness. He felt ten years younger and much more vigorous than in the previous four years.

Charlene welcomed him with a whoop of joy that she muffled with her hand across her mouth. She embraced him and held him tight, beaming with delight.

"I couldn't wait for you to come. Oh, the day was so . . . so dark without you." She placed hungry kisses on his face and neck. "You smell good. I want more. Let me touch your skin."

Alexander lost his clothes to her eager hands, and he helped her out of her nightie. Kissing and laughing, they crossed her room. Happy about her good mood, he took her in his arms, and after fondling and more kissing, they lay down on the bed naked. He pulled the blanket over them.

"You're wonderful to love," Charlene whispered as she traced his lips with her fingertips. "I could stay with you *eight days a week* and feel safe."

Alexander kissed her fingers. His heart was overflowing with love, and at the same time, he was too sad for words. Instead of any half-hearted explanation, Alexander kissed her lips, her throat, and her shoulder. He enjoyed her girlish giggles and smiled as he placed more kisses on her bosom and belly. For the first time in years, he felt alive and was at a place where he was loved and needed. He hadn't imagined that a simple life could be satisfying. A part of his mind reminded him of the mission he had to fulfill and that he hadn't gained much information in the weeks of his employment. Another part of his brain kicked the first part to hell and told him to enjoy life to the fullest and not look back. Here was his future, and he was determined to hold fast.

Charlene's hand was between his legs, gently kneading his

member.

"I want you to take me, my strong lover."

"Hmm, honeyed words this early in the evening? You're generous tonight."

"I'm horny." Charlene tittered and kissed the soft skin around his nipple. "I want to feel you inside me. Take me, or I'll take you."

He looked at her hand around his hard-on. "Quite literally, I see." Alexander lifted her chin for another kiss. "Guess I'd better do as you please."

"Oh, yes. Please, please me."

Nicolas felt Jacklyn's ongoing rebuff deeply, like a pain that hurt him more than any whip ever could. He accepted her being offended, worried, and angry, but he couldn't cope with his lover being distant and reluctant to be touched. Any attempt at explaining his decision had been met by stern reproof for his foolish action with comments about his gullibility to believe he could do any good. Could he even solve a crime while at the mercy of some villagers with criminal intentions and possibly armed to the teeth? She acted as if his fate was already sealed, and that he'd spend his time being tortured for information.

He packed his bag with the clothes Freeman had provided while she worked at her physiotherapy office. Finally he decided there was still a chance to part on good terms.

Sunday morning, Nicolas stood beside Jacklyn's bed, wearing nothing but a blue ribbon around his waist. He kissed her cheek to wake her up.

"Good morning, ma Belle. I wanted to surprise you with a gift before I leave."

Jacklyn looked him up and down. Despite her attempt at being angry, he saw the glimmer of joy in her eyes.

"You made an effort to wrap it up, I see." She put a finger under the ribbon and ripped it off. She inhaled in mock surprise. "Unwrapped. Now I see what you mean." She pulled him close for a kiss. "Let me feel it, too."

Eagerly, Nicolas climbed on the bed to hover with his body above hers, waiting with bated breath for her decision. They kissed, and Jacklyn ran her hands along his arms, exhaling blissfully.

"It's a beautiful gift, well thought out. You might work on the wrapping, though." Jacklyn leaned back on the pillow. "And what does the gift include?"

"Whatever you want to do with me."

Open-mouthed, Jacklyn took a moment before responding. "Are you saying—"

"I mean what I say. I know you've got some role-play ideas in your mind you haven't shown me yet. As long as there's a chance to use the safe word when I can't take it, let's try it."

While he closed his eyes, she caressed his freshly shaven cheek. "This truly is a lovely gift."

"The pillory, then?" Nicolas had anticipated something extraordinary, but his fantasies were only half as good as Jacklyn's imagination, and she surprised him every time.

"The pillory." She lifted the beams between the bedposts and invited him to bend over. When he hesitated, she frowned. "You can still change your mind, Nick, but you said—"

"I know what I said." Bracing for a unique hour, Nicolas put his head and hands in the depressions so she could lower the upper beam. He noticed that she didn't lock the hatches. If he eliminated the only possible way out—being strong enough to lift the upper beam—he was truly trapped. He couldn't move forward or backward, and the spreader bar between his feet restricted him further. By taking deep breaths,

Nicolas calmed himself. It had been his choice, and his mistress — he knew — was only too happy to play with him in this fashion.

Jacklyn kissed his forehead and left the bed. Her hands traveled along his arms, across his shoulders, and down his back to his buttocks. She stood behind him and kneaded his muscles, then reached for his shaft and gave it a lot of attention. Her plan worked. Nicolas forgot about the wood around his neck and how tightly he was bound. His arousal grew within minutes, even more so when she fastened a ring around the base of his cock and used a ball divider. She had him trained to react to her sexual ideas, and he was an apt student.

Once, she had admitted he fired her lust straight to heaven by granting her such power. His current position, restrained in the pillory, brought her the closest she could get to a climax without being penetrated.

He heard her strained breathing, her moans, and knew she was touching herself. The mind game increased his desire. While they played, he had no will of his own. His knees trembled when she lubed his anus, then proceeded to fuck him with a strap-on.

Nicolas groaned. His position was stressful, and yet he wouldn't want it any other way. Jacklyn lived her fantasy, and he was a part of it, enjoying every moment, never doubting her love and devotion. She grabbed his hard cock and stroked up and down in the same rhythm she pushed inside him. The combined sensations were too much to take. Nicolas knew part of the game consisted of his mistress permitting him to come, but he couldn't fight the urge for more than a few heartbeats and spilled himself on the floor.

"Bad boy!" Jacklyn scolded him, but there was laughter in her voice.

Later that day, after a refreshing run through the park and a long shower, Jacklyn asked Nicolas to stay in his bathrobe.

He smiled lopsidedly and set down his coffee mug. "All right, but what's the reason?"

"I want to have access to your perfect body for the rest of the day."

He raised his brows.

"Well, my beast," she murmured, "I'll be deprived of your presence for weeks. I'm not used to that, and I don't know how I can stand it." She opened the belt and parted the bathrobe. "I'm memorizing the way you look." She embraced him at the waist and pressed her body against his. "I'm missing you already."

Nicolas held her tight and kissed her hair. "Don't worry about me, please. How hard can it be to find Thomas, find evidence of the crimes the Turners committed, and come back to you?" When he read doubt in her eyes, he kissed her lips gently. "But you're right. It'll be a hard time."

"Let me love you, Nick."

His smile deepened, and he cocked his head. "Just like that? Without any shackles? I don't know if I can do that."

She used the belt ends to pull him toward the bedroom. "I bet you can."

Samuel leaned back in his chair and wiped his weary eyes. His brothers, Gabriel and Gilead, as well as his sister, Jael, sat at the table with him, keeping their conversation muted. None of them were in a good mood. Their father had decided all important subjects had been dealt with, and he was tired. Consequently, he had left to take a nap. Though his father was still considered the head of the family, he was no longer interested in the financial or judicial details his sons dealt with. As on many occasions before, Solomon Turner, the lawyer of the family and the most ambitious man Samuel knew, was absent, probably in a meeting with his high-strung clients in Richmond.

"You should've told him." Jael looked up from her knitting. Her lips were as thin as the wool she used for the baby shoes. She had a carping tone, worse with every sentence. "It's not right that you undertake investments in other companies, even if they're US-based. It's not right." Obviously infuriated, she worked the needles for another row of plain stitches. "You can't decide on your own where our money goes, not even if you consider it prosperous." Her glare pierced the men at the table. "And we all know that some of your investments were less fortunate than claimed. Our father needs—"

"Our father needs to rest." Samuel sighed, wiping his forehead. He looked at the carafe with brandy and decided he'd have another drink. These days, brandy and scotch were his best friends. The liquor also helped him deal with Jael's constant nagging. The way he saw it, Jael was only really relaxed and happy with children. "He's been out in the corrals the whole afternoon, watching the yearlings and deciding which ones to sell. You know how hard it is for him to sell one mare. It might take days for him to find an answer."

"You shouldn't drink so much," Jael said. "It's bad for your liver."

Samuel ignored both Jael's words and Gabriel's chuckle and nodded toward Gilead. "Rest assured, your investment won't be compromised. Be careful with your choices, though. As I see it, Jael's right—we can't afford another misfortune."

Gilead, his older brother, sat rigidly in his chair. Sweat covered his brow. "I understand." His round face reddened as he adjusted his glasses nervously, then put both hands flat on the table. A moment later, he reached for his glass but didn't drink. "I'm aware that all of you scrutinize my work, while no one could do it better." He looked around the table, his lips drawn to a thin line. He spoke with a growl in his tone. "Maybe you think that the wealth the Turners have always enjoyed will last until eternity. But I can tell you that sustaining the premises, with all its obligations, is like trying to keep water in a bucket with a hole." He scoffed. "Many holes. And you aren't penny pinchers, if you don't mind my saying." He looked around. "The new stereos you bought were high end, not some crap from a flea market. Not to mention, father bought another mare at the auction last month. That beast cost a fortune, but he said —"

"We know that." Gabriel sounded impatient and obviously lacked the desire to polish his words for the sake of diplomacy. "We've dealt with your complaints, and because of that we have forged links" — he gestured with his hand and forced a smile — "that . . . let's say . . . you as the righteous bank manager don't want to know about, okay?"

Jael huffed, but Gabriel continued without glancing at her.

"Samuel and I did what we had to do, and you put the incoming money through the *Florence Town Foundation*, as you've done for years. Are there any other complaints we have to deal with today?" He looked around. "Then I've got one. Samuel, there's been complaints about your son Jebediah. He quarrels a lot and doesn't accept reprimand or follow orders to work. I want you to talk to him. He's way out of line."

Samuel clenched his teeth as he set down his empty glass with more force than necessary. "You're always complaining about Jeb. Is there any time you're not rambling?"

"I said you should talk to him. Remind him that arguments are solved peacefully. With words. I don't like people running around with black eyes, okay? It's bad for our family's reputation."

"Tyrone's a bad influence."

Gilead widened his eyes. "You accuse *my* son of influencing Jeb in a bad way? That's ridiculous!"

"Just because one of your sons is a lawyer doesn't mean the others are without fail."

Gilead sat up straight. His face flushed even more while his hands clenched the armrest. "I don't say that. But the Steward's son, Michael, that weasel is by far worse than—"

Gabriel raised his voice. "Damn your righteousness, Gilead! I don't want this to turn into banter about sons and daughters. We all know about Michael, but he's not my concern. Sam, tell Jebediah he either behaves or will face the consequences."

Samuel felt the weight of command resting on his shoulders as he looked at his elder brother. He tried to keep his response neutral. "Very well. I'll do that."

Gabriel knocked on the table, then struggled to get up. The armrests clung to his portly body as he stood, then the chair thudded on the floor again. "Fine. I've got to go. There's some cattle waiting for me, and I'm late for my next appointment with the farmer from Wilk's land to haggle about hay. He didn't like the price I named. Maybe he's come to his senses." He stood and wobbled out of the room.

Samuel looked at his remaining siblings and sighed. "The town festival is important. We should try to make it count, make our name stand out." He stood, forcing a smile. "So far, we're faring better than last year. Let's work together so that it stays that way."

Nicolas lifted his gaze from the file about Florence Town and its famous inhabitants. "They've lived there for generations? Even their offspring? How come?"

Freeman chuckled, shaking his head. "You don't know much about life in rural areas, huh? Let me tell you this. One family with money — or on the way to making money — settles down, draws workers of all kinds, and invests in the infrastructure because the people need to sleep and eat somewhere. Then the next families move in, and word gets around that there's work and therefore money to make. Soon, the village expands to a town. In this case, the Turners came first, the Reese family second." He tapped the file on the table. "A Turner married a Reese. That was the start. A little later, the Stewards followed, and they, too, invested in the region, erected a small hospital, and became benefactors for Florence Town. Knowledge about their wealth is sketchy, though. They appear to be millionaires without professions, but people like these can't stop making money." Freeman shrugged. "So, my best bet is they invest in the stock market, hidden behind fake companies, and live off the interests."

"That's not illegal." Nicolas had read the reports about the three families and their connections in business as well as their private lives. "Unless they're trying to evade taxes."

"That's still to be proven. We know from Thomas's investigations that at least the Turner family is armed and planning criminal activities. You don't need such special detonators for a simple hole in the ground. He said he'd concentrate his investigation on that premise, but his findings were few." Freeman set down his teacup. "Agent Zutarski — undercover as Alexander Leeland — said the town's inhabitants live happy lives. The top families pay fair wages. The town has an elementary school, a kindergarten, and a nice home for the elderly. Employees of the three big companies don't have to pay for health care, and that's the majority of the townsfolk there. No one lives on the streets, and the unemployment rate is non-existent. Everyone is taken care of." He smiled as he lifted his hands. "Sounds like heaven, doesn't it?"

Nicolas exhaled and pointed at the files and photos. "When did they start thinking about building bombs? Are they truly doing it? Maybe Samuel Turner bought the detonators for someone else as a go-between. I mean, did the families show a tendency to violent acts in the past? It doesn't sound likely."

"Honestly, Nicolas, we don't know. Violence? Yes, but more like brawls and illegal shooting of game. Up to this point, we couldn't connect any family member to any attack on buildings or public attractions. There were several assaults on public buildings in Richmond in the last few years, but nothing supports a theory that the Turners or their neighbors had their hands in them. They look like saints. As I said earlier—we have no right to search incoming truckloads. No judge would support us if we don't show him more than a photo."

"So that's my task then."

Freeman sat back and sighed heavy-heartedly. His big brown eyes rested sympathetically on Nicolas. "To be honest with you—I worry for Thomas and his state of mind. I don't want to think he blew his cover and was killed. I'll hope he's alive until the opposite's proven."

"Excuse my curiosity, but do you two have more in common than being colleagues?"

Freeman emptied his teacup, set it down, and folded his hands in his lap. "Thomas passed all tests with top results, and he impressed me with his work ethics. So his career was gaining speed when I fell sick. No doc could tell me when I'd be fit again, and I spent weeks at the hospital. At that time, I was in the middle of remodeling our house, and I thought that nothing could be done without me. Thomas got wind of it and offered his help. He'd learned a lot during his soldier days. You know—a jack of all trades but master of none. That's him. While I was treated at the hospital, he spent his spare time at my house. I returned to a happy wife and a finished home. Man, I was so happy." Freeman made a face. "I think his marriage went down the drain at the same time. It wasn't long before he told me his wife had filed for divorce. So I returned the favor and helped him as best as I could." He looked lost in his memories. "So, yes, Tagline's a fine agent, and he's a good friend of mine."

"What did you call him?"

Freeman laughed briefly. "He's nuts about the taglines of movies . . . quotes them a lot. You know, the catchy phrases such as *Who ya gonna call?* And everyone answers *Ghostbusters!* That's what I mean. I guess he knows about a hundred of them by heart." He put down the teapot after pouring another cup. "I want you to thoroughly investigate the compound, secure evidence if possible, or inform us of explosives, firearms, detonators, and anything else you find that might tell us about the group's intentions. I also ask that you not risk your life to become a hero. You said you've got a girlfriend. I want you to return to her."

"If she still wants me." Nicolas stared at the pictures in front of him, but he saw Jacklyn's close-lipped expression upon their farewell. "She wasn't amused by my decision to take this assignment."

"Shall I talk to her?"

"You would?"

Freeman curled the corner of his lips, almost to a smile. "You're one of my agents for this mission, and I want you to leave feeling good, not stressed."

Chapter Three

To adapt to his role, Nicolas got a buzz cut and changed his tailor-made wardrobe to old jeans, a worn-out shirt, and a jacket, as well as a pair of work boots. He drove to Virginia in a car that Freeman had borrowed from a friend. The old vehicle's engine stuttered on the last several miles of highway but made it through Belmont without more than a few hiccups.

He was bathed in sweat by the time he reached the Turner farm, where he found the billboard telling him farmhands were still needed. The engine rumbled the last mile toward the first building, and he swore he'd have it checked by a mechanic as soon as possible. He asked a man at the fence to see the person in charge of hiring and was sent to Sebastian Taffner.

The foreman greeted him with a firm handshake. They introduced each other, then Taffner squinted at him, taking in Nicolas's appearance from head to toe. "Ever worked on a farm before?"

"No, but I learn fast."

"What was your last job?"

Nicolas cast down his gaze. "I was a warehouse guard." He tried to sound desperate, and the foreman took the bait.

"What happened? Got caught stealing? Or did you quarrel too much?" Taffner crossed his arms and stood with his legs apart, lips pursed. He scrutinized Nicolas openly.

"No. This wasn't about me breaking the law. Let's say, my private situation went south, and I had to beat feet."

"But Florence Town wasn't your first idea, huh?"

Nicolas gave the man a lopsided smile. "Maybe not. But my car made it here. I need a job, man, really. I'm flat broke."

"Call me *chief*." Taffner smacked his lips and put a cigarette between them. "We work from six in the morning till four in the afternoon. Breakfast and dinner are supplied, but you're responsible for the rest."

"Wow, you serve breakfast?"

Taffner's eyes narrowed. "You'll live in the barracks with the other boys from out of town. Cell phones don't work around here—if you got one—but there's a landline you can use for free. The town's six miles down the road if there's anything you need. You got working gear?"

"Yeah, I've got what I need."

"If not—there's a shop in town. Reasonable prices . . . believe me. No one's gonna rob you here."

"What about weekends?"

Taffner's scowl was a clear indicator that asking for spare time was an insult. "First week is on probation. Either you work hard, or I'll fire you next Sunday. Do you understand that?"

"I understand." Nicolas lifted his hand. "Fine. Do you have a contract I should sign?"

Taffner laughed. "Hell, I don't see you staying here, but if you want one—ask me next Monday, okay?" He pointed toward an elongated building. "I'll show you where you put your stuff and where you sleep." On the way, he turned to look over his shoulder. "You stay in the barracks or work in the fields. The rest of the premises is off-limits, okay? The Turners don't like strangers hanging around their mansion or the stables if you don't work there. If there's anything amiss or you have questions, turn to me. And only to me."

"All right," Nicolas said when Taffner looked as if he wanted confirmation.

"Good. You'll start tomorrow and collect stones in the fields."

"Stones?"

Taffner stopped and turned. "Dude, you do as you're told. If that's not to your liking, you're free to leave. Otherwise, shut your trap."

He walked on, and Nicolas followed, thinking of Jacklyn's remark that he couldn't pose as a farmhand when he'd never worked at any place like a farm, other than the garden of his parents' house.

As always, when he was faced with a new task, Nicolas tried to familiarize himself with the situation as quickly and efficiently as possible. He took in the surroundings and compared reality to the pictures and maps Freeman had shown him. The workers' wooden barracks were simply built, furnished with beds, nightstands, and small wardrobes for each person. The large room smelled freshly scrubbed, and the linen of the bed Taffner showed him was clean.

He stowed his belongings, smiling at the heap of old clothes Freeman had bought at a second-hand shop. Compared to his usual dress code, Nicolas felt like a bum. On second thought, that was exactly the impression he was trying to make — a man who had nowhere to go, had no money, and no perspective. Taffner needed to consider him a simple man who'd do as he was told without being a threat.

Nicolas looked out the window of the barracks across the large yard toward the mansion. A haggard-looking woman appeared leading two small children, one at each hand, down the stairs to play catch in the garden. The evening was chilly, but the children laughed and obviously enjoyed the time outdoors. Judging by the pictures he had been shown, the woman was Jael, Jacob Turner's daughter.

Nicolas stood rooted, caught by the scene. He imagined becoming a father and enjoying the wonders of a new life. How
would it be to hold a baby in his arms? How would it be to
see his son or daughter grow up?

He sighed. Jacklyn had never mentioned any interest in
starting a family, and in his heart, he knew she wouldn't embrace the idea of becoming a mother.

He turned away from the window when a group of farmhands shuffled into the barracks, lamenting about their long
day and the tasks they had accomplished. They looked tired
and dirty, and their interest in a stranger was marginal.

Nicolas introduced himself, learned the men's names, and
followed them when they went to take a shower. He grabbed
a towel and froze when he realized there were no single stalls
but a large room with showers along the wall. The other men
removed their clothes, and when he hesitated looked curi-
ously in his direction. He felt obliged to join them, even
though he disliked the idea. Nicolas felt scrutinized in an intimate way, even more so when a rangy man, about forty-five,
approached him and put a wet hand on his shoulder blade.

"We haven't yet been introduced—I'm Abner. I've been
working here for ten years."

"I'm Nick."

"Fine, Nick. Seeing your build—and whatever else you
have to offer—I need to ask you a question."

Nicolas held his breath, feeling awkward and vulnerable,
but Abner didn't seem to notice.

"Have you thought about becoming a sperm donor? The
Florence Research Center always needs some, and you appear a
perfect man for the task. You should know that the doctors
and nurses that work at the hospital in Florence Town are
paid by the foundation. They only ask for some favors in return." He toweled himself off. "Think about it. You can do
something good and help others." Abner winked at him. "It's

the right idea, you understand?"

"I see." Nicolas turned off the water and hurried to get dressed again. He hadn't expected such a close inspection and hoped there was nothing else he had overlooked.

While walking down the stable aisle, Alexander mulled over what he had heard at the diner an hour ago.

The Steward family boasted of their wealth, and the two sons spent money as if they had a printing machine in the basement. One of the guests stated, in a muted voice, that he'd seen Michael, the youngest son, run around with a new rifle, which looked like those he'd seen in action movies—a weapon a sniper would use. The elder son, Nathaniel, had held a hunting rifle, and while in town shopping, the two of them had bragged that they'd be going into the woods to test them on targets against some trees. One guest worried about the young men's *targets* and quietly hoped there wouldn't be another *accident*. Judging by the older woman's gaze, accidents of this kind were not uncommon.

Though owning weapons wasn't illegal, Alexander wondered whether the siblings had nothing else to do than play with guns. The way the guests had talked, a few were suspicious of what the brothers did when they didn't shoot at targets. He decided to follow up on the leads regarding the weapons during his next visit to the town.

Alexander always sat in a corner booth like a shadow the people overlooked. He had made it a habit to listen to the inhabitants' conversations. That was how, a few weeks before, he had learned about a young truck driver named Gilbert Hanson and heard his complaints about a transport gone wrong for the Reese family. The man had suffered a severe acid burn on his right arm. Though the treatment at the hospital was free, Hanson had stated he'd sue the Reese family since there shouldn't have been more than harmless liquids in the barrels. The other two men at Hanson's table had murmured about the Reese's generosity and that the family would surely pay without asking twice. Hanson had looked around with glee in his eyes as he claimed he'd make the Reese family bleed for their mistake. After all, the barrels should have been properly closed and sealed.

Alexander had found the information interesting and tried looking for Mr. Hanson the following days but didn't see him again.

He snapped out of his musing and couldn't believe his eyes when Charlene came running down the aisle toward the stall where he was checking on a young gelding with a deep scratch along its side.

"Hey, what're you doing here?"

She opened her hands wide, smiling broadly. "I couldn't stay home any longer."

Alexander left the stall and closed the door. "I'm so glad to see you."

Charlene embraced him and held fast.

He kissed her hairline, bewildered at her behavior. "Would you mind explaining what you're gonna do?" Alex asked after a feverish kiss.

"I made the final step, Alex. We can leave now." She was out of breath yet beamed at him. "Just like you wanted all the time."

"Leave?" Alexander tried to make sense out of her exuberant mood. She was wearing her best pants, a woolen sweater, and a matching overcoat. She looked nice enough to pass as a young lady from the city. "I don't understand what—"

She giggled and clapped her hands. "Let's go, Alex. Take me somewhere else, to someplace you told me about—Boston or New York, or even Philadelphia. I want to find out whether I can be more than a waitress in a diner. Maybe a singer."

Alexander took a step back, frowning. He checked to make sure they were alone in the aisle. Visits like these were dangerous, and he was afraid the Turner family might oppose Charlene being here. "But I—"

"Don't be afraid." Charlene lifted and dropped her shoulders, sighing with contentment. "I'm not afraid anymore. You told me I don't have to live here in this rural town all my life. With you, I can do everything—leave this town, start a new life. You said that you'd have no trouble finding work elsewhere. So, why wait?" She pulled him toward the exit. "I've packed what I need. I drove up here so you can grab your stuff, and off we go!"

He followed her out, eager to get her off the premises. Though it was dark, he was certain people were watchful. "You came with your car and parked it here?"

"Yes, of course." She frowned, irritated.

Alexander ran a hand through his short hair. His heart pounded in his chest. "I can't leave right now, Charlene. As much as I want to, I can't."

Charlene's face fell. She stared at him for a moment before saying, "But you said we'd be together. You claimed that you loved me. We've been dreaming about going away, starting a family! You've talked about this constantly these last weeks. Did you lie to me? Was this all a bad joke at my expense?"

"No!" Alexander remembered that she had been talking about a family, but he knew better than to start an argument he wouldn't win. "I want to be with you, but I can't do it right away. Stay a little longer, please, and then—"

They reached the parking lot. She owned a small compact car that had more miles on the odometer than the manufacturers had imagined the engine to last. She took out her suitcase.

"Would you mind . . ."

He opened the trunk of his car and stowed her suitcase

without thinking.

She slammed the lid. "An hour ago, I told my father that he can kiss my sorry ass and that I'm leaving with you, and he can't do anything about it." She crossed the distance and kissed him with feverish urgency. "Please, Alex, that's what you wanted, right? That I stand up against him and my brother and not let them treat me like a maid. Now we're free."

"Charlene, please . . ." He stepped back, trying to wrap his mind around her decision. He had encouraged her to speak her mind and set an hour a day when she would work for the family and not jump at every call, but he couldn't remember telling her to quarrel with her father.

"Are you bailing out?" Her eyes filled with tears. "You're abandoning me?"

Again, he looked around. The possibility of watchers grew with every minute of their argument. "I'm not abandoning you. But I can't go with you. Maybe in a few days."

"A few days? How many? Two? Four? I'm telling you, I'm not going back. I can't!" She stared at him with wide-open eyes. "Who do you think I am? Shall I crawl back and tell my father he was right all along and that you're a good-for-nothing outsider, who'll use me and drop me anyway? And that I'd be much better off with a guy from around like Jeb?"

He handed her eighty dollars, desperate to lift her mood, and salvage the situation. For the life of him, he wouldn't have thought that she'd suddenly put her idea into practice. "Here. That's all I've got on me. If you had told me —"

"I did tell you." She counted the money. "I told you I wanted to leave this place behind. I hate working at the diner. I hate the sleazy bums who think they're the greatest gift to mankind." She looked up. "I won't get far with this."

Alex scribbled a note to Vernon on a piece of paper he pulled from his glovebox and wrote the phone number of his superior on the backside. His heart beat in his throat. He didn't want to lose Charlene, but he couldn't tell her about his covert mission. "Here, take that. It's for a friend of mine, Vernon. I'll call him from Belmont and tell him to fetch you at the next station. If anything goes wrong, you have to call him, no matter from where. Do you hear me? He'll help you."

"Help me with what?"

"Find a place to sleep, give you money. I'll explain every-thing later." He held up a hand to interrupt her protest. "Let's go. We don't have time. I wanna see you catch the next bus. I bet your father already alarmed his vigilantes."

Wistfully, Charlene looked back at the street she had come, and Alexander hoped she'd change her mind. But then she pulled herself together, turned back toward his car, and sat in the passenger seat, waiting for him. Sighing, Alexander slipped behind the wheel and started the engine.

During the ride to Belmont, Charlene continued trying to convince Alexander to join her escape. When she cried again in frustration, he exhaled, making up his mind.

"Charlene, I'm sorry to say, but I've got some unfinished business in town. I'll leave as soon as I can, but not right now, as much as I want to."

"Unfinished business? What kind?"

"I can't tell you, okay? It's not about you. It's got nothing to do with you. Believe me."

"I do believe you, but it's dangerous to stay. You said my father probably called his vigilantes. I think he'll call the Turn-ers first. You aren't safe here anymore."

Alexander didn't mention that she had brought danger to both of them by driving onto the Turner property in the first place. "I can't change that. I'll deal with them."

She looked at him, deep worry in her eyes. "But . . . once this is over, you'll leave, right? You'll find me wherever your friend takes me?"

"Yes, my love, I'll come to you and take you with me. That's a promise."

She bent to kiss him. "But I hate that you're leaving me alone." She got out of the car, and after he retrieved her suitcase, she walked toward the ticket window. "I need you, Alex. Don't you see that?"

"I know. And I'm sorry." Though he didn't say it, he was devastated as well. Being with Charlene was the only thing that made the investigation worthwhile. When Vernon had asked him to infiltrate a small town and find out about the Turner's alleged criminal activities, he had agreed because he had nothing else to do. Now he dreaded the thought of returning to work and mucking out stalls. There would be no one to meet in the evening. No one to kiss and love him and help him forget.

Charlene showed him the ticket. "The bus goes to Richmond, but it has several stops in between."

Alexander looked at the bus stop list and nodded. "I'll call Vernon as soon as you're inside the bus. Let's go."

He felt a kind of itching and looked over his shoulder. As an agent, he trusted his gut feeling even if he didn't see any indicators of a threat. He knew, though, that Charlene's father was friends with the Turners. If anyone could cause trouble, it was one of their younger sons, Jebediah. More than once, Charlene had complained about the man's pushy attempts at flirting with her. Jebediah was the obnoxious guy without honor and a tendency to cause trouble wherever he went. Everyone in town seemed to know of a story in which Jebediah had brawled with another man. Charlene had always told the guy off, claimed his attention wasn't welcome, but Alexander had seen the man's hungry gazes. Where Jebediah's bad behavior was concerned, Charlene's decision to leave was wise, but rash all the same.

They reached the waiting bus, and the driver helped stow the suitcase.

Charlene turned to embrace and kiss him. "Please, please, hurry with whatever you have to do, okay? I'm lost without you, and I'm wondering whether I'm doing the right thing — leaving you alone in this freaky town." She tried to smile, but tears trickled down her cheeks.

"I will do what I can to speed things up, believe me." He kissed her with all the love he felt, pulled her close, and ruined her hairdo. "I love you so much, I don't have words."

She wiped her cheeks with trembling hands. "Just hurry. I'll miss you."

Alexander's heart broke with her soft words. "I'll miss you, too." He kissed her one last time and watched her enter the bus. She took a seat, and the driver closed the door.

The same moment, a man came running through the empty concourse toward the curb. "Hey, you! Stop the bus! Now!"

Alexander turned around, instantly recognizing the dark blond guy.

The bus driver started the engine immediately and began to pull away.

"Damn, fuck!" Jebediah stopped in his tracks, fuming with rage. He drew his gun and aimed at the slowly departing bus.

"No!" Alexander jumped at Jebediah and pushed up his arm the moment the gun was fired. He used the momentum and Jebediah's pain to wrest the weapon from his hands and dropped it.

The young man stumbled but gained his footing quickly and attacked Alexander. "You fucking bastard!"

Alexander evaded the punch to his face and hit back harder. He broke his opponent's nose, and his next, equally strong punch against Jebediah's jawbone sent him to the ground. The man sat whining like a child while blood dripped down his chin.

Tyrone arrived, teeth bared and as angry as his cousin. He thrust the butt of his rifle against Alexander's ribs, pushing him backward. Alexander rode out the pain to undermine Tyrone's attempt to turn the rifle and shoot him. Alexander grabbed the barrel and pulled hard and fast, causing Tyrone to let go. Alexander threw the gun to the side. A quick glance behind him showed the bus rounding the corner and disappearing.

Tyrone went for another ill-timed attack, but Alexander kicked away his supporting leg. When Tyrone stumbled, Alexander hit his sternum with his knuckles. The lanky young man grimaced with pain but still stood. Alexander pulled back his arm for another punch when he heard a gun being cocked.

Deputy Sheriff Gordon Reese crossed the concourse with careful steps, a shotgun directed at Alexander. He sounded breathless. "Stop it! Right now!"

Alexander stepped back from Tyrone and lifted his hands. "Okay, you win."

Tyrone boxed him in the liver hard. "On your knees, you bastard!"

"Okay." Alexander went down in slow motion, watching his opponents, tensing to fight despite the pain in his midsection.

Gordon seemed uncertain of what to do. His juvenile features were tense, obviously torn between the commitment to his profession and the desire to please his friends. His mouth twitched, and a strand of brown hair fell across his eyes.

Jebediah still whined while Tyrone gathered his wits and retrieved his rifle, spluttering curses.

Gordon threw Tyrone a pair of handcuffs. "Shackle him." He turned to Jebediah. "We'd better take him away quickly. Let's move, bro."

"Yeah, yeah, I'm coming." Jebediah rested on his knees, re-learning how to breathe, trying to cope with his pain. Blood smeared his hands, and when he lifted his head, more dripped on his shirt.

Alexander grinned at his opponent's discomfort but quickly cloaked it when Jebediah looked in his direction.

"He'll pay for that." Jebediah got back on his feet and stood on wobbly legs. "The fucking bastard will pay!"

Alexander suffered being cuffed, watching Jebediah, and readying to dodge another attack.

"Up with you!" Tyrone twisted Alexander's arm and forced him to stand.

Jebediah flung himself forward. "I'll teach you not to mess with me!"

Gordon grabbed Jebediah's shoulder and showed more strength than his appearance suggested. "Don't!" He pulled him back hard. "My father will punish him, not you."

Jebediah spun around, making a face. "Oh, yeah, right! He fucked my girlfriend, okay? I'm the one deciding how he's gonna suffer."

Alexander stared at him, angry beyond reason. "Come on! Try it! I whacked shitheads like you when I was fifteen."

Jebediah's eyes narrowed. He took a step forward, fists raised, but Gordon forced him back again, this time blocking him with his body.

"I said my father will take care of him!" Gordon cut off Jebediah's threat and nodded toward Tyrone. "Let's go back to the cars. You take Alexander's. We can't leave it here."

"We'll take him with us," Jebediah insisted, fumbling in his pockets for a handkerchief. "We've got a place where we can lock him up."

"My father—"

"Stop blathering about your dad being the one who calls the shots here." He pushed Alexander toward the exit. "We can talk to him tomorrow, all right? For now, I want that goon locked up where I can see him suffer."

"But the jail's in town, and I'm obliged to take him there."

"Obliged. Fuck me sideways!" Jebediah holstered his gun. "You think you're the big shot here because you carry a badge? Hell, this shithead fucked my girlfriend. Raped her! I wanna see him pay for that!"

"I didn't rape Charlene!" Alexander shouted and wriggled in Tyrone's grip. "She's in love with me! And I love her! Just so you know!"

"She'd never love an outsider." Jebediah pushed Alexander into the police car. "Sit down, shut up." He poked Gordon's shoulder. "Our place. No discussion."

Gordon hesitated. "Where do you want to lock him up? If what you say is true, he'll face a sentence of no less than three years. My father will kill me if I let him escape."

Alexander raised his brows. "Do you really think she'd have let me bring her to Belmont if I had raped her? Are you crazy?"

"Shut up!" Jebediah slammed the door. "Get in!" he urged Gordon. "And drive, for God's sake."

Gordon got behind the wheel and put the car in gear.

"Think about it," Alexander said from the back seat behind the fence. "Jebediah wanted her, but Charlene didn't let him come close. Haven't you seen her? She shooed him away . . . every time."

"Shut up, I'm thinking," Gordon grumbled.

"Jeb's playing you. He wants me blamed. Charlene wanted to leave, okay? I just helped her catch the bus because her car wouldn't make it. Ask her father. They had a fight about her leaving town."

"The fight was about her abandoning her family when they need her the most."

For a moment, Alexander was quiet, mulling over Gordon's words. "You—"

"I said, shut up!" Gordon shouted, his voice cracking with the last word. He drove like a maniac, turned the corners too fast and too reckless. "You made her life miserable, and she saw no other way than to leave town. That's it. End of story."

Alexander was stunned. "I didn't harm her, Gordon. I swear. I'm in love with her."

"Then why did she leave so suddenly, huh?" Gordon looked at Alexander in the rear mirror. "Explain that to me. Explain why she threw a tantrum with her dad, almost causing him a heart attack. She was out of her mind, totally confused. He couldn't get a straight word out of her, and then she ran away." He nodded. "You can't wriggle out of that, Leeland. You'll stand trial for rape, and she'll testify against you."

"This is a rigged game. Jeb put the words in your head, and you're the dickhead who believes everything."

"Shut the fuck up!" Gordon's hands clenched the wheel as he floored the gas pedal.

Alexander saw the man's inner turmoil reflected on his face, contorted with rage but also irritation. However, if he couldn't convince Gordon of his sincerity, he feared he'd be locked up in some dark place, and they would throw away the key.

"Listen to me. You have to take me to town and put me in jail. Your father has to know of the arrest, okay? Do this by the book. Don't get in trouble just because you want to do Jebediah a favor."

Gordon inhaled noisily, and his round face was covered with sweat, his nostrils widened. He glanced at Alexander from time to time without saying another word.

"Mr. Reese, you are the deputy sheriff. You swore an oath to protect the people. You can't bend the law just because—"

"If you don't stop, I'll pull over and gag you. I swear."

Alexander hung his head. "Just don't leave me to the mercy of Jeb and his hoodlums."

Nicolas couldn't sleep. He mulled over his obligation and how he could make contact with the ATF agent. If the man still worked at the Turner farm, they would eventually run into each other, maybe somewhere in the barn. If the man had changed jobs, Nicolas would search the town for him prior to dealing with the case and the bombs the Turners might possess.

A sudden commotion caught his attention. He got up and looked through the window. Three cars were driving recklessly toward the stables, one of them belonging to the sheriff. Intrigued, Nicolas put on pants and shoes and left the barracks quietly without waking anyone. He moved in the shadows quickly, shivering in the cool air.

The cars stopped behind the large barn in front of a weathered building Nicolas figured to be an older stable. It was much smaller than the new one and contained no more than ten stalls. The car doors opened, and three men got out. He recognized Jebediah and Tyrone Turner as they walked toward the police car. The third man was too young to be the sheriff, so Nicolas took him to be the deputy. In the lamplight, the portly deputy looked like a man being taken to a movie he didn't want to watch. The three men had a brief but intense conversation before Jebediah dragged a handcuffed man from the back seat.

Nicolas's eyes widened when he recognized the ATF agent, who was escorted into the old stable. His loud complaints that he wanted to be taken to the jail were ignored. A heated conversation accompanied their walk, and Nicolas hurried to get closer to hear what they were saying.

He made it to the corner of the barn when Taffner walked

out of his cabin, dressed in a bathrobe and slippers. Nicolas slipped into the barn and hid while Taffner passed him by.

"Is that you, Deputy Reese? Why the hell are you here? And what're you doing with Alex?" Taffner called.

"Go back to bed, Sebastian," Jebediah snarled. He lifted his chin and put his hand on his weapon. "We don't need you here, and it's not your concern, okay? Go!"

"Are you locking him up?"

Nicolas peered through the gap and saw Alexander struggle in Tyrone's grip.

"They say I raped Charlene, but I didn't do it!"

Jebediah punched Alexander in the stomach, and Alexander dropped to his knees, groaning.

"Asshole!"

"Shut up! I swear I'm gonna gag you!" Jebediah turned to Taffner. "Yeah, we're locking him up in one of the old stalls."

"Really?" Taffner sounded amused. "Is the jail already filled with bad guys?"

"That's my business." Jebediah pushed Taffner's shoulder. "Now, go, will ya!"

Taffner murmured a curse but turned away, ignoring the prisoner's lament as well as Jebediah's open hostility.

In the shadow, Nicolas pondered his options while the three men pushed the agent into the stable. Quietly, Nicolas left his position to follow. It surprised him that Taffner, who had given the impression of a man who would stand his ground, walked away without an argument.

Nicolas searched for a place to hide and found none around the barn. The old stable had two entrances, but the second one lay on the other side, and he couldn't reach it without crossing the men's line of sight. So he stood pressed against the wall, listening.

"Will Taffner be a problem?"

Nicolas assumed it was the voice of the deputy, the one

who seemed the most insecure and obviously dissatisfied with the situation.

"No. My father would fire him on the spot if I told him to. Taffner knows he'd better turn a blind eye, because he doesn't want to lose his job. He's got nothing else."

"Okay."

"I found a long chain and a few padlocks. That'll do."

That had to be Tyrone, a man with a high voice and an equally unpleasant laugh of a hyena.

"We can put it around the bars."

"And he'll be able to reach the door, you moron. No, we'll use the chain to lock him to the posts inside. Tomorrow, you'll search the basement for some more shackles. I bet we have some in the storage."

The chains clanked, and Jebediah and Tyrone laughed while the deputy mumbled about the chances of the delinquent getting away.

"Deputy," Alexander said, despair in his voice. "Don't let them do this to me! You have to take me to town. You don't know what they'll do once you're gone."

The deputy didn't say a word. Nicolas heard the sound of fists hitting flesh, then Alexander moaning before he became quiet. A moment later, the deputy left the stable and tried several times to light a cigarette. His hands trembled, and he grumbled about a bad night and that he'd rather have stayed home to watch the football game.

Nicolas pressed his body against the wall, cursing that he hadn't thought of being exposed. Slowly, to avoid attention, he moved toward the smaller side of the stable, but now he was out of earshot. Shivering in the cold and constantly looking around, he waited for the three men to depart.

Tyrone parked Alexander's car at the designated spot, then walked with Jebediah through the large garden toward the mansion, chatting like men after a hard workday. The deputy sheriff got in his car and sped off the property, with the engine roaring as if he was trying to undo his deed by running away.

Teeth clattering, Nicolas was about to enter the stable when he heard footsteps.

"You couldn't sleep, huh?" Taffner asked. His eyes narrowed, and his voice was stern. "Curious, city-boy?"

"Indeed." Nicolas straightened. "You were curious, too."

"It's my job to watch over the premises, not yours. Go back to bed."

"What happened here?"

"That's not your business." He lifted his index finger. "And you'd better not make it your business. The Turners do what they think is right. This is their land. Don't forget that, boy, or you'll be back on the street tomorrow. Do you understand?"

"I understand." Nicolas shrugged and shuffled back toward the barracks. He knew Taffner was watching him leave, and he didn't look over his shoulder.

At least he had found the agent alive.

CHAPTER FOUR

Vernon Freeman knew his wife — waiting impatiently at home — would have his butt if she learned about him driving like a maniac. He overtook two trucks so fast he saw a blur in the side window. In his defense, he had blue lights and sirens on and used his right to speed to reach the bus station in Richmond, where Charlene waited for him.

Her tear-choked call two hours earlier had shocked him so much he had stuttered. Still dressed in a pajama top instead of a dress shirt, he had toppled the coffee pot off the counter. He was a lucky man, though. His wife understood haste, anxiety, and the duties of an ATF senior agent. Vernon had promised to reward his outstanding lady in a special way.

When Vernon parked his car in front of the bus station, he gathered his thoughts. Charlene was the first known Florence Town inhabitant who had left her hometown and could be interrogated. He had offered to send a local patrol, but she wouldn't have it, even though she urged him to come quickly. Stubbornly, she had repeated that Alexander Leeland had told her to call this number and wait because Vernon would help her. Vernon had never been in the position of a guardian and felt ill-equipped when he walked through the concourse.

Because of Charlene's self-description, he found her quickly. She stood from a bench, a creased handkerchief in her hands and tearstains on her face. Her reddened eyes full of fear triggered his protective instinct, especially when she looked around as if she was expecting enemies.

"I'm Vernon Freeman. We talked on the phone."

"I'm Charlene." She dropped the tissue in a paper basket and handed him Alexander's letter. "That's for you."

"Thank you." Vernon unfolded the crinkled piece of paper and inhaled sharply. In clipped words, his agent told him to take care of Charlene without revealing who he was. She was a Florence Town resident, probably being followed and in danger. Vernon should talk to no one about her until his agent could join them.

Vernon exhaled as he lowered the piece of paper. "Alex asks me to take you home with me for a few days. Is that okay with you?"

"Yes, yes, of course." She smiled but looked like she'd cry at any moment. She adjusted the strap of her purse. "Please, take me away from this place. It's awful."

"Very well." He took the heavy suitcase and escorted her to his car. "Do you know who might be following you?" he asked when he sat behind the wheel and got the vehicle in motion.

"I'm not sure. Jebediah, Tyrone, some others." She looked through the window. "My father didn't want me to leave. So he'll have called everyone who'd listen to him."

Vernon merged the car into the sparse traffic. "There's something to drink and eat in the glove compartment. Just in case . . ."

Charlene gave him the barest of smiles and shook her head. Her voice was small. "I want Alexander back with me. Can you help him? He didn't tell me exactly what he's got to do in town, but . . . I understand it's important."

"If he said so, it probably is." He glanced at her, curious how the young woman had won Thomas's heart so fast.

She smoothed the belt of her jacket. "He said he'd been a soldier but couldn't go back to life after his return. He wanted something better and different from anything he had done so far, and he loved working with the horses. Was it all a lie?"

Vernon focused on the road ahead, trying to gain time. He didn't want to ruin the picture she had made of him. "He was a soldier all right, but then life turned against him." He remembered Thomas's despair after the divorce. His friend had looked like death warmed over and hadn't had interest in anything. "I think he needed a change. A fresh start."

"He said he loved me. Kissed me goodbye." Charlene nodded, focused on her hands playing in her lap. She sniffled and reached for a tissue to blow her nose. "I thought we'd just get in his car and drive off. You know, like they do in the movies."

"He's a good man," Vernon said when the silence stretched uncomfortably. "And I'm sure he likes you very much. Tell me, please, what happened."

Charlene gathered her strength. Her voice was soft. "We'd talked about leaving town over the last few weeks, and then I had this big fight with my father about doing housework and taking care of him, since he can't manage very well alone. He's in a wheelchair, and my mom doesn't do much at home. It's all on me. Then he said that I shouldn't dare meet with outsiders. He called them scum, all of them. My father claimed he'd heard bad things about Alexander—that he's a bruiser. He went on rambling about the outsiders being criminals, and in the end, he forbade me to meet with Alex." She scoffed and ripped the tissue into tiny pieces. "I know where he got his information." Charlene turned to face him. "He's friends with the Turners and would've loved to see me married to Jebediah. He said that Jeb loves me, would do everything for me. But that's crap. When I couldn't reach Alex on the telephone, I packed my stuff and drove to the Turners to find him. He took me to the bus station." She lowered her gaze, and again tears were trickling down her cheeks. "I heard a shot."

Vernon clenched the wheel, hoping he'd be spared any devastating words.

"I don't know what happened, but the last thing I saw before the bus turned the corner was Alex fighting with another man." She wiped her eyes with the back of her hand. "I think it was Jeb."

She shook her head.

Vernon let go of the breath he'd been holding.

"I don't know what happened next. But usually, Jeb doesn't come alone. I bet he had his friends with him."

Vernon searched for words to console her, but he needed consolation himself. His agent was alive but in trouble. He wished he'd left town with her, mission be damned.

"I'm sure everything will work out." He knew he sounded lame.

Charlene failed to smile. "I want him back. He's the man I've been waiting for."

"That I understand."

Groaning, Alexander got up and stretched to stare through the bars toward the fields. The sun was up, and the day promised to be warm, made for working with the horses. They were gentle creatures, beautiful and wonderful to look at. Though he hadn't had anything to do with horse care prior to this covert mission, he'd cherished being with them from the first day. The love and care a man invested was given back. The horses appeared to understand him, not with words, but with empathy. A fellow groom had laughed and told him he might become a *horse whisperer*. It was true. The horses liked him and calmed down in his presence. Jacob Turner had noticed that, too, and praised him for his good work. Now Alexander was confined, and someone else would take care of them. He pondered whether the old patriarch would notice his absence and investigate his whereabouts.

Frustrated, he turned away, pulling the clinking chain behind him as he walked across his square cell. The night had been awful, and he hadn't caught a wink of sleep in the straw. Now his stomach was rumbling, since none of his captors had thought about providing him with food. He wondered whether Jebediah had even given a thought to his prisoner beyond locking the chains.

Though the chain holding Alexander was just long enough to allow him to open the stall door, he couldn't get out. The chain was attached to the furthest post from the entrance, and the other end was slung around his ankle, tight enough to hurt. Tyrone had emptied his pockets and taken whatever might be useful to try and open the lock.

He tried to set his hopes on one of the grooms showing up during the day. If the guy wouldn't set him free, Alexander might convince him to call the sheriff to have him transferred to Florence Town jail. But the old stable was beyond the large barn and rarely used, so he knew no worker would come here without a reason.

Disheartened, he sat on the floor again.

Alexander wished Charlene was still at his side. Day by day, they had come to know each other better. She had told him of her weak mother, who wouldn't manage the housework but sat on a chair, daydreaming. And about her handicapped father, who constantly complained about everything because he was dissatisfied with the obstacles life had thrown his way.

Then there was her younger brother, Willy, a car mechanic without ambition, a guy easily persuaded by gambling. He used to take Charlene's money to play in poker games, which he lost, always. Charlene suspected the Stewards had a lot of fun ripping her brother off.

When he'd asked about the Stewards, and where their money came from, Charlene had shrugged and changed the subject. He couldn't tell whether she didn't know anything about them or if she preferred not to talk.

During his first days in Florence Town, he had learned that the people always spoke highly of their benefactors without ever mentioning the dark side of their influence. If asked directly, they either changed the subject or looked at him scornfully. Alexander understood instantly he had to be careful with his questions, or he would be taken down by someone who considered him a spy.

The main door of the barn opened, and Taffner approached with measured steps. He opened the stall and handed Alexander a small pot with warm porridge and a spoon. He appeared neither angry nor pleased with the situation.

"Here's something to eat for you. Jebediah has his mind on something else, I suppose."

"Thank you. That's kind." He took a spoonful, relishing the warmth as well as the taste. "I didn't do what I'm accused of. Please, chief, believe me."

"Word is that Charlene abandoned her family and took a bus out of town, leaving her helpless family behind. I know she's got a mind of her own, but she'd never leave so suddenly. So I think you're behind this. You put that crazy idea in her head." He frowned. "So, maybe, you didn't force yourself on her, but you're the reason she's gone. And that's bad enough."

Alexander knew he couldn't break the leverage the Turner family had over the foreman. "Do you know what they plan to do with me?"

Taffner shrugged and obviously didn't care. "As long as they don't tell me otherwise, I'll put you to work. Buckner, that old loser, didn't show up. I bet he's lying somewhere drunk as a skunk. I'll come back later. You'll muck out the pigpen."

The morning passed slowly as Alexander pondered what kind of sentence waited for him. He snapped out of his thoughts when the barn door was opened again, and Tyrone entered, glee shining in his eyes. Jebediah followed behind him, looking like the victim of a tavern brawl and displaying the disheartened expression of the unreasonably punished. His face carried deep purple bruises in addition to the bandage across his broken nose. Even his dark blond hair seemed in disarray. His movements were slow, and he grimaced at every step.

Jebediah thrust shackles through the bars. "Put them on."

"Leg irons?" Alexander stepped forward. "You want me to . . ." He shook his head and gaped at the young man. "*See our family. And I bet you'll feel much better about yours.* You can't make me."

Jebediah's voice sounded ridiculously nasal. "You either put them on, or I'll let you rot in here. No food, no water. See how long you can stand it. Your decision."

"The deputy knows about me being here. He will —"

"Gordon does what we tell him," Jebediah said with a wave of his hand. "His father wouldn't want to know about you, even if he told him."

"So the sheriff's your grandfather's lapdog?"

Jebediah twitched his brows and smirked. "Oh, you don't know anything about what's going on. No one cares about outsiders. And rumor has it that you've been snooping around. Maybe you wanted to get to other women, too." He waggled a finger *no*. His eyes had a hard glint. "In here, you can't do more harm. That's fine with everybody."

"Put 'em on!" Tyrone demanded and banged the bars. "I've got other shackles in store. Michael knows a blacksmith, and he's got a lot of stuff." He laughed in his high tone. "Man, if you don't do as you're told, I'll tie you up like a package."

He mimicked being tied with arms twisted across his torso, grimacing like a man in pain. "Then you'll suffer."

"Is that what you do with all men who don't do your bidding?"

Jebediah's eyes narrowed. He frowned, and his words were cautious. "What're you trying to tell me, fucker?"

"Do your grandfather and father know that you're keeping me here illegally? That you're lying about your relationship with Charlene?"

Tyrone looked at his cousin, then growled that he'd love to fetch more shackles and gags.

Jebediah shook his head. He looked at Alexander but spoke to Tyrone. "No. Not yet. The time will come. For now, the irons will do. Put them on, Alex, or I swear I'll find ways to make you comply."

Jason watched Matthew Montagna switch on Nicolas's computer. After four weeks, he still couldn't shake the oddity of working with the agent from Chicago on a triple murder case, even though he was the same agent Nicolas had worked with to solve the series of bank robberies.

Though Matthew avoided asking questions about Nicolas and didn't compare Jason's way of investigating to Nicolas's, Jason couldn't shake the feeling of being observed and judged. Additionally, the much older agent seemed like a natural-born leader. Whenever he turned his back, Jason felt the itch to check whether Matthew was mocking him.

"You look as if the case isn't getting any better." Matthew fetched a cup of coffee and sat down.

"Well, not since yesterday. We still don't know the identity of the victims found close to Madison, Virginia. Local police think it's a serial killer on the loose, who uses this part of the woods as a burial ground. That's why they dropped it in our laps." He sighed. "Fortunately for the local forest ranger, the search revealed no more bodies, at least not in this area. But the search is ongoing."

"I got that, though I doubt the theory, because of the two different ways of killing." Matthew skimmed through his emails and checked the files on the desk. "I admit it's odd that the bullets were removed from the bodies." He lifted his gaze. "I've never heard of killers retrieving the slugs. He—or they—must fear that the police would be able to trace the weapon. Maybe it was used before. These were planned killings, not accidents."

"That supports the theory of a serial killer, even though the first victim was stabbed."

"I think it's much more effective if we use our resources. Did you tell—"

"Miller from CSU is on it, but the fingerprints of the victims aren't in the system, and the face recognition program didn't deliver any results either. We checked the missing people lists—nada. The paint on the one victim's hands and the remnants of explosives under the other victim's fingernails aren't enough evidence for conclusions. Without the slugs, Miller can't determine the weapons used. The blade belongs to a skinning knife, not a rare piece. The only thing we know is that their time of death dates back at least ten weeks, while the last victim was killed around March fourth."

"So you're with me? We go with the TV announcement?"

Jason glanced at Sullivan's office. "Believe me, I don't like the idea, but . . . yes." Jason dialed Jacklyn's number. From the way she answered, he deduced she wasn't in the best of moods. "How are you holding up?"

Jacklyn snorted. "I'm not *holding up*! How dare you say that? It's not like he's sick at the hospital and awaiting surgery. He decided to leave me for glory, for honor, and for some guy he doesn't even know."

"His job—"

"No, Jason, I don't want a lecture about FBI work ethics or how Nicolas defines his job. I can't stand that, okay? Nicolas left because he thinks he can change something. That he's able to infiltrate a town with a long history of possible corruption and living above the law. That's like walking into an ongoing bank robbery naked and ordering the gangsters to put down their weapons."

Though he liked the comparison, he wouldn't agree with her. It was hard enough to ignore the images forming in his mind. "No, it's not. Jacklyn, I understand you're upset. I want him back, too. But you knew from the beginning he's an agent—"

"You're doing it again. Don't give me this *service to the country* bullshit."

Jason leaned back, redirecting his approach. "Okay. Nicolas told me you're in the middle of moving. Do you need help?"

"Yes, I do need help." Jacklyn sighed. "I need a plumber, a carpenter, a decorator, and a hundred hands to carry the furniture next week. Oh, and not to mention a year's supply of aspirin."

Jason laughed. "I don't know about the aspirin, but as for the rest—I'll call some friends for you."

"Thank you."

In the silence, Jason heard her sigh again. "Jacky—"

"Have you heard from him?"

"No, not yet. But he's only been gone for a couple of days."

"Seems to me he's been gone for half a year. Agent Freeman visited me, you know? He told me the same *country bullshit* stuff. At least he promised me to stand up for Nicolas when Sullivan tries to belittle his work."

"That's clever of you." Jason glanced at Sullivan's office to find him gone. "I'll get back to you once I've got some crafts-men lined up for you."

"Thank you."

Jason put down the phone just as Sullivan stopped at his desk.

The man didn't waste time with formalities. "Any news about the case?"

"A good morning to you, sir," Matthew said with a smile as false as the *Breitling* watch Sullivan wore. "The news is that we need your permission for a nationwide TV search to put name tags on the dead men we found."

"So you have already exhausted your investigative possibilities?"

Matthew leaned back, inhaling. "Sir, if we hadn't done everything in our power to identify the men, I wouldn't ask. Believe me, a public search of such magnitude leads to a lot of calls by people who think they might've seen some look-alike. Hundreds of phone calls will come in without any connection to the case. So, yes, sir, we've tried everything to avoid occupying twenty agents with phone service." He used his fingers to list the evidence. "The cotton fibers on the men's bodies indicate they had worn working gear — simple stuff, nothing expensive. One man had paint on his fingers — used for painting wood, like houses. The remnants of C-four under the first victim's fingernails indicate he'd handled the material. Still, CSU hasn't been able to determine the exact origin of the explosives or the manufacturer so far. They're working with the ATF to —"

"Have you assumed there had been a quarrel among the victims leading to their deaths?"

Jason wished for an excuse to leave the desk. Watching Matthew's deadpan expression without exploding with laughter was a challenge. He couldn't fathom Matthew's outstanding self-control.

"That would indeed be an interesting quarrel, considering the first victim was stabbed, the second one was shot. Neither the slugs nor the weapons were found. The last victim was shot, too, at least four weeks later. And they had taken off their clothes prior to that. You can correct me, sir, but I assume there was a fourth man in this scenario."

Sullivan nodded curtly. "Keep me informed."

As he walked on, Jason fled the open-plan office for the yard behind the building. He doubled over laughing so hard his belly hurt. Matthew followed calmly and lit a cigarette.

"Do you need a medic?" Matthew asked, blowing out smoke. "Or an oxygen tank?"

"Nope." Jason straightened but couldn't meet Matthew's gaze without chuckling. "I thought he'd punch your face."

"I would say he's as dumb as cattle, but that would insult the cattle. Honestly, I think Sullivan might attempt knocking out both of us but would stumble trying to get close enough."

Jason ran a hand through his growing-out hair and shook his head. Slowly, he regained his composure. "Fact is we're still trying to find the origin of the explosives. I hope Agent Freeman will be more successful."

"Agreed."

Matthew stubbed the cigarette, and while they were on the way back to their desks, he shared a possible theory for the crimes. "I've played with this idea for some time—maybe it's nonsense, but think about it for a moment. The men aren't criminals. Otherwise, their fingerprints would be in the system. So how could a respectable citizen come in contact with explosives? And how did the third victim suffer such a severe burn wound, probably caused by some acid? It doesn't fit. But if we consider what Nicolas said about his mission to uncover whether a rich family had built bombs in some rural town in Virginia, this could be somehow connected."

"In what way?" Jason stopped to have a closer look at the

map. He pointed at a location. "Madison is here. What was the town called? Ah, Florence Town." He pointed at the second location. "It's a distance of about forty miles, Matt, on the way to the mountains. And what's your idea?"

"If they'd already built a bomb, wouldn't they have used it by now? What if someone killed the person with the knowledge, and that's why nothing else has happened so far?"

"And the other two bodies?"

"I've got no explanation for them. Witnesses, maybe?"

Jason scoffed. "That's not much. Let's prepare the TV announcement and hope they've got family members who're missing them."

Vernon's wife, Teresa, prepared a guest room for Charlene. His lady was a born hostess—gentle and caring but without being obtrusive. Vernon called himself lucky that this great woman had agreed to marry him.

He kissed Teresa's hairline. "You're an outstanding woman, and today I love you more than ten years ago."

"Which means you expect we're hosting her for what—a week? A month?" She lowered her voice. "Vernon, it's not that I want her out of the house, but she's a troubled young lady. I hear her cry a lot, and I can't do anything about it. Can't you call a psychologist to help her? Your agency has two, I think."

Vernon pulled her into the kitchen and looked her in the eyes. "I need to keep her under the radar. I don't know if the *Big Three* have eyes and ears inside the ATF, and I won't risk Charlene being hunted, okay? I can't order professional help, because that would trigger interest from DC. So don't tell anyone about our guest, and I'll see that this case is solved as soon as possible."

"Bring her back this *Alexander*. She asks me at any given moment whether I know how he's doing." She narrowed her eyes, frowning. "When I asked her to describe her lover, she mentioned a scar on his chin. And I wonder who he might be."

Vernon knew his wife was clever and would smack him if he denied the obvious. "You're right. *Alexander* is Thomas."

Teresa gaped at him. "You sent Thomas to investigate? Alone? Really? Are you out of your mind, Vernon? Why didn't you pull him out right away? If these guys she's talking about are in any way as crazy as Charlene claims, they'll kill him just because he took her to the station without asking for permission."

"I hope they don't. Please, Tess, he decided to take her to the bus station even though he knew of Jebediah's jealousy. I bet he thought this through. And I don't think Jebediah or his friends would kill him."

"You won't bet your income on that statement, my love." Teresa stepped away from him, gesturing angrily. "I've read about such settlements. The ones with the money call the shots, and the others live a great life as long as they don't question the big men's decisions. It's wrong. It's illegal, even without anyone building bombs." She huffed, frustrated. "They play nice to the outside world and are rotten to the core on the inside."

Vernon kissed her shoulder while she cut peppers with the verve of a four-star cook. "You aren't only beautiful, you're smart, too."

"And if these gangsters kill my Thomas, I'll take my bazooka and rough them up."

"And you're aggressive, a trait I admire. Love, *you are amazing*."

Jacklyn invited her girlfriend into the half-empty living room. Most of her belongings were already packed in boxes ready for transport.

"How are you?" Lesley asked after a brief embrace. "You look like someone who's gone too long without sleep and with too much to worry about."

"That sums it up quite nicely. The move is in two days." She sat on the couch and pulled up her feet. "I'm tired of thinking about what's still left to do." She looked around, but the number of boxes hadn't diminished during the last hour, and she hadn't even started emptying the kitchen cabinets. Exhaling, she hung her head.

"Didn't you have help?"

"Jason was great. He sent me a carpenter, a painter, and someone to check the water pipes right away. And they all claimed that they owed Jason a favor."

"So you didn't have to pay." Lesley nodded her appreciation. "Nice. Where's Nicolas?"

"He's gone on an assignment." Jacklyn held the wine glass but didn't drink. She tried without success to keep the longing out of her voice. "I haven't heard a word from him, and I hope every day that he's okay."

"An FBI assignment. Wow. Well, sounds like he's the top dog."

"I didn't want him to take the job, but he's that righteous guy who can't stand back when he's needed." She drank, but as she had learned during the last weeks, alcohol didn't do her any good. Though her pain was numbed for a while, it always returned with a vengeance. "I need to do something, Les. When the move's done, and the pictures are on the walls, I want you—"

"There's always a place for a mistress to live her dreams." Lesley sat up straight and beamed at her. "You can't imagine how happy I am! That's such a great idea! You can come anytime you want. I bet I've got some dresses in the drawer you haven't worn for some time! If you want advertisement, let me know. I can arrange that."

Jacklyn smiled but sadly. "Actually, I don't want a permanent job at your club. You know that. But I can't . . ." She sighed and lowered her head, thinking of Nicolas's firm body and the movement of muscles under his skin. She yearned for the touch of his strong hands like a parched man craves water in the desert. She had watched the video of their fantastic bondage weekend at the cabin, over and over. Her desire for Nicolas had increased with every repetition. "I don't know how long Nicolas will be gone. And that urge . . . I think I'm going crazy."

Lesley tilted her head left and right, pursing her lips. "Well, that, girl, can be helped. I'll just push the young hunks into your dungeon, and you can have fun while thinking of Nicolas and how you'll treat him when he's back."

"*If* he comes back." Jacklyn emptied the glass and put it on the cluttered table. Thinking of the work still on her list made her dizzy. "It's a dangerous job, Les. That's why I didn't want him to leave." She felt an impulse to cry. As long as she was occupied, she could push away thoughts of him being harmed. Her heart beat faster, remembering how weak he had been after a serial killer had kidnapped and hurt him. She didn't want to live through that ordeal again. "He jumped without a net to catch him, and I don't believe a word of that ATF supervisor promising to help him when he needs help." She paused to compose herself. "We know the story. Three families control everything, and their word is law. They're always right and never get punished. It's a small town in a rural area — I looked it up — a nice, friendly place, picture-perfect, so to speak."

"Oh. they have an internet presence?"

"Yes, they do. A lot of great shots of nature. Endless fields, some farms, a small town that provides the inhabitants with everything they need. It's great to look at if you don't know what's behind the façade." She lowered her gaze. "Nicolas didn't say much, but I understood that he can't call for support even if he needs it because it would blow his cover." Her voice sank to a whisper. "And if he needs it, it's too far away. He might get hurt without anyone close by to help him."

Lesley bent to touch Jacklyn's hand and looked her in the eyes. "You know you can count on me. If you want to storm that shitty little town, I'll drive the Hummer and get you there, right through Main Street."

Jacklyn couldn't help but laugh. The idea of her slender friend dressed up in black leather with an arsenal of weapons strapped on while driving toward the marketplace in Florence Town was funny. She knew, though, that Lesley never made hollow promises. If needed, Lesley Gilbert would turn into *Lara Croft* and not give a damn about the consequences.

"Thank you. I really appreciate that."

Lesley turned one of her black curls around her finger, daydreaming. "Gladly. When will you show up? Next week?"

"If you help me move all this stuff? Yes."

Lesley gave her a sly glance. "No, not really, but I know some subs we can drill to do it."

"Wearing nothing but their skin?"

"Oh, you want to draw the neighbors to their windows? Nasty little sister."

"That's what I am."

At noontime, Alexander was sent by Taffner to muck out the pigpen. He had been allowed to change his clothes, but Jebediah insisted on him wearing the leg irons when he left the stall. Taffner didn't argue, obviously cowed by the Turners and in no position to demand anything for the prisoner.

Jebediah sent a vigilante by the name of Ralph to guard Alexander while he worked. The overweight man clearly couldn't run fifty yards to catch an escapee. However, his new-looking rifle was an impressive tool to keep Alexander from trying anything stupid.

The other workers glanced at him but remained at a distance. Their silent rejection intensified Alexander's punishment. He wanted to explain to them that he loved Charlene, that it had been her decision to leave, but the rumors about his *crime* spread faster than he could argue. He knew from different conversations he had overheard, and other incidents on the farm and in town, that neither the Turner's word nor that of a Reese or a Steward descendant was questioned, ever. Whenever Alexander had anticipated opposition, the people found reasons that the family was right, and they went about their businesses. He accepted that a part of this quiet fellowship resulted from the high standing of the families. He couldn't believe that open wrongdoing was tolerated and went unchallenged. He couldn't believe that the inhabitants had made the mutual decision to live under the thumb of the three families without ever acting against them.

Alexander turned around when a truck rolled through the western gate and stopped behind the large guesthouse. He watched four men jump off, but was too far away to see what kind of goods they were unloading. To avoid suspicion, Alexander changed his position one step at a time, shoveled manure into a barrow, and pushed two pigs aside to reach a better observation point. Two men carried a large white sack toward the back entrance, while two other men came out of the house with two wooden boxes. If he had it right, the men were Turner's grandsons and two strangers he had seen around for several days. Alexander propped on the shovel to watch as they all got back in, closed the doors, and drove off.

"Hey! Get back to work, slacker!"

Caught red-handed, Alexander turned around to judge the guard's mood. There was a split second of eye contact, and he knew the man wouldn't give him away. He hastened back to work.

On the way back from the fields to the barracks, Nicolas watched as Alexander shuffled toward the stable. A portly man escorted him with a cattle prod in his belt and a rifle in his hands. Halfway, Alexander turned to glance over his shoulder, and Nicolas read sadness and pain. While he thought about a way to make contact, Abner slapped his shoulder and told him to hurry. It was dinnertime, and he should take a shower before the meals were served.

Nicolas used the time at the table to listen and gather information. The main subject was Alexander's supposed crime, and that no one understood why he had forced himself on Charlene and driven her to leave town. Most of the men knew the waitress and claimed to know that she was Jebediah Turner's girlfriend. A farmhand named Baker mentioned that Jebediah had been furious a few months back when another employee, Milton Roker, had tried to flirt with her.

"Oh, he was out of his mind!" Baker laughed a deep belly laugh and slapped the table. "You know, he's a hothead all day long, but that day he was so furious I thought he'd spit fire. I don't know who told him about this Roker guy and his greedy hands, but, hey, Jebediah would've burned the town to find him."

"Milton left soon afterward," Abner said and made a face so that his wrinkles appeared to deepen. "I bet he couldn't stand Jebediah breathing down his neck every day."

"Yeah, right. Better for him." Baker emptied his plate and his glass. His bearded face sobered as he exchanged glances with the other men around the table, and his voice turned quiet. "Jeb's got his way with people."

"Some of them do." Abner's small eyes switched from one man to the next. "I heard from Gavan that the poker game got out of hand two days ago." He shook his head and tsked. "Michael was so mad about losing, he put his gun on the table prior to the last game." He cackled when the other workers drew in their collective breaths. "Yeah, no one tried to win that game, not even with a royal flush, I bet."

Baker whistled through his teeth. "That's quite an effective way to tip the scale."

"Oh, yes, it is." Abner emptied his glass, squinting at the farmhands. "Well, I'm in a good mood tonight. Does anyone want a drink? I've got a bottle in my drawer, and I'm willing to share."

"Since you ask so nicely," Baker replied with a courteous bow. "I'm willing to accept a glass or two."

The other men laughed, glasses were fetched, and the evening looked much brighter than two minutes prior.

CHAPTER FIVE

The result of the nationwide TV search caused Jason a headache. There had been two hundred calls from neighbors, possible relatives, and other persons claiming knowledge of the three men within four hours after broadcasting. More calls came in after the next morning's short repetition. The agents on duty had taken notes and sent them via email to Matthew and Jason for investigation. Jason figured he'd need an extra night and a bottle of aspirin — or even better a six-pack of his favorite beer — to go through the list of possible clues. He was grateful when Matthew signaled him that they needed to talk.

"We've got a positive ID on the first shooting victim. He goes by the name of Harvey Bronsteen, a runaway from Ohio. On my request, his aunt sent a picture. He left the family farm three years ago. His parents' death was a trauma he couldn't live with. His aunt said he wanted to start over and left. No one has seen him since. He didn't have any address or friends. She said he was a silent boy who loved to see things go up in flames. The only information she had dates five months back. He had told his aunt he was visiting a beautiful small town in Virginia and that he'd found a true friend. He didn't name the town or the friend. The aunt stated she was worried that he'd driven his passion too far and somehow burned himself." Matthew looked up. "That, obviously, was not the case."

"How did he end up in a shallow grave close to Madison?"

Matthew got up to fill his coffee cup.

Jason was grateful the man had brought his own. He

wouldn't have tolerated Matthew using Nicolas's cup if only for a day.

"Now that we know his name — is there anything pinpointing his last location? Where should we start to look?"

"We'll enlarge the search and add his name, see what pops up." Matthew's expression indicated he didn't have a clue how they should solve this riddle.

After another two hours of collecting stones, Nicolas took a break, drank from a water bottle, and walked toward Taffner. The foreman shouted at the wheel loader driver that he was needed elsewhere. The driver nodded, and the big machine rumbled across the field.

"Hey, Taffner!"

The foreman turned around, distrust in his eyes. "Uh, dude, are you telling me you're gonna quit? I thought so."

"Isn't there anything else to do than this shit? I think you're punishing me. I don't know for what, but I don't like it. Name what's bothering you, or gimme another task."

"You don't like the work I give you? Proud little sucker. But, hey, since you ask so nicely, there's a fellow who needs help with the pigpens." He gestured toward the pens, and Nicolas followed him across the yard. "Feel free to join him if you like that better."

Nicolas grimaced, mumbled curses, and put his hands on his hips. Taffner laughed himself silly but kept walking, so he didn't see Nicolas's smile about the easy solution.

After the rainy day, the pigs stood in mud and excrement. Judging by their noises, they were happy as they dug their snouts into the muck. Nicolas smiled, imagining that if Jacklyn could see him right now, she'd laugh all day. The image of his girlfriend dissolved when he glanced at Alexander's pain-filled face.

"Better take off your shoes, pretty city-boy," Taffner shouted. "This'll be a wet and dirty day for you."

Nicolas did his best to look contrite as he snatched the shovel and pushed a cart toward the low fence. "Thanks for the advice."

Taffner laughed heartily, and on the way back to the main path, he waved. "Have fun! Take a slide! You asked for it."

"Yeah, well, I did." Nicolas took off his shoes and rolled up the pants legs. The thick mud looked anything but inviting, and the first minute it was so cold, he thought his toes would freeze.

"Company in the mud?"

Nicolas turned with the same grimace to nod a welcome toward the tall man in leg irons wading through the dirt. He wore knee-length pants and an old long-sleeved shirt but no shoes. His movements were slow, with indications of pain.

"I think I should've kept my mouth shut. I'm Nicolas.

"Alexander. I haven't seen you around. Are you new here?"

"Yep. A farmhand. Thought this would be a nice job, but . . . it's not."

The portly guard outside the fence slapped his leg with a cattle prod. "Start working, bitches!"

"I love Ralph's peaceful manner." Alexander took the shovel after flipping the bird to the guard. "He's a joy to my heart."

Ralph's face turned pink as a pig's skin. His nostrils flared, and he took a step closer to the fence, only to slip in the mud. Nicolas and Alexander laughed as the guard flailed his arms to regain balance.

"You miserable fucker! I'll teach you manners!" Ralph found safe ground three feet away, looking around hastily, but there was no one else to see his clumsiness.

Alexander straightened and lifted his chin. "Well, you'd

have to come in, huh? Be my guest." He shook his head. "It's too bad stupidity isn't painful. He'd scream all day. I can't believe they let men with only two brain cells join the vigilante committee."

"I heard that!" Ralph slapped the cattle prod into his left hand but stayed away from the fence. He obviously saw no way to get into the pen and keep his feet clean.

"You'd better listen." Nicolas lowered his voice as they stood side by side. "He'll wreak his wrath on you later."

"He's putting it on the tab." Alexander shoveled more forcefully. "Besides, it's Tyrone and Jebediah who're trying to settle a score with me. It doesn't matter what I do." He cleared his throat. "What did you do that brought you in the mud?"

"I asked for another job. Taffner didn't take it too well."

Alexander pursed his lips, frowning. "You know that was a bad idea, right? No one fucks with him. He's a Turner lapdog."

"Well, I come from a *galaxy far, far away*, and don't know much about the rules here." Nicolas kept eye contact until he saw the spark of understanding. *"You won't believe your eye,* okay?"

Alexander turned his back to the guard and kept working. Upon his questioning glance, Nicolas mouthed *FBI*. Alexander's eyes widened, and he shook his head while he pushed the full cart toward the dunghill.

They waited until Ralph was tired of watching them work and took a stroll to empty his bladder.

In spite of Ralph's distance, Alexander lowered his voice to a whisper. "Did Vernon send you?"

"Yes. What have you found out so far?"

"What about Charlene? Is she safe?"

"I don't know anything about Charlene. I came here the night you were arrested."

Alexander hung his head. "God, I hope she made it. I can't

stand the idea that Jeb and Ty caught up with her at the next bus station. It's bad enough what they're doing to me, but I couldn't stand her being at those fuckers' mercy." He gathered his wits when Nicolas urged him. "The guesthouse has got a basement. I saw boxes and sacks transported through the tornado doors when I first got here and then more during the last week. I wanted to go searching, but there was a lot of commotion with people coming and going, so I had no chance. Then I was arrested. So it's up to you. The tornado doors aren't locked, but you need a time frame when no one's around to get in there, which is — as I must admit — quite unlikely. They're cautious."

"Why didn't you report your findings to Vernon? He told me you haven't called him for a month."

"The landlines are tapped, and I think I wasn't careful enough when I asked around. Whenever I drove to Belmont, I was followed and interrogated later. It's hard to do anything unnoticed, and I really didn't want to blow my cover."

"Do you know whether they built a bomb?"

"I'm sure of that. Explosives have a certain smell, and I know what I saw. And there was a strange fellow in the compound — Milton — who claimed he'd build a bomb to destroy half of New York. He hung out with Samuel, sometimes with Gabriel. He lived in the guesthouse the whole time. That's not something they grant easily, so he must've had a special connection despite his bad manners toward Charlene." Alexander grimaced. "I'm sure he was the one who used the detonators to build bombs, but then . . . he disappeared."

"What happened?"

"I heard that he had trouble with Jebediah and went away. When I asked more questions, people turned suspicious. So I dropped the subject."

"I can help with that. One of the farmhands said Jebediah went ape when Milton made eyes at Charlene, and that he left to be out of Jebediah's way."

"Okay. But there's more. Milton had a buddy, a guy they called Snakey, and he's gone, too."

"Do you think he went with Milton?"

"Quite possible. They were said to be inseparable. That was almost three months ago." Alexander shook his head. "If Milton knew about building bombs as he claimed, the Turners were delayed in their preparations after he left."

"We've got no proof for that."

"I heard Milton talk. And he talked quite a lot in the beginning. He boasted about his knowledge, and I bet the Turners wouldn't have suffered this guy if it wasn't for his abilities and his willingness to share." He shoveled with more force than before. "Much later, there were four new strangers. I saw the maids deliver food and take out the linens, so they received full service, too. They aren't working on the farm and don't mingle with the rest of us. What does that tell you?"

"They're continuing Milton's work."

"Judging by their looks, they're basically greedy guys with skills. But I've got no proof, not yet." He looked up into the direction of the guesthouse, frowning. "I haven't seen them around, but . . ."

"Do you think they left? Did they have cars parked here?"

"Nick, the compound's huge. They could hide their cars in a distant storage shed and leave through another gate on the eastern side. There's a service path leading back to the main street from there. That's why I didn't order the cavalry immediately. Once the family gets wind of an imminent search, they could take away all the evidence, and no one would know."

"Though it could've proven who's involved in the conspiracy."

"But it wouldn't have brought the Turners to justice, would it?" Alexander stopped to wipe the sweat off his forehead. He stared beyond the pigpen. "Did you meet the goons already? That's Tyrone over there. And he's always one step behind Jeb." He turned to Nicolas. "Never get in trouble with those bastards. You hear me? Never start a quarrel with them, no matter what they do or say. Ralph or the other vigilantes are harmless. They might hit you when they're agitated, but only if they're allowed to do it by the boss—the sheriff, of course. But Jeb's a shithead."

Nicolas took the full barrow to the dunghill, using the time to identify that Jebediah and Tyrone were headed toward the mansion. Jebediah had the gait of a man in charge, looking left and right like he expected his fans to drop to their knees upon his entrance. He wore a gun at his belt, and Nicolas bet he had a knife somewhere, too.

Ralph came back, fastening his pants. Nicolas returned to the cold mud with the company of Alexander and a large drift of pigs, the only ones who relished the situation.

Jason waved a sheet of paper toward Matthew. "We've got another one identified." He confirmed that Sullivan was out for lunch and sat down at his desk. "The man stabbed was identified by his former colleagues. His name's Milton Roker, a former blaster at the Otensky Mining Company in Ohio. When asked, the supervisor said Roker got fired two and a half years ago after using some company-owned dynamite for fun-fishing in the Chesapeake Bay."

Matthew grimaced, and Jason laughed. "Yep, he saw too much *Crocodile Dundee*. Anyway, the supervisor said that Roker had a profound knowledge of several explosives, including C-four. But—and here it comes—the supervisor also said that he expected Roker to be locked up in a nuthouse. He had been unstable, aggressive, and had spoken about bombing away society, with New York as the first target. But the supervisor also said he hadn't appeared to be in any condition to pull this off. At the time of his dismissal, his wife had left him, then he wasn't seen around town anymore."

"So he traveled the country and led a happy life without smashing New York to smithereens until—"

"Until something went wrong, and he ended his life with a knife between his ribs."

"Unstable, hmm? Maybe he decided to blow up someone's home prior to going for the rest of society."

"And the owner learned of it." Jason sighed as he massaged his cramped neck. "We've got to put out another inquiry to find anybody who met him along the way. That's not much."

"Let's hope Nicolas can do better with his job."

"Let's hope Nicolas survives this stupid endeavor and returns home. That's more important than anything else." One glance at Matthew's face made him wish he could take back his words. "I didn't mean—"

"Yes, you did." Matthew stood and grabbed his pack of cigarettes and the lighter. "And you're right. I'll clear the desk the moment he walks through that door. Don't you worry."

Jason watched him leave. "Stupid Jason. Damn, fuck, stupid Jason."

As if on a catwalk, Jacklyn's friend, Lesley, strutted into the dressing room. Her wicked smile and the whip in her hand ruined a part of the stylish impression. She dropped the coil on the low table, then lounged on the couch to open the zippers of her over the knee boots.

"And how was your day?"

Jacklyn slumped onto the second couch and wiggled her naked toes. "Not that bad. The young gun was a fast shooter—or he would've been if I hadn't strictly forbidden him to come for about an eternity. He moaned and groaned and urged me to strike harder. Well, when I did, he screamed. Once. Oh, the collection of gags you have is impressive. My words, not his. He didn't say that much with the rubber between his teeth."

Lesley laughed, discarding her stockings. "He loved it, I know." She took the coke Jacklyn handed her. "Thanks. If you come to my dungeon more often, I'll share my regular customers with you. Most of them don't mind a strict . . . hand." She frowned. "Handling. Treatment. The way we strike their asses and take their money afterward." She pointed at Jacklyn. "By the way, the young gun left a sizeable tip."

"Well . . ." Jacklyn cast down her eyes and played with the can in her hands. "It's a kind offer, and please don't think I wouldn't cherish your generosity —"

"But it's not what you really want." Lesley rolled her eyes and opened the top buttons of her leather corsage. "The move went well, didn't it?"

Jacklyn put the can on the table to take off the tight leather vest she had on. Sighing, she adjusted her bra and took a deep breath.

"Honestly, I feared it would be a disaster. But then you sent so many men . . ." She laughed breathlessly. The memory of eight men in tight jeans carrying her stuff was sweet. When everything had been placed, they had said goodbye with a kiss on her cheek and a request to meet her at the dungeon. "I bet all neighbors stood at their windows and gaped. It was a marvel, really."

"Sounds great."

"You should've been there to take pictures." Jacklyn blew her a kiss. "Thank you."

"You're welcome. Everything is where it should be — including the important part of the furniture?"

"Oh, the spanking bench! You're a nasty girl. Yes, it's

placed where it should be—with a mirror in front of it."

"Now, finally, you've got some space for it." Lesley winked at her. "I'll deliver the rest with my housewarming visit."

"Can't wait for it. But then . . ." Jacklyn's smile lost its shine. "I wished Nicolas was here to celebrate the housewarming with me."

"I know. He'll come back."

"The question is when . . . and I don't know how long I can stand being without him."

"Still no word?"

"No word." Jacklyn sat up and reached for the casual clothes she had draped on the armrest. She changed into jeans and a t-shirt. "I called Jason, I even called this agent from the ATF who assured me that everything was in order, but of course, I don't believe a word." She stopped putting on her sneakers. "What if he's treated badly, and he's like another person when he comes home? What if he's a mental wreck? I'm not good at patience or understanding. I like our relationship as it is, and I don't know whether I can go on if he's not the same man upon his return."

"You've got a depressing view of his work." Lesley stood to search for her clothes and dropped what she wore on the way. "He's a strong character, right? Otherwise, he wouldn't tolerate you being his mistress."

"Funny."

"Not so much. I remember your old lovers. And I mean *old* in the true sense of the meaning. You always had older men around you. One of them was in his late fifties and openly announced his retirement plans. They all knew about bondage and had loved it for many years prior to meeting you. You always played on the safe side. Those guys didn't want anything aside from you being you with a crop and thumbscrews. You dropped the guys if they pushed for anything more, no matter how much money they offered. And now you've fallen in love with a younger man, a thoroughbred, a straight lover with stamina way beyond your imagination."

"Thanks for the summary."

"Don't be grumpy with me." Lesley stood in the altogether, pointing at Jacklyn with her panties. "You're in love, truly, madly in love with this guy. But you pretend there's a distance between him and you. I hear about his dumb decision, his gullibility, and his recklessness as if you are talking in a time warp." She held up a hand to stop Jacklyn's denial. "No, that's true. Believe me. At the same time, you fear for him, then fear even more that he might come under the influence of some shitheads. Get real, sister — even if the mission goes wonky, you won't drop him and move on. You'd be crazy if you did, and I would set you straight." Lesley sighed when Jacklyn remained silent. "You're turning thirty-seven in a few weeks. It's about time that you settle. And he's right for you. He wants you. What more can a guy do for a woman than change his whole lifestyle? Jump off a bridge?"

Jacklyn chuckled, despite her grumpy mood. "I wouldn't tolerate that. I'm afraid of heights and wouldn't dare jump after him."

"Yeah, right." Lesley put on her clothes and reached out for Jacklyn's hand. "Come on, my treat. I need a burrito and a beer. Are you with me?"

"I'm starving."

"That's what I wanted to hear."

Nicolas bought and shared a bottle of whiskey with his mates at the barracks. When most of them were happily asleep, he got up, dressed, and snuck out of the barracks with a flashlight and a set of tools he had kept hidden at the bottom of his bag.

The night was chilly and cloudy, with a chance of rain. During the daytime, he had scoped out the safest route to the guesthouse and now crossed the open space quickly to find shelter under the porch when he heard footsteps approaching. Two guys from the vigilante committee—Donald and Mike—met for a chat and smoke in front of his hiding spot, and he crouched deeper into the shadows. The position was uncomfortable, and his calves cramped, but he couldn't change the situation.

Within two minutes, Nicolas realized the guys weren't the smartest in class, and their interests centered around women, football, and the right choice of beer for a movie night.

"Did you get the job—driving for the Reese family?"

"Yeah, Don, I got it. Man, you don't believe the numbers I read on the paycheck. Really, they're paying a lot. You should try it."

"Me and trucks? No. Some days I've trouble driving my own car. No one would hand me the keys for a truck. But tell me, what do you have to do that's worth so much money?"

"I pick up the cargo in some town, let's say, Blackstone or Madison, and take it to a mine shaft further east. Some guys unload the barrels, and I drive off again. Easy-peasy." Mike hummed his contentment. "My missus at home is thrilled. Finally, we can breathe a little bit easier. She's been looking for a new car for ages."

"And? Will you spend your new fortune on a car?"

"Are you kidding?" Mike laughed. "I'm thinking about really good tickets for the next Redskins game. Be there and not just watch it on TV. And you? Still happy with being a bartender?"

"I wouldn't call it happy, but it's all right. It pays the rent. Mr. Steward is a good boss. Yeah, he's petty sometimes, but if I'm on time, do my work, and don't dawdle too much, he leaves me alone."

Nicolas lowered his head. The description of the bar owner reminded him of his senior agent in charge, Sullivan. He didn't feel a wave of homesickness but wondered whether hiding under a porch in the cold was truly better than facing Sullivan's narrow-mindedness every day. However, when his mind traveled to his beautiful lady waiting at home, he wished the mission was over tomorrow.

Mike and Donald smoked another cigarette, then continued their shift. Slowly, being careful of his cramped muscles, Nicolas crawled into the open and watched the men disappear around a corner. He crept along the guesthouse wall on his hands and knees. He didn't worry about footprints. The weather forecast predicted rain, so by morning, any sign of his adventure would be washed away.

He found the tornado doors, opened one half, and used the small flashlight to light the stairs. Smiling, he entered, avoiding the tripwire on the second step, then noiselessly closed the lid again.

The basement smelled of dry soil, wood, fresh paint, and an intense scent of chemicals that stung in his nostrils. Carefully, Nicolas followed the flashlight beam to avoid stumbling over boxes and canisters. The basement was huge and furnished with rows of shelves and cupboards. Everything the Turners needed to store for later use appeared to have been brought into this basement.

There was a large table to the left, partly covered by papers, boxes, and various tools. Nicolas could distinguish what most of the items were. Still, he paused to examine three different spools of wire, along with some white crumbs and remnants of plastic wrapping. A broken detonator shell lay to the left of one of the spools.

The boxes under the table were empty, aside from more white crumbs. Nicolas didn't find any characteristic blocks of C-4 or any indications that the hoodlums were still building the bombs. He flipped through the papers on the table and was about to unfold a building plan when he heard steps approaching.

Nicolas stopped and switched off the flashlight. In his haste to find evidence, he hadn't memorized the location of the shelves along the walls. He groped in the darkness and found a gap to squeeze in between two, hoping to avoid detection until the last moment. A canister on the shelf slipped and made a hollow sound as it toppled but didn't fall. Nicolas let go of his breath and stayed perfectly still as he waited.

The footsteps stopped, and the tornado door was opened. A man came down, expertly avoiding the tripwire on the steps. He switched on the overhead lights and walked through the aisles, mumbling to himself, repeating some list over and over.

Nicolas held his breath and counted to ten before he moved back toward the table, aware that the nocturnal visitor might return any moment. As fast as he could, Nicolas reached to pull out the building plan but had to sidestep quickly to keep a small book from falling to the floor. He cursed under his breath when the mound of files slipped, too, and hurried to stack them again. He was lifting the top one to look at the contents when the stranger mumbled like a school kid, clicked his tongue, then wandered into the next aisle. Before Nicolas could pull out his cell phone and call up the camera app, there was a loud noise thirty feet into the basement that sounded like something thumped on the ground.

The man cursed. "Shit! Taffner's gonna kill me for that! Ah, fuck!"

A scraping noise followed, and Nicolas got the impression the man was trying to push something that sounded too heavy to handle.

"Damn, that doesn't work," the guy grumbled.

Nicolas listened for sounds outside the basement but

didn't hear anything. Then he tried to determine what the stranger would do next. When the man whined that he couldn't *put the damn barrel back alone,* Nicolas had no choice but to hurry out of the basement before the stranger came back out to call for help.

Hoping that the information he'd gathered would mean something, Nicolas put away his cell phone, left the basement, and quietly closed the door behind him. After checking left and right, he tried to melt into the shadows between the large lampposts illuminating the path to the house. His mouth was dry, and his heartbeat thumped against his ribs. He had no explanation for his presence should a vigilante see him.

"Hey, fella, what're you doin' here?"

Nicolas froze. He was too far away to claim he'd been on his way to the barracks, and yet he had no other clever cover story.

"Turn around, so I can see you."

Nicolas cursed under his breath and turned, swaying like a twig in the wind. "You can see me?" he prattled. "Really, really see me?" He looked around. "I thought I'd be invisible to normal men. Are you a normal man?" Squinting, he smacked his lips, adding a drunken grin. At the same time, he tried to judge the portly vigilante's mood, and whether he'd have a chance to get away without being whacked. He was glad he had stashed his tools in the back of his pants. "You look strange." He pointed at the guy and stuttered, "Al . . . alien."

"I asked what you're doing here." The vigilante shook his head, irritated and obviously annoyed. However, he didn't step closer or level his rifle. "Why did you come here?"

"Where's *here*?" Nicolas looked around wide-eyed as if he hadn't noticed his position. "How did I get here?"

"I can't tell you, man, but you should leave at once. That's private property, okay?"

"Private. Yessssir. Sure. Certainly." Nicolas gave a mock salute, grinning and swaying like a fool. "Very private. Will turn and not come back. Not disturb anybody."

The vigilante's mouth twitched to a smile. "Where did you get that much booze, anyway? Spent the week's pay, huh?"

Behind him, the stranger exited the basement and called out for *Eddy.* The vigilante glanced over his shoulder, but said to Nicolas, "You'd better be sober in the morning, or the chief will have your ass. Now, off you go!"

"Sure. No problem." Nicolas stumbled over his feet, laughed himself silly, and found his way back to the barracks, babbling the whole distance about private quarters, aliens, and that devilish booze that the visitors from outer space had served.

Samuel sipped his brandy as he tried to calm down. He kept an eye out for his father, who was roaming the mansion in order to come up with an epiphany — which mare he'd sell or maybe not. The old man always walked around like a restless spirit when troubled. Whoever he met became a target for his attempts at coming to a decision. He expected helpful insight and didn't accept that his sons and grandchildren had other obligations than helping him solve non-existing problems. It usually came down to praising him for his always wise decisions, if only to get away.

Samuel heard his father on the creaking steps one floor up, mumbling to himself. He sighed when Gabriel approached, and he offered him a glass of brandy.

"No, thanks. Not now." Gabriel listened and apparently decided their father was too far away to hear them talk. "Did you speak with the new guys for the job before they left? Are they up to it? People who know who's in charge, and don't try to hornswoggle us for their own goals? We paid them hard cash, and quite a lot. I really didn't like that the other ones treated us like idiots who'd be lost without their help. I wondered how you could bear them."

"Stop griping about things that can't be changed. I know you didn't like Milton in the first place, but he's no longer a problem, is he?" Samuel wouldn't admit that the same worry had kept him awake for several nights now. "What else do you want?"

"I want to know some details about the men you trust with explosives, for example. I thought that Milton had left finished work, but no—"

"Keep your voice down, damn it! Yes, everything's ready and on its way, and I trust the men we hired. They're experienced, and they claim they did this before. We don't need anyone else for the transport and delivery."

Gabriel's nostrils widened as he voiced his anger. "We wanted this done weeks ago! We can't afford another delay. Gilead—"

"Gilead sweats the moment he wakes up and can't find his pants. Don't say a word to him or—"

"Or he'll wet the pants he can't find?" Gabriel scoffed. "Will he faint when I mention the word *bankruptcy*?" He looked up when Jebediah hurried into the room. "What do *you* want here at this time of night?"

"You look quite agitated," Samuel stated, annoyed at the interruption. Although reluctant to agree with his brother, Gabriel was right about Jebediah's behavior—he was too impetuous. "What's up?"

"I think someone crept into the basement of the guesthouse."

"Do you have proof?"

"No. But Eddy just told me he saw a new farmhand close to the guesthouse—drunk, he said."

"So, he was drunk." Gabriel shook his head and shrugged.

"Hell, these lowlifes get drunk all the time. Leave him be."

"He's right." Samuel felt anger bubble up. "And now that you're here—let me tell you that I'm tired of your escapades. I want you to behave properly and not brawl with every ordinary *schmo*. Do you understand me?"

"I come here to tell you we've got an enemy in the house, and you browbeat me? What the fuck!" Jebediah reached for the bottle of brandy, but Samuel was faster and stopped him with a glare.

Jebediah scoffed. "Fine. No booze, either." He shrugged. "Whatever. You think you're the only one who does what's right?"

Samuel let go of the bottle. "I'm telling you that you've got to lay low after the incident. It was bad for business, and you damn well know that."

Jebediah kept his gaze on the brandy and put his hands in his pockets while he lifted and dropped his shoulders. "Things got out of hand," he said defiantly, but with less vigor than he'd shown earlier. "It wasn't my fault."

Samuel wondered whether killing a man had traumatized his son.

"Killing the guy *was* your fault." Gabriel clenched his fists. "It would've been enough to bash him, tell him his place, keep him in the guesthouse if you had to. But, no, you had to kill him."

Jebediah thrust his chin forward and pressed his lips tight.

Samuel huffed. "I think you understand that you were way out of line. Either behave or—"

"Or *what*?"

Stubbornness was back in Jebediah's eyes, and Samuel got the impression he didn't know his son anymore. He had no idea when his talented, handsome teenager had turned into a rambling adolescent that didn't leave the house unarmed. But then, every man on the Turner premises was armed. He exhaled, frustrated beyond belief.

"Or you'll face the consequences," Gabriel concluded, making eye contact with Samuel. "It might be that you'll be confined to your quarters."

"Oh, really! Try harder."

"What about Alexander?" Samuel demanded to know. He longed for a drink but didn't want to open the bottle while Jebediah was in the room. "Why didn't you let Gordon take him to the town jail?"

"He . . . he misused Charlene. He put ideas into her head, made her run away."

"But it was her decision." Gabriel reached for a glass and poured himself some brandy. "What's the crime?"

"She wouldn't run away on her own! She's in love with *me*." Anger flashed across Jebediah's face. "Alex must've had some leverage against her to make her leave. Maybe she came to him to talk about it."

Gabriel cocked his head. "You're saying she wanted to negotiate?"

"Why not?"

"It doesn't seem likely. Alex has been here for roughly five months, give or take. How could he influence her if you say she's in love with you?"

Jebediah's anger flared even more. "I'm sure he misused her in some way!"

"Do you have any proof?" Samuel asked, tired of the argument. "Did anyone witness anything?"

"Her father saw them together! And he told me that he'd forbidden Charlene to meet with him ever again! He's an outsider, and not good enough for her." Jebediah clenched his jaw so tightly the muscles stood out prominently. "I'm sure Alex forced her to leave. That's what he does. He tries to influence everybody."

Out of the blue, Gabriel laughed. "You're saying you couldn't challenge him to fight with you."

Jebediah's eyes narrowed, but he didn't deny it.

"Well, then . . ." Gabriel raised his glass in a mock salute to Jebediah. "It's time you either charge him or release him."

"He's responsible for Charlene leaving me, and I'll see that he gets punished for it!" Abruptly, Jebediah turned and hurried out of the room.

"He's a handful," Gabriel muttered. "It's annoying that he's turning people against him. And in several cases, against us."

"Yes, sometimes he and his friends run riot." Samuel helped himself to a drink when Gabriel made a face. "What do you want me to say? That our sons aren't peaceful enough to make the Turner family proud and be looked up to at church? You're right. But then we can't afford them being squeamish, right? Not since we started our new business. They do what you and I wouldn't do. Sometimes that comes with a price." Samuel emptied his glass in one gulp. "A heavy price." He longed for another drink or—even better—half a bottle to drown his bad mood in alcohol. "And now I don't want to hear about Jeb and his deeds anymore."

The next morning, Nicolas was shoveling the muck in the pigpen.

"Do you know the best thing I've learned to cherish in this dump?" Alexander asked as he pushed the barrow through the thick mud. "The easy life."

"Is that so?" Nicolas shivered in the cool air and thought about returning to the barracks to fetch a sweater. He spotted a group of vigilantes, but the man who had caught him redhanded the night before wasn't among them.

"Yes. Being a groom. It's a good job. You work with the

horses, learn about their abilities, their characters, their little whims. They recognize you. Their actions differ between the grooms. They know exactly who treats them fairly and who doesn't." He shrugged at Nicolas's incredulous stare. "It's not a job to get rich by, but it's a good and honest job. And you don't get into danger—flying hooves excluded."

"Well, it's not your real job, Alex, is it?"

"Charlene fell in love with me, though I'm not a rich guy. If she wanted a wealthy stud to shower her with gifts, she would've made a different choice."

"That's nice to know, but—"

Alexander stopped with the empty barrow, and honest yearning reflected in his face and his words. "Charlene's a great woman. She isn't a celebrity who wants admiration. She's a human being, honest, caring—a woman to love for life. When I met her and realized she had feelings for me, I suddenly . . ." He sighed heavy-heartedly. "Meeting her was like feeling sunshine on my skin again after years of rain. She's a wonderful woman."

"I hope she'll testify to what she's seen around here."

"If she's got something to say."

Alexander sounded cautious, and Nicolas didn't ask the first question that came to his mind, but he decided to push a little. "She's a waitress."

"She was a waitress. And she's scared."

"As a waitress, she must've seen and heard a lot about what's going on in Florence Town. Bartenders and waitresses are always the best witnesses. They know practically everyone in town."

Alexander lowered his voice to a growl. "I don't want her misused, okay? I told Vernon to keep her safe, not to squeeze her for information."

"Well, you haven't found out much since you got here, have you? I mean, you could've investigated with more—"

He paused when he saw Alexander's hurt expression. "I understand it wasn't your plan to fall in love."

"Right. And you, by the way, haven't done any better so far."

"Point taken." Nicolas didn't mention that Alexander had had months to search the entire compound and half of the town if need be.

"Let's get this done before the chief comes to check on us."

"Any word about how long Jebediah will keep you prisoner here?"

"Not one." Alexander grimaced and doubled over.

Nicolas dropped the shovel to lend Alexander a hand. "Hey! What's wrong?"

Alexander put his hands on his knees, panting. His face reddened, and his eyes bulged. "It's my stomach."

"You need to see a doctor."

"No. It'll be over in a minute. It's just a bout of cramps." He remained in the position until his breathing slowed down to normal. When he straightened, the pain in his eyes was evident. "Don't play nurse, okay? I took some hits the last couple of days. It'll go away."

"Did the vigilantes beat you?"

"Don't think about it." He picked up the shovels and handed one to Nicolas. "Really, don't. I'll make it."

While they worked, a woman of about forty with a fashionable light brown bob left the garden of the mansion through a wooden gate, black binoculars in her hand. She stood in the shadow of a large oak tree dressed like a lady who had just returned from an important company meeting. She wore a cream-colored skirt, a matching jacket, and a dark blue blouse. Her high-heeled shoes were impractical for a relaxing stroll, but she appeared to be perfectly able to walk the soft sandy path until she found a lookout position and lifted the binoculars.

"Do you know her?" Nicolas asked in a quiet tone.

"She's married to the lawyer of the family, Solomon. From what I overheard, Solomon doesn't come here often. He's a fella who loves his work more than anything. I believe he could live without the Turner wealth. Maybe not without the protection, but certainly without financial help." Alexander lifted his gaze cautiously. "She's scrutinizing you."

"That's BS. Why would she do that?"

"That's why she brought the binoculars, dummy. Young, good-looking guy with muscles in all the right places."

"Yeah, and dirt from head to toe." Nicolas shook his head, laughing. "I bet she's amused watching two men playing in the mud."

"We'll see."

CHAPTER SIX

Jason tapped the desk with his fingers while he waited for Agent Freeman to answer his call, eager to get information about Nicolas. The triple murder case from Madison was stuck in the mud, and Sullivan had tasked him and Matthew with other cases, each of them older and considered unsolvable without new evidence. Jason despised checking old information.

Matthew didn't seem bothered. He still spent time investigating the loose ends of the bank robbery he'd worked with Nicolas. He spoke with witnesses, went through files thick as telephone books, and followed every lead on the last bank robber still in hiding. Tom Pinnock, the driver for the gang, had not only testified about the three brothers, who had committed several bank robberies, but also about their sister, Katherine. Matthew had killed Herman, the oldest brother, at a mall, while the younger twins had been arrested and awaited trial. Despite Pinnock's description of the fourth sibling and an intensive search for her on the video footage, Katherine remained undetected. Police and FBI assumed she had left the country for South America.

When Jason asked why he didn't give up on the case, Matthew had explained he needed to stay busy. It helped him forget about his former wife and being stuck in Washington, DC, without a chance to return to Chicago. Matthew claimed his only joy was Bingo, a rescue dog from a shelter, and the reason Matthew tried to leave the office on time.

Every day Jason went home, he couldn't keep his mind off

his best friend's whereabouts and the dangers accompanying Nicolas's current assignment. Jason quarreled with his girl-friend for no good reason, and though Elaine was a patient woman, he knew he'd lose her if he didn't get a grip.

"Agent Freeman," a voice through the phone grabbed his attention.

Startled, Jason stuttered. "Sir, I've been trying to reach you for days. Doesn't your secretary hand you messages?"

"I got them."

Jason waited, but Freeman was obviously a clam. "Fine. You didn't call me back. So my question is still the same. I want to know about the whereabouts of my colleague, Agent Hayes. He's been away for three weeks now, without any —"

"Do you know the *Parkland Grill* overlooking the Poto-mac?" Freeman cut him short.

"Yes." Jason waited for more information.

"I usually have lunch at thirteen hundred." Freeman hung up.

Jason stared at the phone, wondering if he would have to pick out information from Freeman's words the same way one picked his teeth.

Jason sat down at the table opposite to Agent Freeman. The waitress asked for their orders, and when Jason opened his mouth to turn her down, Freeman lifted his hand.

"The trout's really great here. Not to mention they make a very good ribeye steak, if that's more to your liking."

"I didn't come here —"

"I know. Place your order." Freeman smiled at the woman. "The trout, please. And another tonic water."

Jason pursed his lips, ordered the same meal, and the wait-ress left.

"Just two colleagues meeting for lunch, or what? You dodge my calls. You don't give me any information. I don't like this, Agent Freeman."

Freeman folded his arms on the table. "I like your concern for Nicolas. I really appreciate it."

"It doesn't help him that much if I can't do anything for him, right?"

Freeman winced. "So far, I haven't heard from him, but that doesn't mean anything. He has to get acquainted with his new job." Freeman tried and failed to look positive. "It's not unusual for a covert mission."

Jason ran a hand through his hair. "What about the explosives? Any news of their origin?"

"Characteristics show it's US-made but bought with charges that can't be traced back to a certain dealer. We have surveillance tapes of several illegal transactions within the last six months, and we're working on the identification of the customers. Another task force is checking companies with permits to handle C-four. We're checking their suppliers, but that takes time. What about the three dead men?"

"If you read your emails, you'd know that two of them have name tags by now. Milton Roker was a former blaster. We assume he helped the Turners build a bomb, if there is one. The shooting victim is Harvey Bronsteen, a runaway from Ohio. His last information said he was in a small town in Virginia and had met a true friend. We couldn't identify the second young man. I sent you the pictures."

"Where did you find them?"

"In the woods close to Madison, Virginia, buried, but not deep enough. They were found in the same area, but not in the same grave. A search dog in training had a field day. The owner's pretty proud, though he threw up at the crime scene — the owner, not the dog. Which wasn't so pretty, and the medical examiner said some harsh words about it."

"You think the deaths are related?"

"We don't know. Roker and Bronsteen don't have anything

in common, and as long as we can't name the third victim, we don't have anything to go on. My partner assumes Roker could've been the one who was building the bomb for the Turners, but then he was killed, and the project was thrown back. He bases his argument on the fact that the Turners haven't yet detonated a bomb anywhere." Grudgingly, Jason added, "Our boss has handed us other cases. He thinks we can't solve this one."

Freeman pressed his lips together and pondered for a long time. "If I have it right, Madison's not that far from Florence Town. Maybe . . ." He hesitated once more. "I might get you an answer. But there's one condition—you can't talk about this to anyone. Don't reveal your source. Don't share the information with your partner."

"Nick's in a hell hole in Virginia." Jason bristled. "So, yes, I'll keep this to myself. Who's gonna help me?"

Freeman looked him in the eyes. "Thomas accompanied a young woman to the bus station in Belmont so that she could leave town the same night Nicolas got there. She had my number, and I fetched her quicker than she could be followed. She told me that Thomas got into a fight after the bus had departed."

Freeman tried to stop him, but this time Jason was too upset to remain quiet.

"Are you saying you are hiding a witness of a crime? That you've got information about the Turners and their doings? About things going on in Florence Town? Why don't you use this to accuse the Turners and let Nick and your agent return home? What did you do? Help her leave the country?"

"No. Calm down. We wouldn't be sitting here if I wasn't willing to share information. And I don't think she witnessed any crime." Freeman sighed. "Charlene is young, about twenty years old maybe. She was a waitress at the town diner.

I suppose Thomas was like a saint for her, because he promised to take her away from the small town and show her the big world. I don't know if that was the reason she adores him so much. Anyway, she fell in love with him, but then—and here the context is sketchy—she suddenly decided to leave town without him. She doesn't reveal any background, only that she expects Thomas to come through the door any day now. Thomas helped her catch the bus, and she thinks he was punished for doing so. Now she's worried about what happened to him. And this worry is eating her up so much that she acts irrationally. I don't want to upset her further." Freeman sipped his tonic water and looked like a father learning of his only child's car accident. "I want to protect her, Agent Beckham. I want to keep her safe until Thomas comes back."

Jason refused to be touched by the story. "She's an insider. She can probably reveal something about what's going on in the town. And it's worth a try to show her the pictures. If she knew one of the victims, we could go to the town and ask questions."

"All right. I'll see what I can do." Freeman shook his head and stopped with the cutlery in his hands. "I must explain to her why I've got the pictures."

"You didn't reveal that you're with the ATF?"

"No. I don't trust anyone. Charlene might decide tomorrow that she wants to go back and live with Thomas in Florence Town. After all, she's got family there, and they might be friends with members of the *Big Three*. Who knows?" He resumed eating.

"Fine, think of a story, tell her whatever you want." Jason's mood didn't improve. He was still angry that he hadn't known there was a first-class witness. "Agent Freeman, I have three dead bodies found in the woods in Virginia. Their murderer is still around, and it is possible they're linked. It's the right thing to ask this woman what she knows about them.

Maybe she knows their killer, too."

Agent Freeman took his time to answer. "My agent trusted me to keep the young woman safe, and that's what I'm going to do."

Jason held the knife tight in his hand, trying to control his temper. "The young woman is safe, my friend is not."

Freeman glared at him from across the table. "*My* friend's probably in deep trouble, too. So don't think I take this lightly."

Tired and yet determined to get valuable information into the right hands, Nicolas drove his aging car to Belmont. He checked the rearview mirror frequently but couldn't make out any followers. Relieved that his short trip might go unnoticed, he went to the town bank, withdrew some money, and searched for a public phone. He dialed Vernon's number from memory.

"Freeman."

"It's me." Nicolas turned to the wall and lowered his voice. "The packages are on the way, all wrapped up. Nothing's left."

"When?"

"I can't tell, but the men doing the job haven't been around for at least two days."

"Destination?"

"One will be delivered to a company in Silver Spring. Last letters *t-i-c-s*."

"Company with a name ending with *t-i-c-s*. In Silver Spring. Any idea about the kind of company?"

"No." He refrained from calling Freeman *sir* at the last moment. He glanced over his shoulder and spotted several pedestrians walking down the sidewalk, entering and exiting stores, stopping for a chat with others. No one appeared to be part of the vigilantes from Florence Town. "Check the information you got from the drones. They departed in a van, I think."

"No can do. The drone was shot down." Vernon huffed. "There are a lot of people heavily armed in that town."

"Damn it." Nicolas glanced over his shoulder again. He had the feeling he was being watched, and that would be bad. It might be crazy nerves, but he didn't think so. "There were more building plans, at least three, but I couldn't put my hands on them. There wasn't enough time to study them, either, but it's a sure bet there will be at least four targets."

"Any remnants you could seize as evidence?"

"I couldn't take anything with me, if that's what you mean. In case of a trial, it wouldn't suffice as evidence, anyway."

"Go back and try to take pictures, at least. We've got to have something in our hands if we want to nail those bastards. Are you okay?"

"Yes. And Alexander, too . . . in a way. What about Charlene?"

"She's with my wife and me." Vernon sighed. "I hope for her sake that this mission won't take too long. Charlene can't wait to see her boyfriend again."

Nicolas kept to himself how Alexander was being treated. Behind him, two men moved closer, playing with quarters in their hands. Nicolas lowered his voice even more. "I'll see what I can do. By the way, the phones in Florence Town are probably tapped. I'm in Belmont right now, but I don't know whether I can make such a trip regularly. Alex—Thomas claimed that he'd been followed when he drove here. I've got to go."

"I understand. Keep your head up, Nick, and good luck."

"Thank you, sir." He hung up, hanging his head as he realized he had addressed Freeman as if he were his superior.

When Nicolas turned around, the two men he'd spotted

earlier were still there. They looked his way and didn't break eye contact. In their thirties, wearing baseball caps and worker's gear, they had chatted during the time he was on the phone. He didn't like their curiosity and couldn't determine the reason for it.

When he turned and walked away, one of the men went to the phone while the other kept watching him. Without haste, he went down the street and bought two Danishes with apple filling in a bakery. He slipped behind the wheel of his car, hoping it would make it back to Florence Town without more than the few hiccups it had shown so far. He decided to look into the services of the local garage for a thorough checkup — if he needed to escape, the vehicle wouldn't outrun a bicycle.

On the country road between Belmont and Florence Town, Nicolas couldn't shake the notion he was being followed. He ate a Danish and was licking his fingers clean when the sheriff's car overtook him with blue lights and siren wailing. The vehicle swerved into the right lane in front of him, signaling him to stop. Nicolas braked behind the car and waited, his hands on the steering wheel.

Two men exited, neither wearing a uniform but both carrying holstered guns at their belts. The driver was about thirty years old. He wore jeans, boots, and a black leather jacket that looked expensive. He put on a Stetson and a stern face. The man riding shotgun appeared five years older than the driver. His clothing consisted of cowboy boots, tight-fitting jeans, and a checkered, dark red shirt with rolled-up sleeves. Though they looked like working clothes, the quality was much better. He threw away a cigarette stub and blew out the rest of the smoke as he approached Nicolas's car.

Nicolas opened the window. "Anything wrong?"

"Yes," the driver replied. "Would you mind stepping out of the car, please?"

"Yes, I would. You don't look as if you work for the sheriff, but it's his car. And this isn't Florence Town but Belmont. So what's your jurisdiction here, if there's any?"

The driver laughed and turned to the second man. "I told ya, Nate, he's a tough cookie." When he lowered his face to the window again, the amusement was gone from his eyes. "Get out, fucker, or I'll make you." He put his left hand on the butt of his weapon. "My bro has got the same piece already trained on you, and he's a damn good shot."

"He's not lying," Nate said from behind his gun.

Nicolas realized he was about to meet Michael Steward and his brother, Nathaniel, and not just for a friendly chat among neighbors.

"You followed me to Belmont?" he asked as he got out of his car. He tried to put Michael in the line of fire to have a chance for a successful defense but didn't succeed. Nathaniel apparently had military experience in keeping people in check.

"We followed you, all right, but we didn't have to. We've got contacts there, some folk reporting directly to us." Michael slammed the door and pressed Nicolas's chest against the car. "Hands behind your back." His breath smelled of tobacco. "Don't make a fuss."

"You aren't sheriffs!" Nicolas protested the hard grip, but when Nathaniel came around the hood, his gun still trained at him, he stopped resisting. "Are you arresting me? For what? Driving through town?"

Michael pulled handcuffs from his belt. "For snooping around, fucker. You were seen in the restricted area on the Turner premises yesterday. You'll have to answer some questions."

"I don't know about any restricted area. I was totally sloshed yesterday."

Cars passed them by, but none of the drivers seemed interested in the scene. While some regions had people so curious they'd cause accidents just to see what was happening on the shoulder, this town's citizens preferred to look the other way to avoid getting involved.

Nicolas suffered being cuffed. "Now what? Do you take me to town? Show me to the sheriff?" He groaned when Michael twisted his arm behind his back and pushed him toward the sheriff's car. "Make up some more accusations?"

Nathaniel holstered his gun and went on a quick search through Nicolas's pockets. He found and opened his wallet. "One hundred and fifty dollars? That's a lot of money for a lowlife who claims to be flat broke." He helped his brother push Nicolas into the back seat of the sheriff's car, then got behind the wheel while Michael took over driving Nicolas's car. "You bought that car recently. You parted with your girlfriend recently, and you left your hometown recently." He glanced into the rearview mirror. "Makes me wonder. Why did you come here? Just for the fresh air?"

"I tried to get away from trouble."

"Ah!" Nathaniel laughed without humor. "We need to talk about that."

"You've got nothing against me that's worth an arrest. Let me go."

"Not so quick." Nathaniel's eyes narrowed, and Nicolas recognized the man's savagery, as if a cold hand had tightened around his neck.

Samuel joined Gabriel on the porch overlooking the mansion's garden. He handed his brother a glass of iced tea, and they sat for a while in quiet contemplation. Jael was sitting in the shade of the garden, knitting and humming a song. It was a picture full of tranquility.

Samuel enjoyed the quietness of the warm day but knew, by Gabriel's intake of breath, he hadn't come to laze in the peace of the afternoon.

"You didn't say it, but judging by the old Loman's frustration, I assume Charlene got away." Gabriel turned his way. "Could there be trouble ahead?"

"Beyond Jeb running around in circles because his *beloved* is out of reach? No."

"What about the bodies the FBI found? I heard they had a nationwide call for their IDs."

"I know. They identified Snakey, and by now, they know about Milton, too, but that doesn't concern us."

"*Doesn't concern us*?" Gabriel sat up straight, iced tea splashing across his knee. "Damn it! And if they can trace them back to us?"

"Lower your voice!" Samuel shot him an angry glare and checked whether Jael was paying attention to their argument. "If you knew better, why didn't you take care of disposing of the bodies? To answer your question—I was assured that the FBI has only naked bodies without bullets. They could identify two of them, yes, but that's it. Their investigation will lead nowhere."

"Charlene—"

"She saw them around, so what? Even if she tells the FBI that the men were here, we can still claim they left us. Nothing connects us to those bodies."

"We should've sent some vigilantes after her to bring her back."

Samuel changed position to glare directly at Gabriel's angry face. "How? Alex took her to the bus station, and she took off. Yes, supposedly, she took the bus to Richmond, but what could be done? She wouldn't have accompanied anyone back here, and no one could risk her screaming and alarming the police. That would've been more harmful than her leaving town."

Gabriel shook his head, and after a while, said, "Why not get rid of Alex? From what I've heard, he's been sneaking around and watching people like he's collecting information. I don't like that."

Samuel lowered his chin and shrugged his shoulders. "Because our father takes a great fancy to him, claims he's a horse whisperer." He scoffed when Gabriel rolled his eyes. "We can't fire him without risking Father's fury. Additionally, Alexander has got friends here, and even the chief likes him. They might question the accusations Jebediah blurted out like a schoolboy, and they would certainly ask about his whereabouts if we removed him by force. No, we can't get rid of him right now." He sighed. "I thought about him being locked up. For the moment, it's the best solution and gives us time to think. Maybe he'll give up and ask for his dismissal, anyway. A stall in the stable is not the most comfortable abode."

Gabriel set back on the large swing more at ease. "What about our transport?"

"On time and in position. What about your friends from the south?"

"They got their goods, and I got the money. So this time, Gilead should be happy." He lifted his glass. "Here's to hoping the year will provide us with more fortunate deals."

Samuel raised his glass. "I'll drink to that."

Nicolas feared the worst on the ride back to Florence Town and tried in vain to slip out of the handcuffs. He had met criminals in many shades, from acting calmly despite their murderous actions to cruel and agitated on the brink of a nervous breakdown. Nathaniel Steward obviously belonged to the group that enjoyed their acts. Every step of the crime was a feast for him — the more crushing, the better. Even though the man might be able to pass as a normal citizen and behave in his surroundings, there was no denying his brutal streak. He watched Nicolas with the interest of a hunter tracking potential prey, and this ride was merely a prelude for the actions to follow. No doubt both brothers would enjoy a manhunt through the vast woodlands with the prospect of killing the victim in the end.

"What's your job?" Nicolas asked to start a conversation.

Nathaniel's voice was soft yet haunting. "I'm the solution to many puzzles."

"You consider me a puzzle?"

Nathaniel scoffed, smiling. "I consider you the smallest of pieces. No one will truly notice whether you fit your spot or not." One hand on the steering wheel, he lit a cigarette and inhaled deeply. "Where did you get the money?"

"Not your concern."

"I think you're a nasty little dropout with a lot of lies up your sleeve." Nathaniel glanced into the rearview mirror. His small brown eyes held a hard glare. "You tell one story here, one story there, but nothing's real."

"Isn't that what you do? You don't have a job but run around with a gun, drive the sheriff's car, and arrest harmless citizens, who are simply enjoying a sunny afternoon. I still have a Danish in my car I'd like to eat."

"We'll make you talk," Nathaniel said defiantly. "Try to be a smartass, but you'll talk."

"So that's your job then—torturer for the Turner family?"

Nathaniel's eyes narrowed and his mouth pulled into a thin line.

Nicolas plowed on. "They want someone eliminated, and you do the dirty work? For money? For fun? Because you've got nothing else to do?"

"Stop babbling."

"You're the one who removes unpleasant obstacles, huh?

You've got no connection to the victim, so everyone's fine."

Nicolas saw the truth in the man's eyes, and it frightened him to the core. In that moment, he hated that he was right. He was tied up and unarmed, and he didn't know what the next hour held in store for him.

CHAPTER SEVEN

"What did she say?" Jason demanded, pressing the phone against his ear. "Agent Freeman, I'm not the most patient man these days, so why don't you tell me?"

"When I showed her the pictures, she recognized Milton Roker and the third man. It's Gilbert Hanson, twenty-five, a Florence Town resident. He was a truck driver for *Suitable Disposal Solutions* — a Reese company — before he disappeared. Charlene told me that some time ago, Gilbert had suffered a minor accident on one of his runs and had to be treated for an acid burn wound on his right arm."

Jason growled but regained his composure quickly. "So we have a clear reason to investigate in Florence Town."

"You know the people will deny any knowledge, and you don't want to endanger our agents, right?" Freeman sounded cautious.

Jason tapped the desk until Matthew looked up, clearly annoyed. "Yes, I know. That doesn't keep me from pestering them."

"One more thing. Nicolas called me. He's okay, still investigating. He told me that probably four bombs have left the premises. One's heading for Silver Spring, destined for a company ending with the letter *t-i-c-s*. Does that ring a bell?"

"*Cosmetics* comes to my mind, but that's just a shot from the hip. I'll go searching."

"My men are on it, too."

"Anything about the other bombs?"

"No. He didn't have time."

"Thank you." Jason hung up and sat with his elbows on his knees and his hands covering his face. Whatever might happen next, he was beyond relieved that his partner was alive and obviously doing well. Up to that moment, he hadn't realized the depth of his worry. He relished the relief until Matthew softly asked whether there was anything amiss.

"Quite the opposite." Jason let go of his breath and wiped his face. "Matthew, we're gonna take a ride to southern Virginia."

He picked up the phone to deliver the good news to Jacky.

Nicolas looked out the window when Nathaniel stopped the sheriff's car a mile away from the main road near the ruin of an old barn. Green fields surrounded the building, and there was no one in sight. The sun was setting, and the wind had calmed down. Under different circumstances, Nicolas would've considered this a romantic location to take his lover on a dreamy rendezvous. Briefly, he thought of Jacklyn, but then the door was opened, and he looked up into Nathaniel's angry face.

"Get out!"

"And what if I don't? Will you kill me right here and hastily bury me?"

Nathaniel grabbed his upper arm. "I said get out!"

Michael joined them, scrutinizing the surrounding area as if he was expecting an unwanted witness. His fingers twitched nervously as he set his hand on the butt of his gun. "He said he'd come."

"Yeah, he will. You know he's never on time."

Nathaniel dragged Nicolas toward the barn entrance. Inside, the semi-darkness gave the place a mystical touch, enhanced by the last rays of sunshine falling through the holes in the wooden walls. There were remnants of straw and hay still stacked along the walls and on the ground. The ground was covered with sand and the residue of the many animals that probably roamed the neglected space. A flock of birds stirred from their nests and flew away under loud protest.

"You're waiting for the one who calls the shots, huh?" Nicolas asked, looking back toward the parked cars. "Can you close your fly without help?" He could get away if he could get rid of the two brothers quickly and effectively. Though they might be trained in combat, Nicolas bet they had spent the last years terrorizing unarmed civilians.

Michael punched him hard in the stomach. "Shut up!"

Nicolas's knees buckled, and he groaned but managed to remain upright, unwilling to grant his captor an easy success. "I've known losers like you all my life." He sucked in air. "You'll always be just stooges." He grinned, though it cost him.

When Michael swung for another punch, Nicolas side-stepped and kicked him hard enough to force the man to the ground. In a fluid motion, he brought up his knee, and Michael fell backward, screaming in pain with blood gushing from his nose. Immediately, Nicolas turned to kick Nathaniel's midsection before he could pull his gun, but his opponent anticipated the attack and rammed his fist against the side of Nicolas's head.

"Bastard!"

When Nicolas stumbled, Nathaniel pushed his back so hard Nicolas fell prone into the sand, panting, coping with the unexpected pain. His chance to beat his captors had passed, his efforts wasted.

"Get up, bro!" Nathaniel ordered and helped Michael stand. "Are you okay?"

"I will kill that asshole!" He wiped his nose and reached for his handkerchief.

"Not yet." Nathaniel crouched beside Nicolas's head. "So

you've got some fighting skills. Who are you, bastard?"

"A farmhand." Nicolas looked up, trying to determine Nathaniel's next move. His head hurt, and he was dizzy. "So far, I've only mucked pigpens. If you don't believe me, ask the chief. He'll tell you." He tried to get on his feet, but Nathaniel put a boot between his shoulder blades.

"Nah, I'm not convinced." Nathaniel turned his head when Jebediah Turner entered, closely followed by Tyrone, whose high-pitched laughter filled the barn.

"Oh, now lookee here!" Tyrone hooted. "The spy we've been looking for!" Then he noticed Michael's blood-smeared face and scoffed. "Fuck! What happened to you?"

"Not your concern!" Michael turned away to wipe his face, cursing under his breath.

"Pull him up!" Jebediah ordered, and Tyrone was only too eager to execute the command when Nathaniel made room.

Bracing for more maltreatment, Nicolas stood, swaying and feeling light-headed. He eyed the Turner offspring and found the same glee in Tyrone's eyes he had seen in Nathaniel's earlier.

"What were you searching for the other night?" Jebediah pulled his gun and twirled it around his finger like a gunslinger.

"I wasn't searching anything. I was drunk."

Tyrone delivered a punch to Nicolas's midsection, but it lacked the strength to cause harm. Nicolas tensed his abs and breathed through the pain. Without the other men standing by, Nicolas would've bested the lanky youngster within thirty seconds.

"I can't tell you anything else." He stepped backward, out of Tyrone's range. "No! Don't hit me again! Please! I can't even remember where I was! I only know that I was in my bed this morning."

"Eddy said he found you close to the guesthouse. That's

quite a distance from the barracks where you should be at night. Once more — what did you want there?"

"I wandered off." Nicolas shook his head, pretending despair. "Honestly, I don't know what you want from me! I drank too much. I know I shouldn't do that, and I feel lousy. I don't want to lose my job."

Michael scoffed. "He's got more than a hundred bucks on him."

"More than a hundred?" Jebediah stepped closer. "From who? Who pays you, and for what?"

"A friend lent me the money. My car's a total wreck. I need some repairs and can't pay for them. Okay? I didn't lie that I'm broke."

"The car's a piece of shit," Michael confirmed behind his handkerchief. "Won't make it far."

Jebediah's eyes narrowed as he waved his finger *no*, his gaze fixed on Nicolas's face. "I don't believe you. What did you do in Belmont?"

"Fetched the money."

"There's a bank in Florence Town, you moron."

"Really? I didn't know."

"And then you called someone. There's a phone in the barracks. Why didn't you use it?"

"Because I was in Belmont, and I saw the telephone booth."

"Smartass!" Tyrone was about to swing for Nicolas's face, but Jebediah intercepted the move.

"Not his face, dummy. Not yet."

"You don't wanna whack him?" Michael asked, stepping closer to Jebediah. He had stuffed pieces of the handkerchief into his nose, so he sounded nasal. "That was the deal, wasn't it?"

"A deal?" Nicolas asked. "You make a contract to beat up other people? How crazy is that?"

"Shut up!" Nathaniel yelled, pushing Nicolas's shoulder.

Nicolas stumbled over a stack of hay and fell on his butt, glad to be out of range.

Quickly, Tyrone reached to grab him, but Nicolas stopped him with a kick to his thighs. Tyrone stumbled, arms flailing, much to the other men's entertainment.

Nicolas rolled backward and managed to stand up again. His shoulders and arms hurt from wearing the cuffs so long, and he felt like a trapped mouse that the cat would kill sooner than later. He checked the empty space behind him, but there was no use in running. He couldn't outrun the four men, and he wouldn't escape their guns.

Tyrone was after him, but Nathaniel was the one who pushed Nicolas back to where Jebediah waited, impatiently swirling the gun.

"I bet we can use him as a punching bag, but it won't get us anywhere." Jebediah put the gun back in its holster. His eyes narrowed to small slits, his expression one of pure malevolence. "I called Gordon before I left. He'll deliver what I want."

"Let's finish him," Michael hissed, limping closer to Jebediah. "Whatever he saw, it won't matter when he's dead. We've solved other problems — we'll solve this one."

Jebediah smirked, and for a moment, Nicolas assumed the gun would reappear to *finish* Michael, but Jebediah stepped to the side, shaking his head. "I need to know what he did in Belmont. I bet he'll keep telling us he phoned his friend about the money. Right, sucker?"

Nicolas nodded rapidly. "Yes, I thanked him for the money and told him I'll pay it back next month."

"Ah." Jebediah's gaze remained locked on Nicolas. "Do you always call your friends *sir*?"

"He did?" Michael growled.

Jebediah nodded, one eyebrow raised, his gaze still fixed on Nicolas. "There's more to this fucking guy than meets the eye, but . . ." He turned to Michael. "It's like playing hide and seek. I need to know who he called, and why he drove the long way to Belmont when everything he needed is right around the corner."

Michael turned away, obviously frustrated. "Next time you'd better make up your mind more quickly. I'm not your errand boy, you got that?"

Nicolas laughed out loud. "See? I told you you'll always be a stooge for others."

While Jebediah's brows furrowed in confusion, Michael swung around faster than expected and punched Nicolas in the face.

"Damn it!" Jebediah pushed Michael's shoulders. "Don't you ever listen? I need him to talk!"

"He called me dumb!" Michael protested and returned the push. "And I'm not dumb! And if you, prissy boy, treat me like dirt, I won't lift a finger for you anymore. It's much easier working for the Reese family."

Jebediah looked as if he wanted to join Nicolas's argument but checked himself the last moment. "You can whack him another time, okay? Just help me take him to our place. I bet you'll like what I've got in mind."

Nicolas ran his tongue across his bleeding lips. He could hardly believe his luck that the goons would be letting him live a little longer.

An explosion on the twelfth floor of the *Natural Beauty Cosmetics Company* building in Silver Spring, Maryland, destroyed a renovated conference room and claimed the lives of eight managers just finishing their monthly briefing. Pieces of wood and metal shot like missiles through the room, piercing arms, legs, and chests as well as chairs and walls. Three larger pieces shattered the windows, raining shards down to the street below. Four more people, close to the door, were severely injured, and only survived because they were outside of the main blast area.

Colleagues who first arrived at the crime scene stumbled back in horror. It was a young mail delivery trainee who had started working that day that collected his wits enough to call for an ambulance and the police. The young man withstood the stomach-churning sight of injured and dead people and delivered first aid wherever possible. He was clever enough to leave nails and thicker metal chunks in the wounds to avoid further bleeding.

Agent Freeman learned of the explosion and its consequences from the officer-in-charge of the local fire department, fifteen minutes after it occurred. As he readied his team to move out, reports of two more explosions came in, making it hard to set priorities. Freeman decided to hand one case to his colleague, Bert Thompson. He wanted to keep his focus on the attack in Silver Spring because of the information he'd received from Nicolas. He cursed the terrorists for their apt timing. Then cursed even harder when he determined he would need more than the twenty men he could deploy immediately.

The second bomb had detonated in a fertilizer factory west of Gillanburg, leaving three people dead. Freeman contacted the local authorities, who said they had the situation under control. The factory had been completely destroyed due to secondary explosions and the spreading of liquid fertilizer. Firefighters were taking precautions to contain the fires and prevent them from flashing over to other buildings. Thick smoke clouded a radius of a mile around the plant, and nearby residents had been ordered to stay home and keep their windows shut.

The third explosion had taken place in a large research center in Richmond, Virginia, destroying data of sperm donors and the entire inventory of sperm stored at the facility. Five hand-sized bombs had targeted different areas in the building, and the blasts had caused maximal damage to sensitive equipment and electronic devices. The management claimed the destruction also included expensive machines used to freeze and store sperm for transport. The company would be out of business for at least a year if the repairs couldn't be financed quickly. One of the directors had suffered a heart attack learning of the news and was transported to the nearest hospital for treatment. So far, he was the only casualty reported.

Freeman contacted Homeland Security and informed them of what he knew about the bombings. He reviewed the reports again, and shook his head, trying and failing to find a link between the three attacks. On the ride to Silver Spring, he pulled up the information he had about the Turners and their businesses, hoping to find a clear connection. The assaults on the fertilizer factory, the research center, and the cosmetics company didn't make sense.

"Why now?" Freeman mumbled. "Why not a year ago?"

The management for *Natural Beauty Cosmetics Company* claimed they ran their company strictly by natural standards and manufactured products no other competitor brought to the market. They produced cosmetics and cleansers made of organic substances. Their slogan announced customers would *prolong their lives in harmony with nature's resources and live more happily*. Though this looked like an obvious lie, it was no reason to bomb the company out of business.

All three companies had been in business without changing their locations or products for years. Even the research center had been located in Richmond for more than six years.

Freeman checked the background information on the research center Thompson had sent. There was an undeniable increase in dealing with frozen sperm since the nineteen-nineties. Apparently, a homey family was no longer a preference for everyone, and a growing number of women preferred sperm from men they didn't know to conceive perfect babies. In consequence, such centers sold sperm on the open market. Freeman whistled through his teeth, seeing the increase in sales over recent years.

Within five minutes, Freeman collected a list of other research centers dealing with sperm and test-tube fertilization on the east coast. Homeland Security offered a team to inform the centers about the possible threat of a terrorist attack and help establish their precautions.

The company selling liquid fertilizer had steady sales over the years, no criminal record of any kind, and a good standing in southern Virginia. It served the local farmers and was proud of its customer base beyond the state borders. However, the management had changed last year, and the new owners tried to enlarge the company and appeal to wealthier customers by offering specialized products for different soils.

Freeman called Thompson and asked him to check the backgrounds of former employees and competitors.

Pursing his lips, he dug into details once more, knowing he was up for a long week of investigation.

During the ride back to the Turner premises, Nicolas couldn't believe his luck that he hadn't ended his life in a shallow grave beside the barn outside of town. When he was pulled out of the sheriff's car and dragged toward the old stable, he wasn't convinced he'd be cheering his survival for long.

Tyrone had taken a detour with Jebediah's large SUV and arrived a step behind Michael and Nathaniel, out of breath and beaming with glee. "See what I've got!" He waved a piece of leather and metal in his hand like a trophy. "If he doesn't want to talk, he won't—with no one!"

"What's that?" Jebediah asked, irritated, and still cranky.

Nicolas could only assume the young man's day had been bad. He probably hoped his prisoner would break down and whine for forgiveness to make up for anything he'd suffered.

"It's a lockable gag."

Jebediah snatched it from Tyrone's hand. "Where did you find this? It looks spiffy."

"It is. See here . . . It's got a little metal piece that'll press down the tongue. Better than duct tape." Tyrone seesawed, grinning like a fool. "I got it from Lizzy. She's got a lot of that stuff."

The Steward brothers burst out laughing. Nathaniel sobered to ask, "She's hoarding bondage stuff? For who?"

"I don't give a fuck. I know that for the right price, she'll give us other items." Tyrone took back the gag. "Get him to kneel down."

Michael approached with a malevolent expression, but Nicolas was smart enough to obey without being pushed.

Michael grinned. "You're learning."

"Why are you doing this to me?" Nicolas evaded the gag as long as possible. "This is against the law! You're imprisoning me without a reason! I did nothing wrong!"

"Open up!" Tyrone ordered. "Maybe a night with this piece in your mouth will change your mind."

Tyrone didn't possess the strength to force Nicolas, but Michael was willing to lend a hand and stretched Nicolas's head back. Nicolas clenched his teeth against the gag, but Michael slammed his knee against Nicolas's back, and the sudden pain broke his resistance. The gag slipped between Nicolas's teeth, and Tyrone hurried to close the buckle.

"Done. It's locked," Tyrone stated, satisfied. "He can't get rid of it alone."

Nicolas choked on the oval piece of metal that lay on his tongue. A leather strap pressed on the bridge of his nose while another one around his chin kept his mouth shut. Pain from the pressure caused Nicolas's eyes to tear up.

Tyrone laughed like a hyena as he bent to look into Nicolas's eyes. "Oh, this is good. Now you feel what it means to anger my friend." He straightened and turned to Jebediah. "Shall we lock him up in the stall?"

"For now." Jebediah looked down the empty stable aisle in a rage. "Where's Gordon, damn it?"

"Maybe on some sheriff mission." Tyrone pushed Nicolas into the stall and unlocked the handcuffs.

Nicolas immediately inspected his surroundings, searching for any way out.

Tyrone was equally quick. "Yeah, no climbing, Mr. Sportsman. The fence is soldered to the stable walls. There is no escape."

Nicolas swiveled around to smash Tyrone in the face, even if it was a fruitless attack and wouldn't help him escape. But the goon must have sensed his intention and quickly slammed the door and fastened the padlock. Nicolas stepped back, grimacing. He was more than frustrated that he had gotten himself into this situation.

"No witty comeback this time?" Nathaniel teased. "I miss your complaints already." He banged the door and turned to leave. "Hey, Jeb, grab a beer with us? You owe me one — or at least Mike here. He looks like the survivor of a bad tavern brawl."

"Funny," Michael replied, still sounding like he'd been hit by a severe cold.

"I'll wait for Gordon." Jebediah cast a last glare at Nicolas and followed his friends out of the stable. "I'll drop by later."

"By then, you'd better bring your own beer."

Tyrone's laughter resounded through the stable. "If you don't have enough, I bet your father has it on tap."

CHAPTER EIGHT

A lexander despised the sound of the heavy chains between his ankles as he shuffled from the groom's bunkhouse toward the old stable. He had been allowed to shower, shave, and change clothes, guarded by two of Jebediah's most trusted vigilantes the whole time. The only thing worse than feeling the heavy shackles restricting his every move was the sight of his feet in them. Looking at his bare feet locked into the cruel restraints brought home how much of his freedom had been lost. Alexander had never been in captivity before, not as a soldier, and not as an agent. He had accepted the mission in Florence Town, aware he might get hurt. Still, he hadn't anticipated spending his time in captivity as a prisoner of Jebediah's injustice.

Alexander had pondered how he could escape, but somehow Jebediah had anticipated the move. Consequently, Tyrone had instructed Chief Taffner and the men guarding him that he wasn't allowed to walk without leg irons anymore. As he shuffled through the aisle, he dreaded another night in shackles, alone in the darkness of a straw-filled stall with only a single blanket against the cold. He dreamed of his escape but knew he had to plan carefully. Though the vigilantes obeyed Jebediah's orders, he had friends among the grooms, if only he could reach them. And then there was Nicolas. If everything else failed, the FBI agent would assist him, even if it ruined his cover.

Alexander snapped out of his reverie when the guard

pushed him into the stall. He was about to lie down and wallow in misery when he noticed another inmate.

"Nick? What the hell are you doing here?" It took him a moment to figure out that Nicolas couldn't talk. He flinched at the sight of the gag and waited for the guards to leave. "Can I help you get this off?"

Nicolas turned his head, and Alexander saw the lock.

"Why were you arrested, and what the fuck have they done to you? No, forget the questions." He lifted a hand and shook his head. "Dumb idea. Let's do this differently." Alexander chuckled when Nicolas nodded vigorously. "Okay, first of all — was it worth the lockup?"

Nicolas nodded again.

"Okay. Concerning the investigation?"

Another nod.

Alexander grinned. *"There is no gene for the human spirit.* And the Turners caught you red-handed?"

Nicolas shook his head.

"Okay, no, probably not." Alexander made a face. "But you were caught doing something they thought was suspicious? Fine. You wanted to tell Vernon and . . ."

Nicolas widened his eyes and nodded emphatically.

"Ah. You delivered the message but were caught right after. Then someone gave you a beating, and now you can't sit and —"

Alexander chortled when Nicolas turned and pulled down his pants for a short glimpse. When he faced Alexander again, he made the sign for *talking.*

"Well . . . your ass is still in prime condition, but you did a lot of talking? No. Your sign was for *no talking* from now on? Ah, that and . . ."

Nicolas put his palms together.

"You're praying for me to understand? Yes, I'm with you. No, just kidding. Don't kill me over such a cheap joke."

Nicolas tapped his left arm and showed Alexander one finger.

"You've been here for an hour? Okay, so this is your punishment?"

Nicolas moved his head left and right and looked around the stall.

"In a way?"

Nicolas nodded, then grimaced.

"You fear it could get worse?"

Again, Nicolas nodded and huffed in frustration.

"Who brought you here? Jebediah?"

Nicolas lifted four fingers.

"Damn! Jeb sent four men to catch you? They were pretty afraid of your strength, huh?"

Nicolas showed him the abrasions around his wrists.

"I see. The men pointed their guns at you and then cuffed your hands. Okay, Jeb and Tyrone, right? And the other two? From the vigilante committee? No."

Nicolas posed like he was firing a rifle.

"The Steward siblings? Bad company. How do they fit?" Alexander pondered while Nicolas pantomimed more shooting actions. "They shot more people? I supposed that much. But they aren't working alone? Yes, neither appears to have the brightest mind. From the conversations I overheard, I already concluded that the Stewards fidget a lot with their weapons. Who knows how many bodies they've buried?"

Nicolas mimicked spinning a revolver in his hand.

"Yes, they might act like gunslingers. I had thought about investigating in that direction when I heard someone whine about the Stewards and their hunting habits. Could mean anything, though."

Nicolas pointed toward Alexander's stomach.

"Yeah, it's not getting better. I think it's gastritis, and

this . . . accommodation doesn't make it any better. I'll survive. No, I won't go into details, so don't ask. Okay, bad joke. Aside from being gagged with that . . . thing that looks like it hurts, are you okay?"

Nicolas rolled his eyes and exhaled noisily.

"Yeah, I don't like being locked up here, either." Alexander grimaced. "Try to sleep. I'm worn out. I . . . I have to lie down."

Samuel knew it was the wrong time to speak with his father, but seeing Jacob's contentment, and hearing him hum a song upon entering the house, was the last straw. After Gilead had announced the latest numbers of the offshore accounts, the siblings — Jael excluded — were so angered they had no words.

Gabriel had stormed off, as usual, to find peace in the fields. Gilead had sweated so heavily he needed a shower and more than a glass of whiskey to calm down. Samuel merely opened a fresh bottle of his favorite brandy.

He emptied yet another glass, put it down on the table with an audible thud, and approached his father with steps that were no longer stable and lifted a finger. "Before you retire after your hard workday, let me ask you one question."

Jacob looked at Samuel benevolently, a gesture that angered Samuel more than harsh words would have done.

"Now, what do you want to know?"

Samuel narrowed his eyes, gazing into the blue ones of his father. There was no doubt Jacob was the role model for every mayor across the eastern states. He was the incarnation of a man willing to go the extra mile to find a suitable solution for everyone — a King Solomon of modern times. During his campaign, Jacob had sat with the elderly, the ladies from the bingo group, and local moms and dads. All of them had agreed that Jacob Turner would listen to their problems and find ways to solve them. Turner senior had won the election by a landslide.

Samuel felt like retching. "You spend money on your horses, you give money to the poor, you finance the hospital — really stupid moves, if you ask me. Why, for God's sake? Do you think the citizens will kneel at your feet? Is that what you want?"

Jacob just smiled as he smoothed his long white beard. "No, I want to give something back to the people. Our ancestors obtained much of the money we possess illegally. Didn't you know that? They took land and then declared it rightfully theirs, years later, with the help of fellow judges that our forefathers called *friends*. Of course, those *friends* got their share while many simple farmers were robbed of their homes and left with nothing. Their claims were never negotiated." He flung his arms wide. "The wealth we enjoy was built on the poor shoulders of farmers, who lost their possession to our greedy family a century ago. There isn't much I can do to fix the past. But I'll do what's in my power to help now."

"A crusade, huh? Yeah, fine, whatever. It would be great if you spent less on the critters, then. I just saw the bill for some highly decorated broodmare that'll be delivered tomorrow. A hundred and twenty thousand dollars? Seriously?" He didn't wait for an answer. His mouth was dry, so he turned to pour another drink. "It would be fine if you sold yearlings or foals for a good price to counter the cost. But, no, you hoard the animals as if they were rare antiquities."

"You drank too much already, Sam." Jacob's voice was quiet, but laced with anger.

Samuel hated himself for being cowed, but he couldn't deny the sudden pins and needles along his back.

"You don't know what you're talking about anymore." Jacob chose a chair and sat down slowly. "Breeding horses is not like science. You can't calculate exactly. It's more like a feeling. You need to know the right time to part with a foal or a yearling, and the customer needs to be right. All the animals are different—as are the people. They have their own rhythm."

Samuel turned with his full glass in hand. "Rhythm, huh? Our accounts tell me that you'd better sell a tad faster, or we'll run into bankruptcy much sooner than later. There isn't that much of the old Turner wealth left if you get my meaning."

Jacob cocked his head. His expression was sly. "Oh, and that's my fault now? You were born into wealth. You never needed to work hard your entire life. You enjoyed a private school, a fine college, a university of your choice. Now you run the business, I'll give you that. That's very noble. And we've got a banker in the family, the most squeamish man ever born, if you ask me. But look at what you're doing. Your new car, the new stereo, and the many other expenses you had last year don't count? Don't look at me as if I am the only one to blame." He shook his head. "Solomon had the guts to leave the house and say no to my money, but you? Neither Gabriel nor Jael or you turn down a dime if you want something. You just buy what you want or go to expensive restaurants in Richmond to dine with the rich and famous. And only a few months ago, a large amount of money was spent on sacks and boxes with unknown contents, which were quickly stowed in the basement of the guesthouse."

Samuel swallowed and started coughing. "You know?"

Jacob huffed. "You thought I wouldn't notice?" He exhaled a heavy sigh. "Of course I know. I'm an old man. I don't need much sleep. Some nights, I wander through the house like a restless spirit. I hear and see a lot of things."

Samuel didn't know how much his father had put together, and he didn't want to provoke him. "I understand."

Jacob nodded and stood slowly with a soft groan. "I will retire now and think about the brazen brats I brought into this world. Or maybe not." He straightened. "Maybe thinking about another honest mare and her stallion foal will be a much better thought for the night."

Samuel watched his father leave, more worried than before. Hastily, he emptied his glass, but the sting of imminent doom remained.

Nicolas stirred from a restless, uncomfortable slumber when the fluorescent lights came to life. He made it to his feet and saw Jebediah, Tyrone, and a third man in a sheriff's uniform pushing a metal cage on a dolly along the aisle. The uniformed guy didn't look happy, but he refrained from comments until the cage came to rest in front of Nicolas's stall.

"If you had told me what you wanted to do with this, I had—"

"Shut your trap, Gordon!" Tyrone yelled. "It's here, and we're gonna use it. End of story."

Gordon glanced at Nicolas but quickly turned away. "This is a cage that measures fifty by thirty inches. He's more than six feet tall, damn it!"

"The more uncomfortable he'll be, right?" Jebediah growled and forced Gordon back with his stare. "If you don't stop whining, I'll tell your father about the little bunnies you entertain in Madison."

Gordon's face lost its color as he stumbled a step and shook his head vehemently. "You wouldn't."

Jebediah shrugged and ordered Tyrone to unlock the stall. "I would, but only if I have to."

"Bastard."

Footsteps approached from the end of the aisle, and Nathaniel joined them, thumbs in his belt and an expectant grin on his face. "Did I miss anything?"

"Not yet." Jebediah pointed his gun at Nicolas as he spoke to Tyrone. "Are you ready?"

"I'm right here." Tyrone opened the stall door and pushed the metal cage inside.

"Cage him, huh?" Nathaniel clicked his tongue. "That's truly something I hadn't anticipated. Too bad Mike didn't want to come. Looks . . . tight."

"I told ya," Jebediah replied without taking his eyes off Nicolas.

Nicolas moved back against the wall, panting, fearing, and yet already knowing what Jebediah had in mind. His heart pounded against his ribs. He dreaded the man's viciousness and knew he should either escape right now or be doomed. If he misjudged Jebediah's decisiveness, his life would end in this stall.

"Gimme a hand!" Tyrone demanded, and Gordon helped him put the large cage on the ground.

In the other stall, Alexander got up and stood at the fence with a shocked expression. "What's your plan, Jeb? What're you up to?"

"What does it look like?" Tyrone snarled.

Alexander banged the bars. "You can't put him in there! This is torture, you miserable fucker!"

Jebediah pointed his weapon at Alexander's head. "Gimme a reason, asshole, why I shouldn't shoot you right here."

Alexander's eyes widened, and he lifted his hands in defense even though it wouldn't mean anything if Jebediah snapped and pulled the trigger.

"Don't do anything you'll regret later." Jebediah's sneer was pure evil.

Nathaniel nodded in mock appreciation. "You've got another one locked up? Hell, you've been a busy beaver."

"If you shot him in the head, there would be brains all over the place," Tyrone said with a mock shiver.

Jebediah laughed and lowered the gun, pointing a finger at his cousin. "Quite right. What a mess!"

Tyrone joined the laughter. "And he shouldn't mess with you. You've proven what you can do with a knife. What more could you do with—"

"Enough!" Jebediah barked so ferociously, Tyrone's head snapped back. "I don't wanna hear anymore." The gun was back up, this time pointing at Nicolas. "Step into the cage!"

"No!" Alexander rattled the bars. "Jebediah! You can't do that! Gordon, hey! You cannot let them do this! You're with the sheriff's office. Does your father know—"

"Shut up, Alex, or I'll find another gag for you!" Tyrone shouted, then turned to Nicolas. "You! Get in there, or I'll make you!"

"Now this is getting interesting." Nathaniel crossed his arms and leaned against the stall with a grin.

While Alexander still protested, Nicolas stared down the muzzle of the gun, trying to assess whether Jebediah would actually shoot him. Though Tyrone and Nathaniel would cheer Jebediah on, Gordon looked like a crime witness who wanted to be anywhere but in the same room with the criminals. However, Gordon didn't protest or tried to stop Jebediah. Instead, he glanced around nervously.

Jebediah's finger tightened around the trigger. "Get in, or I'll put a bullet in your shoulder, asshole! And then I'll watch you bleed. Do you want that?"

Nicolas shook his head. His heart felt like it was in his throat, but for the life of him, he couldn't take a step in the direction of the cage. It was big enough to transport a large dog but too small for a human being.

"Get in!" Tyrone grabbed for him but wasn't fast enough.

Nicolas got hold of Tyrone's wrist and twisted it hard, forcing the screaming man to the ground before he knocked him out with a jab against his temple. Tyrone dropped, unconscious.

Nathaniel grunted. "Sucker."

"Shithead!" Jebediah hesitated for a second, but then holstered the gun. "Gordon!"

Without a moment's delay, Gordon—who looked strong enough to be a serious opponent—joined Jebediah in the stall.

Nicolas readied for a pit fight. His first goal was to knock out Jebediah, then have time to deal with Gordon.

Jebediah was rash and attacked without control—an easy target for Nicolas's fists. Jebediah crashed against the bars, out for the count. Nicolas turned to Gordon just in time to see the man's oncoming fist, dodged the blow, and punched Gordon's side with all he had. The guy grunted but stood his ground—he had a lot of muscles and fat beneath the shirt.

Gordon's next jab was so fast that all Nicolas saw was a blur before he felt the impact on his cheek and chin. He stumbled but had no room to maneuver. Nathaniel took Jebediah's place, going for Nicolas's stomach with his fist. The hit hurt, and then Gordon swung for yet another punch. Nicolas pulled up his arms to block, but the blow was forceful and broke through his defense. Nicolas's consciousness reeled, and when Nathaniel used the butt of his gun on Nicolas's head, he collapsed, his head throbbing with pain.

Through the pulsing of his blood, he heard angry voices around him. One belonged to a seething Jebediah, the other to Gordon, who argued that he'd never again help Jebediah.

Every breath was agony, and Nicolas felt boneless. He had no strength left to resist Gordon and Nathaniel as they dragged him toward the cage and pushed him in. He didn't make it easy for them, and they cursed him the whole time, but they managed to get him inside and fasten a padlock on the door.

Through a thick fog, Nicolas watched as Tyrone stood on wobbly legs and shuffled out of the stall, assisted by a thin-lipped Jebediah, who groaned when he tried to straighten. Tyrone whined about his painful wrist, then the stall door slammed shut, and the muffled voices ebbed away. Nathaniel whooped with joy, the only one happy with the situation.

"Nick! Nick, hey, buddy! Can you hear me?" Alexander shouted.

Nicolas nodded, but then, as if the one move was too much, he passed out.

CHAPTER NINE

Jason felt like he was riding to the rescue. It wasn't quite true, and — if he was honest — he didn't know whether he would even see Nicolas on their trip to Florence Town. But that hope spiced up the task and made him feel better. He didn't say a word to Matthew — partly because he feared the older agent wouldn't understand his motivation, and partly because it felt childish. Nicolas was a seasoned agent, a man who would fight his way out of every situation. A man who knew about danger and handled it professionally.

At least, Jason had used those and similar words to console Jacklyn on the phone. Even though she kept her head high and pretended not to care, he knew she worried far more than usual when her beloved Nicolas dealt with a case.

"We should start with the diner," Matthew said, pointing toward the glass front on the other side of the street.

Like the other shops in town, *Loman's Diner* was well kept and looked like something from a movie of the sixties. The impression intensified when Jason followed Matthew into the large dining area. Cozy bright red upholstery covered the booths, and a long counter — spick and span — with bar stools took up most of one side.

A red-haired waitress in her forties, with glasses and a bobbing ponytail, approached them with a beaming smile. Her name tag said *Irene*. "What can I do for you, gents?"

Her smile withered when both Jason and Matthew showed their IDs.

"We have some questions concerning guests of this establishment." Jason showed Irene the DMV pictures of the three dead men. "Do you recognize them, miss?"

Irene adjusted her glasses and looked around the half-empty room before she bit her lips and nodded. "Yes, I've seen them around. Roker is the worn-out looking guy, then that's Snakey — I don't know his real name. The last one is Gilbert Hanson, the younger of the Hanson brothers." She looked up. "Why are you here? Are they missing?"

"No, Irene," Jason replied while carefully studying her expression. "They're dead."

"Dead?" Irene put a hand across her mouth, stifling a cry. "But how?"

The cook came through the swinging doors, wiping his hands on a towel. "Is there anything amiss? Irene, what's wrong? Are these guys bothering you?"

"We're with the FBI." Matthew showed his ID once more. "Do you know these men, mister?"

"Duke. Call me Duke. And, yes, I know the Hanson fella. Gilbert, isn't it? The other two? They might've been here, but I don't remember. I don't see all the guests."

"When was the last time Mr. Hanson came in here?"

"I can't say for sure." Irene wiped her eyes with a handkerchief. "But it's been some weeks." She sniffled. "His father said Gilbert would be away for some time, traveling. I remember that he'd always wanted to see the world — go places, you know — but lacked the money. Now he seemed to have it." She shook her head, sobbing louder now, causing other guests to turn their heads. "I thought that he'd come back with a lot of stories from amusement parks or cities he'd seen."

"Gilbert is dead?" a guest asked as he approached the counter. He looked like the survivor of a serious car accident, who couldn't believe he was the only one.

"Yes, sir." Jason turned around. "Did you know him?"

"We all knew him." The man made a face as if it was self-explanatory that the inhabitants were a big family. "Where did you find him?"

"Do you know when he was last seen in town?"

"About the end of February, I guess. He had trouble with his car. Wouldn't start because it was so freakin' cold."

Before Jason had a chance for another question, the man turned around and ran out of the diner.

"I know where he's going," Matthew mumbled. "Damn it."

Jason kept his expression blank. "Irene, do you know who gave Gilbert Hanson money for his journey?"

"No. But his father didn't appear happy. I think he didn't want him to leave. After all, the Hansons have lived here a long time, never went away. He seemed worried what might happen to his son outside of Florence Town." She tried and failed to smile. "You know, we all are like that. We know what we've got here."

"Duke? Anything else about Gilbert Hanson?"

"I know he worked for one of the Reese companies as a driver. That's it. Nice fella. Never started a brawl. He wasn't like some other folk that come here looking for a fight." He snorted and went back to the kitchen.

"The FBI put out a nationwide TV bulletin with the pictures of the victims between April nineteen and April twenty-two. Don't you watch the news here?"

Irene glanced toward the entrance. A group of four men in working gear entered the diner, chatting about the lousy streets and the many potholes on the road to Madison. They chose a booth close to the exit and signaled Irene to come over.

"Cable TV doesn't work properly, and I think it was the time the overhead lines were damaged after a truck accident on route thirty." She shrugged. "It happens." She reached for her notebook and pen.

Jason put his calling card on the counter. "If you remember anything else, please, give us a call."

"You're from Washington?" Irene's eyes widened, and she obviously forgot about the guests. "How is life there? Is it really a big city? Do people get killed there every day?"

"I wouldn't say every day," Matthew replied with his winning smile. "Sometimes, we can save the good guys and arrest the bad ones."

Outside the diner, Jason let go of his breath and pulled out his keys. He jerked when Matthew slapped the file with the victims' pictures on the hood of the vehicle and was astonished when Matthew pushed him back against the car door.

"Hey, how dare you?"

"*How I dare*?" Matthew's face was close to his. "How dare *you* keep back information from me? How did you know about Gilbert Hanson? Who told you?"

Jason headed toward the trunk of the car, aware that Matthew was older, stronger, and in better shape. He didn't want to start a fight with the man. He didn't know how Matthew had figured out he already knew about Gilbert, but it didn't matter now.

"I'm not supposed to share my source. It's enough that we know the name of the victim. That's all that counts."

"Damn you, Jason, you sent me in there blind? You take me into an interrogation without telling me that you already identified the last victim? How long have you known about Hanson?"

Jason thrust out his chin and didn't respond.

Matthew put his hands on his hips.

For a heartbeat, Jason feared he'd get punched in his face, but his colleague turned away abruptly and pulled out his pack of cigarettes. He spoke with one between his lips. "You know, until my wife turned traitor, I was a happy agent in

Chicago. I had friends, I had a great job, and a high rate of success. Within six months, nothing was left, and my boss urged me to change field offices and start over." He faced Jason again, blowing out smoke. His brows were knitted, and he spat the words. "Nicolas treated me fairly. He wasn't looking for a new partner, but he accepted me and how I work. You . . . I'm not so sure. Get in the car. This'll be a long day."

In the cage, Nicolas could only sit or kneel. There was no room to lie down or stretch out his legs. During the night, he had tried shifting his position in every possible direction. No matter what he did, he still couldn't get rid of the muscle cramps in his shoulders and legs, which worsened through the chilly night. He had tried in vain to pull out the gag. His tongue hurt so much that he wanted to cry out but could only moan his misery with saliva dribbling down his chin. He was thirsty and hungry and knew he couldn't withstand Jebediah's viciousness for another day. If there was a way out of this situation by telling the man another lie, he would take it.

To distract himself, Nicolas thought about the last day with Jacklyn before his departure for Virginia. That afternoon, Jacklyn had taken him to bed, showered him with kisses, and caressed his body. He had waited for her to tie him down, but it didn't happen. Though she tried to conceal it, Nicolas had seen the sadness in her eyes, and he loved her more than ever.

Kissing and fondling had led to lovemaking, more intimate and attentive than ever before. Jacklyn had made him turn on his back and smiled when he put his hands on her breasts. More than anything, Nicolas wanted to make her happy, wanted to see joy in her eyes, and wanted her to know that he would be hers forever. He had kissed away her tears and held her close to him. Never before had he felt that deep kind of emotion for a woman. He would do anything for her, even promise her to come back unharmed though he knew it might be a lie.

In the next stall, Alexander stirred when Taffner and a guy from the vigilante committee appeared to fetch him for work. He got up, groaning, then looked in Nicolas's direction.

Alexander grimaced, then turned to Taffner. "Chief, help him, please! He's been in that cage the whole night! That's torture! Do you want to be an accomplice to this crime? Or should I say, to yet another crime Jeb and his goons commit?"

"Shut up and get to work!" the vigilante snapped.

Nicolas couldn't see Taffner's reaction but knew the foreman wouldn't act against Jebediah. He knew Taffner didn't want to lose his job — he might also fear ending up in a similar predicament.

After Alexander was gone, Nicolas listened to the sounds around, hoping that someone would come looking. The staff on the farm switched on the machines, people walked by in the distance, chatting with each other. He hadn't felt so lonely for a long time — abandoned in a way that hurt him both physically and psychologically.

He didn't know how long he would have to suffer in this cage before Jebediah and Tyrone came to release him. He could be waiting for hours without anyone daring to rescue him. The realization that his torment might not end that morning when the minions were up and going about their businesses took his breath away. Once more, he pulled up his knees to gain leverage and pushed on the cage door. Once more, the door resisted.

"Ah, the dog's awake!" Tyrone opened the stall door and swaggered through. "How was your night? Oh, right, you can't tell me."

Jebediah entered the stall, appearing less stressed than the night before, and yet still malevolent. He had a certain smell on him that Nicolas knew but couldn't place, but he knew it wasn't perfume.

"Let's see if he wants to tell us the truth today." Tyrone fumbled with the small padlock on the gag.

The moment the lock was gone, Nicolas pulled out the gag, retching and coughing. His tongue and the roof of his mouth felt numb, and he dreaded the pain that would follow when feeling returned to both. He wanted to swear but couldn't. His tongue lay like lead in his mouth, and even swallowing was difficult.

Jebediah knelt beside the cage and pursed his lips like a scientist observing an interesting specimen. "How did you like being locked up like this? Was it a . . . cleansing experience? Did you think about the meaning of life and whether there's life on other planets?" He chuckled.

Nicolas attempted to curse but could only groan. He rattled the bars, trying to make Jebediah understand he wanted out of this prison.

Jebediah looked up at Tyrone, and the slumbering anger was back in his voice. "You turned him into a slavering vegetable, you dimwit!" He clenched his fists. "Damn it, Ty, what did you do? I wanted to interrogate him, not see him drool all over the floor! Look at him!"

Tyrone shrugged. "I don't know. Guess you have a wait a while. I have no experience with this stuff, just thought it was a cool idea." He swiveled around. "Shit. The old man's coming."

"What?" Jebediah stood so quickly he stumbled toward the door. "What's he doing here?"

"Someone talked," Tyrone whispered. "And I know it wasn't the dog."

From his position in the cage, Nicolas couldn't see the patriarch approach, but he tried to make a sound in his throat, not caring why Jacob Turner had decided to enter the old stable.

"Taffner," Jebediah growled. "That old fart will pay for this."

Jason hung his head as he sat behind the wheel of the car again. The Hansons weren't home. The neighbors reported that a man had come to their house and shouted something about a terrible accident. Five minutes later, Mr. Hanson had left with his wife and his second son in their car. According to the witness, the woman had looked stricken, and Jason knew exactly why.

Matthew's careful question as to where the Hansons might've gone was answered with a shrug and a hint to try the hospital, because Mrs. Hanson had looked *truly terrible*.

"Well, who wouldn't look terrible after receiving such news. Damn it." Matthew stood beside the open passenger door, smoking. "We should've started with the Hansons and avoid this. It should've been our task to deliver the bad news." He stubbed his cigarette and slipped onto the seat, obviously suppressing his anger. "The hospital, then."

"No one at the diner seemed upset about Roker and *Snakey* Bronsteen being dead," Jason stated. "Only Hanson triggered that effect. Why?"

"Because Hanson was a local guy, and the others were from out of town?"

Jason started the engine. "That's one explanation. It might be they weren't the most favorite guys around."

They drove back through town, and Matthew pointed out two men on the sidewalk carrying guns in their holsters. "Looks like the Old West around here. Everyone's armed and proud of it."

"I want to talk with the sheriff later. He should explain how easily they give licenses in this town."

Matthew snorted.

"What? Do you think he won't answer the FBI?"

"I think he'll laugh in your face and claim that everyone's got a right to wear a piece. You just passed by the hospital parking lot."

"Damn!" Jason turned the car around and parked close to the entrance. "Let's see if we can salvage the situation and get some answers about Gilbert Hanson."

"Salvaging the situation sounds good to me," Matthew growled.

His glare sent shivers down Jason's spine.

Nicolas began to hope when Jacob Tuner's face appeared at the stall door and his eyes widened. His expression changed from curious to angry in a heartbeat.

Jacob's voice boomed through the barn, interrupting his grandson's attempt to explain the situation. "Jebediah! Let this man out of this dreadful cage, now!" He turned to Tyrone. "And you will tell my driver to bring my car around! Go, before I tan your hide like I did when you were a kid!"

Tyrone's head vanished, and from the sound of his footsteps, he ran down the aisle.

"Don't tell me he's been in there all night! Jebediah Elmer Clarence Turner, you've got a lot to explain!"

"Grandpa, no, you don't know what he's done!" Jebediah stepped in Jacob's way. "He's a thief, and I need to know what he's stolen!"

"You need your head examined!" He pushed the stall door so wide open that it crashed in its hinges.

"He must've hidden the stuff somewhere!"

Jacob made another threatening step forward. "Open the cage, or I swear you will spend several days locked up in a cell at the sheriff station."

"But—"

"Now!" Jacob seemed to grow in size as his voice rose to its full volume.

In spite of Jebediah's influence on his accomplices, he clearly stood no chance against the patriarch's will. Growling curses about Taffner the miserable traitor, Jebediah opened the cage door and stepped away.

Nicolas turned so he could crawl out on his hands and knees, relieved to be able to move at last. But he was in so much pain he had to pause before he made it out onto the straw. His shoulder muscles were in agony. He couldn't stretch out, but slumped to the ground on his side, groaning. His hope that he would feel better once he left the cage was shattered by cramps that didn't let up. Though he hadn't made it far, the effort left him sweating.

"That was your idea of punishing a thief?" Jacob asked. "I wouldn't mind putting you in there just to contemplate your doings. Don't you dare run away!"

Nicolas lifted his head and saw Jebediah slip out of the stall and hurry down the aisle, sputtering curses. He hoped Taffner would be too far away to be found.

"That was not the last word in that matter!" Jacob shouted out to his grandson. He turned back and tried to crouch but gave up, grimacing. "Oh, the age — my knees. This is a bad way to start the day, believe me." He waited until Nicolas made eye contact. "I apologize for my grandson's behavior. He tends to exaggerate."

Nicolas snorted when words still failed him. Trembling, he waited for his strength to return. His weakness frightened him. If Jebediah returned with more men in tow, he was in no condition to defend himself.

Jacob narrowed his eyes. "I was told you're one of the new farmhands. Well, let's see what I can do about that." He straightened and slowly turned his head. "The cavalry is approaching. I'll take you to the hospital for a checkup. You look like you need it."

The large, black limousine stopped close to Jacob, and the driver got out to help Nicolas stand, then slowly, carefully, guided him toward the back seat of the vehicle. Nicolas hardly felt his legs and feet, and every step was a fight to stay upright. He was lucky the driver was a beefy guy.

Jacob sat on the other side and poured a glass of water. "Here, son, you look like you need it."

Nicolas held the glass with both hands, careful not to spill the contents when the car rolled through the aisle and across the yard toward the street. He drank in small sips and relished the cool liquid in his mouth.

Jacob watched him intently, mumbling to himself, yet refrained from any conversation. It was all the same to Nicolas. He was grateful for his rescue and grateful that Jebediah wasn't around to torment him further. If it wasn't for the mission, he'd have asked Jacob to take him to the nearest bus station to leave this damned town behind for good.

He handed the old man the empty glass.

Luckily, the limousine was fast, and the ride to the hospital only took ten minutes. Obviously, the Turner car was known, so the driver parked right in front of the entrance, then got out and signaled two orderlies to bring a stretcher.

Nicolas marveled at the speed and efficiency of the staff as they helped him lie down. The pain of stretching his legs took his breath away, and he bit down hard to not cry out.

On the way to the ER, one of the orderlies held a conversation with Jacob, who didn't go into detail about the cause of Nicolas's injuries, but demanded that he be taken care of immediately. The Turners would, of course, cover the bill.

Nicolas didn't know why Jacob Turner had shown up at the old stable, but he couldn't imagine a better start to the day.

Jason looked around the lobby of the *Florence Town Medical Center* while Matthew used his charm on the portly nurse at the counter. In accordance with the appearance of the rest of the town, the building was new, or at least recently renovated. The equipment was state of the art, and the hospital employed sufficient staff so that no patient had to wait long. Though it was a small town, there was an impressive list of medical specialists next to the entrance.

He remembered what the waitress had said about how they didn't like to leave town because they knew what they had here. Maybe there was truth to it. It reminded him of a spoiled kid that didn't want to leave his parents' home, where he got everything he needed, no matter his behavior.

Matthew returned and pointed to the right. "Mrs. Hanson suffered a severe shock and is still in treatment, but we can talk with her husband."

When Jason turned his head, he saw a man on a stretcher being taken to the ER. Judging by his size and the blond crew cut, he thought it could be Nicolas and started to head in that direction.

Matthew grabbed his arm and gently but persistently pulled him in the other direction. "You stay here and lead the interrogation," he whispered. "No snooping around, Agent Beckham, or you will get yourself in trouble."

Though Jason knew his partner was right, it galled him that he had to walk the other way. Upon entering the waiting room, he was touched by Mr. Hanson's grief. He appeared to have shrunken on the armchair, his face covered with his calloused hands, and sobbing quietly.

The man wiped his eyes as he looked up. "Can I help you?"

"We're with the FBI." Jason and Matthew showed their IDs. "My condolences for the loss of your son, Mr. Hanson. Though this is a terrible time, we're obliged to ask you some questions, since your son didn't die of a natural cause."

"He was killed? I thought he had an accident. Oh, my God. I knew something was wrong when he didn't call anymore." The man wrung his hands. "How did he die?"

"He was shot." Jason watched Mr. Hanson's reaction carefully, but the grieving father only revealed shock and sadness. "His body was found close to Madison. Do you have any idea whether he was in that area? Do you know of any enemies your son had?"

"Enemies? No. He was a good kid, never got in trouble. Worked hard." Mr. Hanson swallowed and closed his eyes, taking a deep breath. "I don't know where he went after he left our home. He . . . he had so many plans. Do you know when he was killed?"

"In the first week of March. Please, Mr. Hanson, tell us why your son left Florence Town."

Mr. Hanson wiped his brow, then stood and went to the window. "He had an accident on one of his routes close after Christmas — nothing bad, at least that's what he said. But he stood up against the company and told them he had the right to compensation. He got it. Mrs. Reese didn't make a fuss, and Gilbert was happy." He turned around. "Finally, he had money to travel, so he said. He packed his car and left, excited to see the world like a teenager running away from home."

"Did he tell you where he wanted to go to?" Matthew asked as he took down notes.

"Not exactly, but he'd always wanted to see the ocean." Mr. Hanson hesitated.

"Was there anything odd about his departure?"

"Well, he had a thick envelope and blushed when it dropped out of his jacket. I thought such compensation would be paid to his account, but . . . I think he had a stack of bills in there."

"Did he tell you when he'd be back?"

"No, but I urged him to call us once a week, and he said

he'd do it." Mr. Hanson's eyes filled with unshed tears. "He was such a good boy."

A man of about thirty years entered the room, the spitting image of Mr. Hanson, approached and stood behind Mr. Hanson, placing a hand on the older man's shoulder.

"Anything wrong, dad?" the young man asked.

"These are FBI agents. They are investigating your brother's murder."

"Murder?" Mr. Hanson's son stared at Jason and Matthew with a confused expression. "My brother was killed? But he was on a pleasure cruise. He wanted to go to New York, see the east coast. How is it possible? Do you know who did this?"

"We're still investigating," Jason said. "Can you tell us about your brother's activities prior to his departure? As we learned, he left in a rush with a lot of money."

"Yes, he'd dreamed for so long of traveling, he couldn't wait another day. I admit I didn't understand why he wanted to get away so badly. It's a good living here, and he had a well-paying job."

"Do you know any of his friends, who might help us find a connection to his killer?"

"He's got some friends among the drivers, but . . . I couldn't name anyone in particular. He was at home most of the time when he wasn't working. Driving large trucks is a stressful job."

"Do you drive for the Reese Company, too?"

"No, I'm an orderly here. My shift starts in about an hour."

"Do I have it right that he packed a suitcase and took his car?" Matthew asked.

"Sure. I helped him pack." His sudden smile was replaced by sadness. "I'm much better at packing stuff. He drove off and didn't look back. When I think about it, he wasn't as happy as he should've been to finally get away."

"When did he leave?"

"March second."

Jason had a feeling that Gilbert had tried to escape out of town only to be killed the same day. His killer had probably already been waiting for him along the road.

"He should've stayed," Mr. Hanson stated quietly and sobbed again.

CHAPTER TEN

The estate of the Reese family resembled an old English castle. It was a rather ostentatious replica, with gargoyles, little towers, and balustrades, which were pleasant to look at but didn't fit the era. Jason was mesmerized by the demonstration of wealth that surrounded him. When he parked the car and got out, he caught a glimpse of a woman with wavy brown hair standing on a large balcony on the second floor. She had one hand on the banister, the other around a shimmering glass.

Matthew's voice suddenly ripped Jason from the trance he had fallen in.

"Like in the old movies, I know. Let's see how much of an actress she is." Matthew buttoned his jacket and straightened the cuffs of his white dress shirt. "I wouldn't be surprised if she greeted us like Samantha Lord in *High Society*."

Jason, who restricted watching TV to news and football — and a chick flick if Elaine urged him — glared at Matthew, irritated to have been caught off guard. "I'm still thinking about Hanson's car and his belongings. What did the killer do with it? Did he drive it farther away, or deep-six it in a lake?"

"Questions for later. Here comes the lady of the house."

Jason could tell by Matthew's sudden intake of breath that his partner was impressed. And though he didn't want to, Jason found Mrs. Reese's appearance impressive as well. She was in her sixties, of average height, slender, and bore her age well. Her blue skirt and jacket looked tailored to her frame, and though she was at home, she wore classic pumps with a moderate heel. Her blouse was a shade lighter than the jacket, and her jewelry — necklace, ring, and bracelet — matched the colors of her attire. Her face was powdered, her nails polished in a soft rose color, and when she came down the stairs, she put on a smile of greeting.

Jason distrusted people who appeared all too friendly.

He and Matthew introduced themselves, and Mrs. Reese — owner of two companies in her name — invited them into the parlor, which was bigger than his entire apartment. A butler came in and quietly left with the lady's orders for coffee and cake.

Mrs. Reese had a limp she tried to conceal, and Jason would bet she didn't use a crutch out of vanity. She sat down and invited him and Matthew to have a seat on the broad couch on the other side of a marble table.

"What can I do for you, gentlemen? I hope nothing is amiss with my family."

"No, Mrs. Reese. We're here to investigate the death of Gilbert Hanson. He died in the first week of March."

"I remember him." She sounded sympathetic. "He worked as a driver for my company. Very reliable man."

"We were told that Mr. Hanson received compensation for an accidental injury while working for you."

Her smile withered, replaced by caution. "That is correct. He claimed that one of the barrels hadn't been sealed." She waved a hand. "I didn't ask for proof and explained to him that compensation for such a minor injury was highly unusual. After all, the job description reflects the responsibility that comes with the high wages. But I want my employees to give their best. Therefore, I will, of course, in any case, pay for their hospital stay and compensate for the setbacks or rehab measures. It has always been my credo that the employees are like a big family." Her smile was back. "But that much you didn't want to know. To cut a long story short, I paid him ten thousand dollars."

"That is a lot of money for a minor injury," Matthew replied in a honeyed voice.

"Indeed. But I prefer seeing my employees happy rather than annoyed. Mr. Hanson took the money and declared he'd use it for a trip to the east coast. May I ask whether he died on his trip? Did he have an accident?"

"No, he was shot."

"Shot? Victim of a crime, then?" Her eyes widened, and her tone was incredulous. "Because of the money he carried?"

"Why did you pay him cash, Mrs. Reese?"

She lifted her chin and studied Jason and Matthew for a moment. "I asked him, and he said he'd prefer cash because he didn't know whether there would be a bank along his way." She shrugged elegantly and put her palms together. "He might've had other reasons, but they were not my concern."

"I had a look into your financials," Jason said and opened his notebook. "You didn't log the expenses for the compensation on any of your company accounts." He looked up. "Would you mind explaining your procedure?"

"Agent Beckham, if you looked closely, my companies make at least twenty million dollars a year. Each. I didn't log it because I paid him cash from my safe."

She held his stare, and Jason got the impression she considered herself above him because she made ten thousand dollars sound like it was peanuts for her. Besides, she probably had another twenty thousand dollars in a drawer for her butler's daily expenses.

"Which means you paid him privately."

Mrs. Reese parted her palms with a shrug and put them back together. "It was the easiest and the fastest way to settle the claim."

Matthew cocked his head, smiling. "You're saying that Gilbert Hanson had reason to demand compensation and that it would've cost you much more if he had litigated."

For a moment, Mrs. Reese's smile was replaced by the hard expression of a seasoned executive who would bite her competitor's ear off if it helped make a profit. Then the moment was over, and she was back to her former sweetness. "I talked with him and explained that, although he might eventually — and it wasn't a certainty — receive more money as a result of a court order, it would take him years to fight for it."

"A bird in the hand is worth two in the bush?"

"So to speak."

The butler delivered coffee, cake, and small butter cookies that smelled delicious. Against bureau rules, Jason decided to indulge in a snack. He accepted the cup of coffee while Matthew continued the questioning.

"Do you always settle such demands privately?"

Mrs. Reese's eyes narrowed, and she cocked her head slightly. "Don't try to imply that I'm making illegal payments for my company. It's not true. To answer the question behind yours — there haven't been other such claims in the past. The accidents that have occurred in the company have been limited to car accidents with material damage."

Matthew acknowledged the statement with a curt nod. "Did Mr. Hanson threaten you to come back for more? After all, he must've known that ten thousand dollars was nothing for you."

"He accepted the payment and left my office, Agent Montagna. There was nothing more to it."

"Did you fire him?"

"No. I agreed as a part of the compensation that I'd employ him again after his journey, no matter how long he was gone." She simpered. "I can always use a good driver. He didn't need to convince me."

"Didn't you fear he'd uncover, say, sloppy handling of toxic waste within your company?"

"No, not at all. Because there is no sloppy handling." She glared at Matthew with growing anger that showed in her eyes but not in her words. "Everything goes by the book. But I can't guarantee complete and absolute safety, because that's impossible. Accidents happen. It's my duty as the company owner to compensate. That's all."

Matthew asked about where the toxic waste came from and where it was delivered while Jason munched cookies and enjoyed the strong coffee. He had to admit he hadn't had a decent cup of coffee in a long time. If he hadn't been there for the investigation, he'd have stayed until the cookie plate was empty.

"Did you order Gilbert Hanson to be murdered?"

"Pardon?" Mrs. Reese looked shocked, and the folded hands on her lap trembled. "What are you saying?" She gasped. "I told you I consider my employees my family. I'd never . . ." She took a deep breath, pausing for a moment. "Agents, that is a horrible accusation."

"It was a question," Matthew stated in his no-nonsense voice. "If there was a chance that Gilbert Hanson decided to blackmail you, you wouldn't get away with a mere ten thousand dollars. He'd come back for more, and if you refused payment, he could have accused your company in public — either for your company's sloppy handling with toxic material or for silencing him with money. Bad press would harm you, wouldn't it? After all, we were told he likes to travel. With your money, he'd have a chance to see the world, not only places on the east coast."

Her voice sank to a trembling whisper. "It's horrible that you assume I might be so cold-hearted to have such a nice young man killed. It's . . . I don't have words." She swallowed, and her face paled beneath the powder. "Please, get out. If you have more questions, feel free to contact my lawyer, but I . . ." She shook her head and gestured Matthew and Jason to leave. "You don't know . . . This is plainly outrageous."

Jason and Matthew stood next to their car in the driveway.

"You dug into her finances?" Matthew asked as he lit a cigarette. "Really? When?"

Jason opened the driver's door and stopped. He chose his words carefully when he saw anger in Matthew's eyes. "Yes. I pulled files about all the wealthy families living here. It's a money jungle."

"Once again, Jason, didn't you think I was worth sharing the information with? No, don't roll your eyes. You didn't tell me about the Hanson identification, and now I learn that you have files I needed to see, too. What's wrong with you?"

"Agent Freeman sent them."

"Oh, really. It's getting better and better. What else didn't you tell me?" He eyed Jason through the smoke. "You'd better work with me, Jason. I'm not some rookie you can lead by the nose."

When Nicolas opened his eyes, he felt weightless, as if floating through a thick mist in which the surroundings appeared slowly, and objects became visible piece by piece. Even the sounds around him seemed distant. The pain in his limbs and shoulders was dim, lurking under the surface. He turned his head to see the IV needle in his left arm. Someone had exchanged his soiled clothes for a fresh hospital gown and covered his body with a thick blanket. He was still shivering.

He was lying in a single-bed room, surrounded by medical equipment. Beyond the quiet beeping of the heart monitor,

Nicolas heard voices in the corridor and a muted announcement over speakers. He couldn't remember when he had passed out, and his watch lay on the small nightstand he couldn't reach. Slowly, carefully, he moved his tongue around his mouth.

"Getting better," he whispered, then smiled at the first sounds he had made for what felt like forever.

Staring at the landscape painting on the opposite wall, Nicolas pondered how to proceed once he left the hospital. There was a chance that Jebediah would be lurking behind the next corner to attack before Nicolas could reach the barracks to collect his stuff and leave this marvelous town behind. But if he left in a rush, he'd have to admit that his investigation hadn't revealed anything useful. And he wouldn't be able to assist Alexander in any other way beyond freeing him at night and carrying him away. He felt like a loser who ruined his first covert mission within a week. Jacklyn's words came back to him — *Sullivan hopes you won't find out anything or don't come back.*

Jacob Turner entered the room, followed by a doctor, who checked Nicolas's vitals, told him he'd be released that same afternoon, and left, closing the door behind him. As if they had known each other for more than a few minutes, Jacob pulled a chair and sat beside the bed. He folded his hands in his lap, and his look was benevolent.

"The doc's given you a drug to relieve the pain and something to relax your muscles. You should be okay in a few hours."

"Thank you."

"Ah, words at last." Jacob chuckled. "This might be a small town, but we've got good doctors." He looked Nicolas in the eyes for a long time. Finally, he furrowed his thick brows. "I don't know what you did, Nick, and I don't care. If you tried to steal something, there were no indications that you hid it anywhere. Yes, I had your belongings checked. No one found a single dime or anything you took from my family. Whatever accusations Jebediah made, they don't hold up." He cleared his throat, exhaled, and ran a hand through his beard. "I'm glad that Joanne, my daughter-in-law, told me she hadn't seen you around and that I could help you out of your predicament. I don't know whether you're willing to stay after that awful night. If you do, I'll pay you a sizeable compensation for your imprisonment, and employ you as a groom. If not, you're free to pack your belongings and leave." He waited for a reaction, and when Nicolas frowned, he stood and clasped his hands behind his back. "Be that as it may. You don't have to decide right away, just let me know when you do."

"Jebediah won't—"

"Leave my grandson to me." His eyes narrowed, and his voice was suddenly stern. "I will handle him. He won't bother you again, but I tell you this. Don't you dare touch him."

"I did nothing wrong, but he put me in a cage. Where's my compensation for that?"

Jacob growled as he turned toward the door. "I told you, take the money or leave. It's up to you."

"What about Alexander?"

"What about him?" Jacob stopped with his hand on the knob.

"He's been imprisoned by Jebediah for a week. He treats him like a slave."

The old patriarch stroked his beard. His look was adamant, on the verge of anger. "Old Loman told me how Alexander urged Charlene to leave and threatened her with what he'd do to her if she didn't." He shook his head. "She left her parents alone in a time of need. He pays for that crime."

"She wanted to leave."

"You cannot know that. It's not your business, and you'd better not interfere."

"If he committed a crime, why's he not in custody at the

sheriff's office?"

"Don't you listen? You're new here. I'm offering you a chance for a good job and money. Take it." Without waiting for a reply, Jacob left the room, slamming the door behind him.

Nicolas wished for nothing more than to free his fellow agent and leave this town behind. However, as he lay recovering, Nicolas summed up what he had found out so far — there were leads but no proof. He had overheard conversations that might mean something, but nothing beyond a few statements that might connect the Turner or the Reese offspring — even the Steward brothers — to the bombs. By now, the remnants of C-4 and other materials needed to build the bombs would've been removed from the basement. And no one had seen the blasters leave or witnessed them as they placed the bombs. Whole buildings might be damaged, and people could die because he wasn't clever enough to hand Freeman tangible evidence.

Sullivan hopes you won't find out anything or don't come back.

Sighing heavily, Nicolas decided he'd take up the challenge with Jebediah and the old man's offer. Although he didn't have a clue about horses, he would play along.

Jason sat across from Sheriff Alan Reese, a man in his late fifties with a gray crew cut and the bearing of a former soldier. The man obviously expected everyone to respect him as if he were still wearing the military uniform. The sheriff explained he had seen Roker and Snakey — he also didn't know Snakey's real name — in town, and of course, he had known Gilbert Hanson since the young man was born. He didn't know anything about their disappearance or their murderers. He couldn't imagine anyone bearing a grudge against the men and didn't know of any citizens with former convictions who had returned to town to cause trouble. None of the men had been in brawls or part of any criminal activity, as far as he could tell. He couldn't name friends or relatives who might be able to shed light on what the men had been doing or why they'd been killed.

In a tone of voice that made it clear he considered the conversation over, the sheriff declared it wasn't his business to check on all inhabitants and guests from outside, but he'd do all he could to speed the FBI investigation. If he could help with anything, he'd gladly do it. From his stance, Jason knew the sheriff wouldn't lift a finger if it might lead to accusing one of his friends or even relatives. He got the impression that the moment they left the house, the sheriff would be calling everyone in town to warn them of the agents snooping around.

As he drove up the driveway of the Turner estate, Jason's mood hit rock bottom. The main house was as large as that of the Reese family and looked even older. He had learned that the Turners had been the first to settle in Florence Town. If the legend was to be trusted, the town had been named after the wife of the first Turner who built a home in the middle of nowhere. Within three generations, the Turners had piled up wealth with their farm products and later with selling fertile lands to aspiring farmers. The reasons why their income increased so rapidly were sketchy, but no one had ever found the family guilty of under the table dealings. The Turners still owned hundreds of acres of land, which was mostly leased to farmers and other company owners. Their name was known across county borders, and Jason imagined the family would have a good standing wherever they went.

Matthew had called ahead, so they were welcomed into the home right away. The butler asked them to wait for Mr. Solomon Turner, the family lawyer, in one of the large offices on the second floor. Jason exhaled, trying to get a grip on his anger, which was directed at no one in particular. The amount of wealth annoyed him, if only because they had more than they needed, while others lived in poverty.

Solomon Turner's office was as neat and tidy as a man free of sins. The furniture was made of conservative walnut, and the absence of any knickknacks gave the space the aura of aloofness. Shelves along the walls were filled with volumes of judicial books, indicating the office owner had his focus solely on his cases. The view from the window, across the well-tended garden, soothed the senses.

Jason stood in the center of the room, looking around and disliking that Turner was keeping Matthew and him waiting. He assumed the lawyer wanted to demonstrate how busy he was, and that he couldn't afford time to talk with the FBI. Jason decided to browbeat the man for disregarding the importance of the visit, but when the lawyer entered the office, Jason found it difficult to keep a straight face.

Solomon Turner — a man with a spotless reputation and an excellent diploma — wore his brown toupee slightly off-center, ruining the effect of the rest of his appearance in a tailored suit, expensive shirt, and tie. In spite of his polite greeting and invitation to sit opposite his massive desk, Jason didn't know where to look and what to say.

Matthew handed the photographs of Milton Roker, Harvey Bronsteen, and Gilbert Hanson across the desk. His voice was down to business. "As you might've heard in the news, the FBI is searching for the murderer of these men. They were found in the woods close to Madison, Virginia, on March tenth. Can you tell us anything about them?"

"No." Solomon looked up and pushed the pictures back across the desk. He shrugged as if the matter was solved. "I'm the lawyer of the Turner family and not a permanent resident. I have a law firm in Richmond."

"So you don't live here." Jason smiled amiably, staring into the lawyer's blue eyes behind his black-rimmed glasses. "I'm sure — in this case — you won't mind if we talk with other members of the family who can tell us about them."

"Then why —" He glanced at the door and hummed with a nod and a frown. "The family's very busy at the moment."

"We assume Mr. Roker lived on the premises, at least for a while." Jason put away the pictures. "So it's necessary that we talk with all members of your family who might've seen him or talked with him. The same goes for Mr. Bronsteen."

Solomon didn't twitch or show any sign of unrest. His eyes narrowed. "There is no evidence that connects our family to the crime, so I don't see the relevance of —"

"If you don't ask your brothers and sister as well as your father to show up in this room right away, my partner and I will spend the day on your premises and interrogate them where we find them. And we'll need to talk to the staff as well."

Solomon grumbled under his breath about the obtrusive practice of the investigation and made a few calls, explaining that the FBI insisted on speaking to every family member. Still angry, he sat back and steepled his fingers. "They'll be here in a few minutes. As you'll understand, I'll be present throughout your interrogation."

"Is there a reason, Mr. Turner? Do you think one of your siblings committed a crime?" Matthew almost managed to leave the sarcasm out of his voice.

"No, I don't." Solomon asserted. "However, experience shows that the police tend to be rash when it comes to blaming innocent citizens of capital crimes."

"You have experience with the police investigating the doings of the Turner family?"

"I didn't say that."

"Once again. Do you have reason to believe that one of

your family members might've committed a crime?"

"Of course not." Solomon squirmed on his seat. The corners of his mouth twitched, and sweat suddenly beaded his brow. "You can ask who you want — the Turners are the foundation of this town." He nodded emphatically. "Hard-working men and women who do a lot for the people. My father is mayor of Florence Town, as you surely know. He won the last election with a large majority."

"I did know." Matthew cocked his head, making direct eye contact with Solomon. "However, my experience shows that wealth tends to corrupt people. And corruption leads to crime."

Solomon didn't have to respond, because Jacob Turner entered the room, filling it with his presence. Jason watched as Solomon turned from stern lawyer to obedient son in a heartbeat. He hastily stood and introduced the agents, then allocated his office chair to his father.

Jacob looked at Solomon with mild amusement. "Get that thing on your head examined. It tries to wander off."

Jason had a hard time holding back a laugh when Solomon blushed and hurried out of the room.

"Agent Freeman? We've got something for you."

"I need some good news," Freeman mumbled as he treaded his way through the debris at the Silver Spring bombing site. One of his men knelt beside the remnants of the mahogany table. "What's up?"

"I secured some small remnants of the C-four used. The rest is ash and won't suffice for any identification. The detonator's a standard industrial issue, nothing hand made. If you've got an intact one, you can compare it to this. Sorry, boss, but that's all I can tell you."

Freeman nodded. "Now we can compare your findings to

the ones we got off the dead man in Madison and see whether they match." He straightened and surveyed the blast scene. Though he had been on his job for thirteen years, he was still shocked by the outburst of terror criminals evoked. He couldn't imagine anyone being so driven by malevolence to murder innocent people.

Outside the destruction area, he called the FBI bureau and promised Agent Miller from the CSU, who took the call, to send the evidence to his laboratory for examination. Both agreed on their hope that the attacks would stop.

Jason sat back and observed Jacob Turner as he settled in behind the desk. The man acted like he didn't have a care in the world.

"Excuse Solomon — the lawyer is an overzealous bureaucrat." Jacob rocked the chair, still smiling. "What can I do for you, agents? Besides offering you a tour through town. I'm the mayor, so I might show you some treasures you haven't seen so far."

"A kind offer, but we have to decline," Matthew said and offered a diplomatic smile in return. "We learned that Mr. Roker and Mr. Bronsteen were guests of the house before they disappeared, only to show up as dead bodies in the woods close to Madison. They were murdered in cold blood."

Jason considered his partner's approach bold but knew Matthew had his way of provoking people.

Jacob frowned, but didn't appear offended, shocked, or sad. "Mr. Roker — that haggard guy with a mouth that never stood still, right?"

Jason provided the photographs once more.

"Yeah, right, the chatterbox. And the other one . . . Oh, you mean Snakey or Snake-eye. Yes, I've seen them both around from time to time. They looked to me as if one couldn't walk without the other — if you get my meaning." Jacob wiggled his brows, then shrugged. "Not my friends, not my guests. How were the men murdered? When?"

"When did you see them the last time?" Matthew asked.

Jacob Turner leaned forward and consulted the calendar on the desk. He took his time turning back the pages while he was mumbling to himself. "In January, I think." He looked up. "Forgive an old man. I'm not fast, and I can't see as good as I did when I was young. And then there's the arthritis that's bothering me. But I'm rambling. Excuse me. What else do you want to know?"

"What were these men doing on the premises?"

"I don't have the slightest idea. As I already said, I didn't have anything to do with them. I breed horses. I spend my days at the stables and out in the corrals, watching the mares and the foals. I've got some very promising stallions, too. You must always know which stallion fits a mare and hope for the best — concerning the foals, I mean. You know horse breeding is not a science, it's more a feeling." He rubbed his fingers against the thumbs. "You need to know them intimately before you decide which horse is right for a customer. I've got a lot of requests, but I don't sell to everyone." He sat back again and folded his hands on his belly. He was the convincing image of Santa Clause waiting for a child to have a seat on his lap. "Are you riding in your spare time, agents? It's a wonderful hobby."

"Where were the two men accommodated? Here? In your house?" Jason asked.

"My God, no." Jacob scoffed. "We've got a guesthouse, Agent Beckham. We like our privacy as a family very much, and I wouldn't tolerate strangers roaming this building my ancestors erected. It's two hundred years old." He looked around and sighed. "Solomon used to practice law in this office. I think it's a pity he left to make big money in Richmond.

His wife's most unhappy about this." He tsked as he made a face. "Joanne deserves more than a husband who appears on fewer occasions every year. Don't you agree? I suppose you're married, both of you?"

"Does it happen often that you allow guests to stay in the guesthouse as long as they want?"

"It happens, yes. We are generous when it comes to that, and we all have friends, haven't we?"

"Your entire family lives here, on the premises?" Matthew asked.

Jacob's expression turned sly. "The manor has fifty-five rooms, three kitchens, bathrooms — I don't know how many — and many other features you dream about. There's enough room for sons and daughters, daughters-in-law, and a bunch of kids." He continued rocking the chair. "To answer your question — yes, most members of my family live here, Solomon excluded, of course."

"Have you noticed anything unusual on your premises — like trucks and vans coming or leaving? Strangers visiting? Unusual activities at night?"

Jacob laughed out loud. "You really think that I run around day and night and watch like a hawk? Seriously, agents, I'm an old man. I've got security staff that deal with intruders if there are any. I'm not one to carry a rifle and shoot buckshot at strangers' asses." He wiggled his brows again. "Though on some occasions, it might be helpful."

"There are a lot of people carrying guns in this town," Jason said quietly.

"Yeah, that's right." Jacob nodded, still behaving as if the FBI had come to entertain him. "I stand for liberal rights to carry a firearm. It's in the constitution, and it has never harmed anyone who didn't deserve it." He lifted a hand to stop Jason's objection. "Yes, there are several handguns registered to my family members. You can see their licenses if you have to and the weapons, ammunition, and whatever else. But they're for self-defense only. Never shot a soul around here. It's a peaceful town, agents, and you won't find proof of anything else."

Matthew raised his brows. "The deaths of Roker and Bronsteen and also of the young Hanson speak a different language, sir."

Jacob huffed but didn't argue.

CHAPTER ELEVEN

Jason sat with his elbows on his knees, reviewing his notes on the Turner interviews so far.

Gilead Turner had appeared nervous throughout the interview and had started sweating when asked about any knowledge of the murders. He had denied involvement, but Jason made a note to check the man's background.

Jael Turner had been calm and soft-spoken, claiming she saw strangers on the premises every day, but then all the workers, farmhands, and grooms were strangers to her. She hadn't known Roker or Snakey and despised the idea that she could've been in contact with one of them. Her bearing had indicated that she considered strangers to be bacteria-carrying extraterrestrials she avoided at all costs. She spent her days teaching at the elementary school, doing housework, or playing with her nieces and nephews. She had a grown son, but he was handicapped and couldn't participate in the happy family life. Before she could break into tears, Matthew had declared the interrogation over.

Two of the grandsons of the family were either indifferent or angry at being accused of having anything to do with a crime. Tyrone Turner had tried to weasel himself out of the interrogation, made fun of the questions, and appeared as serious as a clown on drugs. Jebediah had been down to business, quiet, and reluctant to speak about his position on the farm. It became clear as glass that both young men had nothing to do but fill their days with games and driving around town. Matthew had agreed when Jason concluded that Tyrone and Jebediah were scalawags with a tendency to stir up trouble. In spite of their behavior, they had made no mistakes during the interrogation that would link them to the crimes.

Matthew leaned back on the armchair, groaning. "This is frustrating."

"I agree with that."

The next person on their list, Samuel Turner, took off his muck-soiled boots in front of the carpeted room and entered on socks, a broad grin on his face. Though the shoes stayed by the doorway, Jason still detected an overwhelming stench of mud and animal excrement. He wished he could leave or at least sit by an open window.

"This is going nowhere," Matthew mumbled and wiped his face while Jason sipped the cold water a close-lipped butler had delivered. "We should come back with our guys from the CSU and have this place turned upside down."

"I wish you luck getting a court order for that."

Matthew fell silent as Samuel crossed the room to stand behind the desk.

"I sold a bunch of pigs this morning," Samuel declared happily and wiped his face with the back of his hand, leaving smears of dirt. His flannel shirt carried stains of mud as well, not to mention his dark brown cords. "The Black family from next town want to breed — pigs, I mean — and they needed a good start." He put his hat on the desk, looked at his dirty hands, and laughed. "Sorry, gents, my brother's call sounded urgent, so I didn't take time to shower." He used a handkerchief to wipe off the dirt. "I hope you don't mind." He stood behind the office chair like a hard-working man who could hardly afford to leave the barn for a chat and a meal. "Now that Gabriel's on a business trip, catching pigs is part of my daily duties."

Matthew asked the same list of questions, and Samuel

pursed his lips and nodded to every one of them.

"Yep, Milton is . . . was a friend of mine." He paused as if realizing that mourning his dead friend was required. "We met way back. He was from around here but then became a blaster in Ohio. I don't know what he wanted there, but, hey, it's life, huh? When he lost his job, he asked me whether he could stay with us until he found a new one."

Jason consulted his notes about Roker and checked the small map with the settlements close to Florence Town. Samuel was right, and Jason was angry with himself that he had overlooked the detail of where Roker was born.

"He lost his job two and a half years ago. Did he live here all that time?"

"My God, no. He came to town in November last year."

"So you let him stay here. What did he do? How did he spend his time?"

Samuel cracked his neck left and right and scratched his head, groaning. "Reading, I guess. Or filling out job applications. He went out from time to time. I don't know exactly where he went—maybe he had interviews for a new job." He unscrewed a water bottle and drank. "We met occasionally, but he didn't have to tell me how he spent his days. As you see, I've got a full-time job running the family business. I wasn't with him all the time."

"You knew that he was a former blaster, a man working with explosives?"

"Yes, certainly. He told me about it and how he was fired— pardon the pun. People said he was unstable, but I don't think so. He was troubled, yes, but his new friend was good for him." Samuel made a face. "I admit I wouldn't have allowed Snakey to stay if it wasn't for Milton's sake. He brought him here because neither of them could afford Snakey living at a motel." He sniffled and set down the bottle. "Anything else?"

"Did they argue with anyone on your staff or in your family?" Matthew asked. "As we learned, he boasted about destroying New York with a bomb. Did you know about that?"

"He was angry that he lost his job. He had a hard time after that. He had burned his fingers in an accident but didn't want to go into detail about that. But a bomb to destroy New York? Never heard of it."

"Did anyone have a reason to kill Roker or Bronsteen?"

"Kill them? No. Milton was loud, he tended to argue a lot, but if you got to know him better, he was a great guy." Samuel paused with a sad look on his face before he said, "I really liked him. He was a fine guy."

"With whom did he argue?"

"I can't remember. Maybe some of the farmhands, the house staff . . . I don't know."

"And about what?"

"Jobs, the future, his political position. He had an opinion about everything and enough time to read every bit of news." He shrugged and gestured with his hands. "That opens the door to a lot of arguments."

"And his companion?"

"Snakey didn't say much. He was clever, though, and I wondered why he had no job. Milton told me that Snakey had lost his parents and somehow lost his balance in life. He wasn't able to . . . function in a company, no matter which one. He was happy to hang around with Milton."

"Did they have money to pay for daily expenses?"

Samuel's mood darkened, and he shook his head. "No, not really. I helped with meals and with some money for clothes, but they didn't want much."

"Why did they leave the premises? Or didn't they, and their belongings are still here?"

"No, they packed up and left. Milton said he wouldn't exploit my hospitality, and I respected that. When he took off,

Snakey went with him. That was at the end of January. I haven't seen them since." He sighed deeply. "Now I know why."

"You don't appear overly shocked by the news," Matthew said.

"Forgive me, Agent Montagna, but I'm a man used to dealing with unpleasant news. I don't tend to break into tears easily."

Jason interjected. "If you don't mind, I'd like to see the guesthouse."

"I don't mind at all." Samuel put his hat back on and slipped into his boots as they left the room. "Please, follow me."

Jason despised the onslaught of mud stench and the man's peculiar officiousness, and he could tell from Matthew's expression that he felt the same way.

When the time had come for Nicolas to leave the hospital, Jacob Turner's driver—obviously butler and organizer, too—delivered fresh clothes. Then without any explanation, he handed him the wallet he had lost to the Steward brothers. Without answering the questions at hand, the driver left with the advice to call the manor should he need a ride back to the premises. The calling card was already on the nightstand.

Nicolas shook his head and was about to get dressed when a nurse of about twenty years entered his room. She was smiling like a teenager who was sent to deliver a basket with cookies to the slightly weird neighbor.

"Do you have a moment?" she asked and closed the door. "I'm Crystal, and I work here, and I . . . would like to make you an offer." She blushed deeply but continued. "It's not my offer, it's more like an offer the hospital makes." She handed him the clipboard she had pressed against her tiny bosom, desperately trying not to look at his bare chest. "If you don't mind . . ."

Nicolas dropped the t-shirt to the side, trying not to smile at the girl's reaction, and read about the *Florence Research Center*, and that they offered good money to sperm donors. The form claimed it was an *easy procedure and healthy for men of all ages*.

He gave it back with an apologetic smile. "No, thanks, I'm not interested."

Crystal's light brown eyes lost their shine. She bit her lower lip, holding the clipboard halfway between them. "Are you sure? I mean, many men do it. It's . . . um, healthy, you know? After all, a part of the clinic here is financed by the research center's profits."

"I read that, too, and, no, I'm not interested."

"You don't need money? I mean, you look like . . ." She broke off, blushing more deeply.

"I look like I need money? Maybe, yes, but not like this." He put on his t-shirt and pants, and Crystal stood beside the bed, seesawing. "Is there anything else I can help you with?"

"No."

Nicolas saw uneasiness in her eyes. "Ah, I see. The doctor sent you to convince me, right? He thought he was clever to choose a young female nurse who might influence my decision in a different way. Sorry."

Crystal pressed the clipboard against her bosom again and lowered her voice. "The treatment's free, but . . . there's a kind of snag to it. We all know that the hospital wouldn't be here like this if it wasn't for the research center. That's what we're told. The staff, the equipment, and the center — it all belongs together."

Nicolas tied the shoelaces. "I heard the Stewards finance the hospital. What happened?"

She shook her head so that her brown curls danced around

her pretty face. "They built it, but then . . . I don't know. Something happened. The papers wrote that the Turners took over covering the expenses. It was the mayor's decision." She nodded emphatically. "He's a good man, really. He does a lot for the citizens. So . . . do you really think you don't want to contribute to the greater good? Help others getting treated here?"

Nicolas smiled at her mischievous attempt to convince him. "I like to know what's happening with my sperm. It's a personal matter." He laughed, seeing her hardly suppressed shock. "Oh, that came out wrong. I just can't imagine it . . . delivering it to a strange woman so she can have a baby I'd never know. I wouldn't know her or the child. That's too strange for me."

Crystal sighed. "I understand. Or, no, I don't, but I see that I can't change your mind. I'll crawl out in shame and deliver the bad news to the doc. He won't be happy with me."

"He should be unhappy with me, not you. You did your best."

"Really? I don't think so."

"You were kind and charming and . . ."

"And you're in a relationship," she said, then smiled sadly.

"I'm not," Nicolas snapped, alarmed by her comment. "Why do you think so?"

She cocked her head and smiled whimsically. "You need to ask? The men coming here take every chance to . . . help themselves, and they're thievishly happy to collect money for it. Because if you don't drive waste for the Reese Company, you don't make much money in this town without having at least a college degree. So forgive me, but I don't buy your moral act, Nick. But, hey, I'm just a nurse." She wished him a good day and left the room.

Jason and Matthew retreated to the diner for lunch. While munching on burgers and fries, Jason looked through the window. If it wasn't for the modern cars, he would've sworn he'd time-traveled back to the sixties. The streets were clean, the windows polished. The people's clothes weren't fashionable, and everyone seemed to have time to stop and chat on the sidewalk, since most citizens appeared to know each other. Jason assumed that in a small town like this, nothing could stay hidden. "And nothing comes to light if they don't want it to."

"Pardon?" Matthew wiped his plate with his last French fries.

"Sorry. Daydreaming. What have we got?"

Matthew wiped his chin with a napkin and opened his notebook. "I don't trust Mrs. Reese's act about Gilbert Hanson. After meeting her husband, I don't think she's the honest businesswoman she claims or that she'd allow a truck driver to walk all over her."

"Right. Even though she might not have ordered Hanson's death, her husband might've considered it necessary to keep his wife's company out of the headlines."

"Question is . . . who pulled the trigger? The sheriff? Someone from out of town? Or one of the vigilante committee he praised as *being very helpful to keep order*? It's interesting how many men serve the committee while everyone praises this peaceful town. Not to mention the large number of weapons." Matthew consulted his notes. "It's obvious the Turners are hiding the most. They're friendly and helpful and yet cautious. And the young ones have too much time on their hands. Only a few have regular jobs." He lifted his gaze. "They live off the Turner wealth, obviously."

"Jebediah behaved so . . . goody-goody. That had to be an act."

"Agreed. From what we heard from people around, Jebediah is known to start a brawl rather than end it." Matthew turned a page. "The basement of the guesthouse looked clean as a whistle. I've never before seen such a room so . . . polished. Like they had a competition in town." He rolled his eyes. "I bet, in a town like this, it's possible they have a *clean-your-basement* day, and the jury consists of a bunch of old frumps."

"The furnishing was partly new."

"Yes, I noticed. Old furniture and carpet in one room and the next one had a new carpet and at least a new table. And there was the stench of smoke, a cheap brand. I assume someone wanted to cover the smell of the new carpet — or another odor." Matthew looked up. "I'd like to have CSU check the floorboards. I bet we would find blood."

"We need a definite connection." Jason checked his cell phone. "No service. Damn."

The waitress approached and refilled their coffee cups. "They don't work here. The mayor didn't give permission for a radio tower, said it would ruin the beautiful landscape. The other towns around did the same." She shrugged. "On some days we don't have TV, either. But we know how to live. That's more important, don't you think?"

Jason thanked her for the coffee, and when she went back to the counter, lowered his voice to whisper, "We can't risk using the phones here."

"Oh, another important piece of information you didn't think worth sharing?" Matthew sipped the hot coffee and put a pack of cigarettes and a lighter on the table. His eyes narrowed. "What else do we have? Old Jacob Turner played us — I bet he's not as senile as he appears. Gilead knows something about the family's skeletons in the closet. If interrogated with more vigor, he'd break and tell us everything. Forget Jael. She's living in never-never land and doesn't want to have any part of reality. Samuel . . ."

"He played the goody-two-shoes convincingly — the youngest son that runs the business and wades in the mud. A classic. If he showed up in one of those TV shows — farmer searching for a good woman — he'd win the ladies' hearts by storm." Jason emptied his cup and stood to pay the bill. "If you ask me, he knew that Roker loved to work with explosives, no matter the target, and he exploited his former friend. I bet more money than just peanuts for meals and clothes changed hands."

They left the diner so Matthew could smoke.

"The basement is the ideal place to fabricate stuff no one should see." Matthew looked down the street. "But the evidence is gone . . . if there was any. We need to check all weapons used by the Turners."

"And what good would it do if you can't compare them? The bodies had no bullets, if you remember, and the ME's guess was vague. He claimed it was a rifle shot rather than a small caliber. But that's not specific, since the killer used forceps or something similar to retrieve the bullets." He shook his head. "You can't build a case without the slugs."

Matthew sniffled as he stubbed the cigarette and threw it in a trash can. "Back to the Turners?"

"Yeah, let's talk to the staff." Jason sighed, looking at his watch. "We'd better book a room at the motel and stay overnight."

"If you snore, I'll pull the cover."

"If they don't have two single rooms, I'd prefer sleeping in the car."

"You deserve it."

Jason knew better than to start another argument.

To stick to his cover, Nicolas accepted the ride back to the

Turner premises and drove his car to the garage at the other end of town. The young mechanic — Willy Loman, as his name tag claimed — sighed and told him even an oil change on the old clunker would take at least two hours. Nicolas decided to have a drink at the bar a block away.

The overweight barkeeper in his sixties greeted him with open reluctance and a disgusted expression, then turned and continued wiping the countertop without looking up again. He had little hair on his head, but more around his chin and down to his chest. His dress shirt, with rolled-up sleeves, was expensive. As was the golden watch around his wrist. From Alexander's notes, Nicolas knew he was meeting with Herbert Steward, son of a family of miners who had made their fortune a century earlier. The exclusive interior of the bar indicated that Steward considered the bar a valuable showcase, not just a place where he made money by selling liquor.

Finally Mr. Steward turned and glared at him. "What do you want?"

Nicolas understood how outsiders felt. "Beer. Draft, if you have one."

Mr. Steward responded with a grunt and an angry glare but took a glass to fill it. "You're not from around here, are you?"

"I moved here recently." He sat on the barstool and opened his leather jacket. His muscles still protested every unusual move, but he worked to hide his pain. "You've got a nice place here."

Mr. Steward set the glass on a coaster, still glaring at him. "It's a nice place when real customers arrive. I hope you can pay for the beer."

The door opened, and a lady of about forty years with a fashionable light brown bob entered the room. She smiled amiably as she took off her gloves and adjusted the purse on her left arm.

Mr. Steward's face lit up with a genuine smile. "Hello, Jo-anne, nice to see you."

"You, too, Herb."

"You're early today."

"I guess so. The usual, please." She pointed toward a table further down the room but came to the bar to stand beside Nicolas. "And his drinks are on me."

Her smile was an invitation and a challenge—a tempting mix of class and sexiness. Nicolas had seen her from afar, but up close, she was a good-looking woman, neither overweight nor slender, with carefully applied lipstick and eyeliner. She scrutinized Nicolas's face for a few moments with the interest of an adventurer looking for a new quest.

"Thanks, but . . . why?" Nicolas asked.

"Come with me, and I'll explain." She made a gesture to-ward her table. Mr. Steward was already on his way to deliver a cocktail with mint on top in a highball glass. Nicolas took his beer and set the glass down quickly enough to move the chair for her.

"Oh, I'm surprised. And impressed." She sat down and put her gloves and the purse on the side of the table. "I hadn't expected manners in such a boorish place." She winked at Mr. Steward, whose forced smile didn't reach his eyes. She added in a mock whisper, "No, he won't be my friend tonight."

Nicolas took the chair on the other side of the small table. "I'm Nick—"

"Murray, I know." She lifted her glass. "Here's to you be-ing here with me and not in lockup."

Nicolas raised his beer, surprised at the revelation. "I'll drink to that—my savior, obviously."

"Not really, but I'll take the compliment anyway." She licked her upper lip, and he could tell by her glance she was out for more than a quick drink at the bar.

"Would you mind explaining—"

"Of course not." Her smile brightened the entire room. She put her elbows on the table and rested her chin on her folded hands as she studied him. "I watched you work, as you might've noticed, and then the next day, you were gone. I wondered what happened, and I asked around." She shrugged elegantly. "It wasn't hard to get the right answers."

"You're friends with the staff?"

Joanne waved her hand. "I'm friends with everybody. If you treat people like valuable human beings and not like dirt, they respect you. I needed about fifteen minutes to find out where you'd been taken."

"You told old man Turner about me."

Joanne chuckled. "Never call Jacob an old man. He would still father children if Mary was still alive. He considers himself at a fantastic age. Yes, he's got arthritis, but his mind is sharp as ever."

"My apologies, Mrs. Turner."

"Joanne. Jo, for my friends." She appeared to be enjoying the conversation as she sipped her drink and stared at him. "You might call me Jo." When he didn't reply, she set down the glass and cocked her head. "Tell me what happened. And be honest. I put some pieces together, but I'd like to hear the story from you."

Nicolas frowned. "Why do you want to know anything about me?"

"The circumstances are self-explanatory." She waved away his question. "Please, tell me what happened to you."

"I was accused of stealing, but the accusation didn't hold up. Jebediah didn't believe me and locked me up in a stall in the old stable."

Joanne frowned and pointed at his chafed wrists. "That's a cheap and much too short story. I bet there's more to it. You look like you caught some punches, and from what I've heard, you offered them quite a fight and almost won."

Nicolas lowered his gaze and exhaled, both hands around the cold beer glass. The memory of the night in the cage haunted his mind like a weight on his shoulder that was gone but still tangible.

"You twisted Tyrone's wrist. It's not broken, but bandaged nevertheless. He won't be using it for weeks." Joanne shrugged. "He's whining like an old man. Jeb took some hits, too, but doesn't talk about it. He runs around bearing a grudge the size of Richmond, and quarrels with everyone." She cocked an eyebrow. "I'd recommend you lie low for a while."

"Mr. Turner said he'd talk with Jeb."

"Oh, that's good." She nodded so vehemently that her golden earrings danced. "If the old man . . . pardon, the lively, vigorous patriarch takes charge, there's no denial, no back talk, and no delay. Jebediah will follow his order. That means you're safe."

"Why does Jacob have such an influence? After all, he's more than seventy years old, and couldn't wrestle Jebediah to the ground."

"No, but it looks like you tried that. Anyway," she said with a wave of her hand. "He's the one who leads this family, and he can get really pissed. Pardon my French. He had a dis-agreement with my husband, and instead of enduring Jacob's permanent browbeating, Solomon opened a law firm in Rich-mond. He said it's for the best to keep a distance. That tells you something about my father-in-law." She sighed and tried to cover her sadness with her drink. "These days, my hus-band's home for about three weeks a year. By the way, this is a Gin-Gin Mule. I learned to love it in New York." Another, even deeper sigh. "Those were the days. If you want to try one, I can order it for you."

"I'll stick with beer."

"But you aren't drinking."

"I'm listening." Nicolas smiled encouragingly.

Joanne took the invitation like a lost girl in the street that's cheered by a friendly stranger. "That's flattering." Joanne took another sip of her drink. "You're wondering why I didn't move with my husband."

"That's right."

"I'm the daughter of Alan Reese, the sheriff. I was born and raised in this town and couldn't leave it. Yes, Solomon urged me to come with him after the fallout, and I tried. But he's at the office twelve sometimes fifteen hours a day, so I'm alone and don't know a soul." She shrugged. "I prefer living here, in Florence Town, where I know everybody." She paused and cocked her head to the side. "And you? What made a guy like you move here to become a farmhand?"

"I had trouble at home . . . with my girlfriend . . . with my job." Nicolas drank his beer, portraying the young dude who had no choice but to leave everything behind and start over. He didn't look up when she touched his hand gently.

"I understand. Sometimes life sucks."

Jason wanted to ignore FBI protocol and break some people's noses to get the answers he needed to solve the case. His gut feeling said that something terrible had happened on the Turner premises, but his duty demanded that he asked the staff friendly questions without accusing anyone of lying to him.

Most of the farmhands and grooms denied knowing Roker or Bronsteen. The pictures didn't help much. Matthew and Jason's questions were rewarded with shrugs and blank faces, culminating in two oversized and slightly drunk farmhands threatening them to leave or face the consequences. Jason kept Matthew from drawing his gun, finished the interrogation, and sent his partner outside to cool down.

When he followed three minutes later, Matthew was talking with a man in his late forties who was smoking something that smelled as bad as the mud from the pigpen. Jason paused to listen.

"So, Abner, you say there was a commotion at the guesthouse?" Matthew offered the older man one of his cigarettes.

"Thanks." Abner nodded so emphatically that his loose chin wobbled. "Yeah, yeah. Roker has quite a temper. You wouldn't think that he was a blaster once, right? Those men should be able to control themselves better, I think. But he was blurting out how he could build bombs like *MacGyver*." Abner chuckled, then coughed badly. "Anyway, he was suddenly gone and his sidekick with him. I guess the Turners had enough of them — and that means the boss had enough." Abner winked at Matthew. "The old one. Jacob Turner."

"He still calls the shots?"

"He's got a voice that fills a riding arena. Believe me. The man shouts, and the horses obey. I've seen it." He nodded emphatically. "It's the same with the grooms and the farmhands. Everybody snaps to attention when the old man wants something. That's why Chief Taffner is so hard on us. He doesn't want anyone to anger the old man."

"But his family? He wouldn't browbeat his family, would he?"

Abner cackled, then coughed again. Jason wondered if he should fetch a glass of water for him, but then remained in the shadow.

"Even Jebediah, who's a hothead and easy to provoke, doesn't mess with his grandfather." Abner nodded with his words. "The same goes for all the others. No one butts heads with Jacob Turner. That's a rule."

Jason made a mental note. It seemed Jebediah's act of the well-behaved young man was in stark contrast to his reputation.

"Tell me more about Roker and Bronsteen. Did you see them work in the guesthouse or its basement?"

"Bronsteen? Ah, you mean Snakey. Well, they seemed to have something to do down there, but I don't know what. When they were gone, there were four other guys that showed up much later." Abner scratched his head as he looked longingly toward the pack of cigarettes, and Matthew offered another one. "Thanks. They went downstairs as well. You see—don't think I'm ratting on someone here, okay? I don't know the other guys, and you didn't hear it from me. They put stuff in a van and then, whoosh, they were gone, just three days ago. Haven't been around since." He blew out smoke and rubbed his stubbly chin. "Maybe Jacob had enough of them, too. Who knows? I don't mind that they're gone." Longing crept into his voice. "Since last year, things have changed around here. It was always good working for the Turners, you know. I've been on this job for years, so I know what I'm talking about. Good payment, good lodging, friendly people around. But then . . ." He shrugged and made a face. "Samuel and Gabriel seem on edge, short-tempered. It's not the same anymore." He drew on the cigarette, then stubbed it out. "All this talk about being a big family. Nah, that's BS."

"Do you know what kind of van the men drove or the license plate?"

Abner cackled heartily. "Good joke!" He slapped his thigh and stopped when another coughing fit racked his body. "Oh, well, a good laugh at last." He wiped tears from his eyes. "Okay, okay, I'm game. Let me think about it. A gray van. Silver-gray." He closed his eyes. "Not a really new one, but not an old model, either. I mean, it's got no scratches or dents. A *Chevy*. A long vehicle with two doors at the side that opened like a cupboard. Passenger window and three windows on each side."

"An *Express Cargo*," Jason said, stepping out of the shadow. "Do you have a part of the plate, maybe? The state?"

"Blue against white and the state was in red. But I can't remember . . ."

"North Carolina or South Dakota. Were the letters in a fancy script?"

Abner frowned, then said, "Nah."

"So it's North Carolina." Matthew grinned. "That's great, Abner, thanks a lot."

"Sure, I'm glad I could help." He smiled even more brightly when Matthew handed him his pack of cigarettes and the lighter.

Nicolas nursed his beer while he listened to Joanne.

She ordered another Gin-Gin Mule and chatted about her glorious childhood, and that her family had favored the aspiring Solomon Turner as her husband. As it was a daughter's duty, she had wed the young man and moved into Turner manor without hesitation. She was lucky—so she claimed—that the old patriarch took a fondness to her that didn't waver when Solomon moved to Richmond. Quite the opposite. Jacob had lost his wife to a fight with cancer and asked Joanne to be the woman at his side during public events while he ran for mayor. She fulfilled her duty as she had done at her husband's side and was rewarded with Jacob's love.

"A love in good faith, Nick, really." She set down the glass and played a finger on its rim. "He's a generous person, more like his forefathers, who built this town. He wants the best for everyone, but that doesn't mean that he bends the rules he set years ago. No, there's a kind of . . . positive sternness to him. He's a conservative man with strict values." She looked up and found Nicolas staring at her. "Are you really such a good listener, or are you playing me for a fool?"

"I like listening to you," Nicolas replied, giving her a tentative smile.

As he had expected, it appeared to be the answer she had hoped for. She lowered her gaze, sighing, and sipping from her cocktail before she went back to her memories.

"You see, Jacob ran the campaign promising the citizens good healthcare for everyone—an improvement of what we had. Originally, the Stewards built and financed the hospital, but then—" Joanne's gaze switched to the counter.

Two guests sat down and placed their orders. Mr. Steward obviously knew them, put small glasses on the counter, and poured whiskey, instantly lost in conversation.

"Jacob counted on the Stewards to keep their word and sustain the hospital, but . . . I don't know for sure, but it's a good guess that Jacob and Herbert quarreled. In the end, the Turners had to take over financing the hospital to avoid its closing. The Stewards are out of business, and Jacob won the election."

"Did it mean so much to him?"

"His campaign? No. But the ongoing healthcare? Yes."

"Was Mr. Steward his competitor?"

"No, Herb wouldn't stand a chance against Jacob when it comes to voter preferences, but—" She stopped and frowned. "That's a good point. Maybe Herb was pissed that Jacob would win with what the Stewards had represented for years." She nodded in appreciation. "You're clever, Nick Murray. Much more than some people would give you credit for. Will you stay in town?"

Nicolas read anxiety in her expression and relief when he nodded. He wished he could tell her who he was. He had the urge to unburden his heart, for Joanne reminded him of Jacklyn in a way that was painful. Joanne was a wonderful, warmhearted woman with lots of love to give, a true gift for a worthy husband. It was a pity she had made the wrong decision in her youth. When he asked about the possibility of a divorce, Joanne politely declined. She stated Solomon was a good and faithful husband, and they had a successful daughter, who — much to her chagrin — was more like her father and on her way to becoming a company lawyer in Boston.

However, Nicolas didn't know what would come out if he dared to reveal the truth, so he cloaked his thoughts behind an encouraging smile. "The old man . . . Pardon, the lively, vigorous patriarch, offered me a position as a groom in the stables."

"Do you know anything about horses?"

"Unfortunately, not." He emptied his glass. "But I'm a fast learner."

"*That* I don't doubt." Joanne's voice had an undertone that sent shivers down his spine.

Jason drove to Belmont as if the devil was right behind him to claim his soul if he didn't arrive yesterday. Matthew was quiet on the ride and exhaled loudly when he got out in the large parking lot of a restaurant.

"If you want to invite me for dinner as compensation, I'll take it. In an hour. Right now, my stomach is a tight knot. That'll take time and a strong drink."

Jason slammed the car door. "You ride with Nick and don't complain." He entered the restaurant and glanced over his shoulder. "So why now?"

"He's a racecar driver. Or he was in his first life. You drove like you couldn't find the brakes anymore." He wiped his brow with the back of his hand. "Phew, I'm just happy to be alive."

"I'll buy you a drink. Will that do?"

Matthew widened his eyes. "Seriously? Did Elaine grant you pocket change for the trip?"

"If you don't shut up, I'll revoke the offer and drink alone. I really need it."

Matthew laughed. "All right. You go and call your beloved, and I'll place the order."

Jason called Vernon Freeman and summed up their findings, including the possible work in the basement and the suspects of the Turner and Reese family. Vernon reported about Nicolas's call and the three explosions.

"As soon as I got the information about the C-four, we knew Roker had to be the one who built the bombs."

"And yet we know he wasn't the one placing them, because he was already dead. Damn. We still need to find his murderer, and the four men who transported the bombs."

"At least I can assign my men to search traffic camera footage from the day the van left the Turner premises. We'll take it from here. Good work, Agent Beckham."

Jason thought of Senior Agent Sullivan's grumpy face and wasn't convinced he was doing good enough work. "It might be that Bronsteen was killed because he asked questions about Roker's whereabouts, but that doesn't help me with the third victim. I've got no clue who killed Gilbert Hanson. The Reese family seems suspicious, but I have nothing to go on."

"Did you talk with the entire Turner staff?"

"Yes, and all family members present."

"What about Alexander Leeland? Did you meet with him, too?"

"No, he wasn't among the farmhands and grooms, and we couldn't ask for him specifically or would've given away his cover. The same goes for Nick. I didn't see him, either."

"Damn it. Where are they?"

Jason didn't put his worry into words that there might be more bodies hidden somewhere in the woods.

CHAPTER TWELVE

"I heard some . . . crude stories about a crazy guy who lived on the Turner premises. Do you know him?" Nicolas knew the question was risky, so he kept his tone casual.

Joanne raised her brows. "The chatterbox that claimed he'd blow up New York?" She made a dismissive gesture. "Oh, well, yes, I heard the stories, and I saw him from time to time. Samuel's old buddy — or so he said." She lowered her voice. "Not even Claudia — that's his wife — knew him. I don't know why he wanted the guy around. They weren't best buddies if you ask me, but Sam and Gabriel wanted something from the guy. I don't know what, and I wasn't interested." She scrunched her face in disgust. "He was also a lecher. That's why I kept a distance. He approached several women of the house staff. I urged Jacob to give him a piece of his mind, but before he could do that, both the chatterbox and his close-mouthed friend were gone."

"Do you know where they went?"

"No, but I know that the FBI found their dead bodies near Madison in March."

"They're dead?" Nicolas was so surprised he almost forgot his cover and had to force his body to remain seated. "How?"

"Well, they didn't die of old age, or the FBI wouldn't be interested, right?" Joanne emptied her drink and wiped her lips with a small napkin. While she searched her purse, she asked, "Why do you wanna know? Did you know him?"

"No, not at all. He seemed like an odd person. How did you get to know about their murders?"

"It was on TV. I was in Richmond, visiting Solomon for a few days. There was another report—oh, yes, the third man found was a local from Florence Town, Gilbert Hanson." She reapplied her lipstick and checked her look in a small mirror. "You look stricken, Nick. What's wrong? Did you hope to meet the fella and his sidekick?"

"Not really. I was just curious." Nicolas's mind was racing. So far, Roker and Bronsteen appeared to have left the Turner premises for unknown reasons, but now events had taken another turn. It was obvious Roker had done something that angered someone so much, he ended up murdered. He thought of Nathaniel's claim to be the solver of riddles. If anyone was able and willing to commit murder, the Steward brothers were first on his list. He had to meet with them again to find out what they knew about the blaster's death.

"All right." She tapped against the empty glass. "I had two drinks, and I feel kinda tipsy. Would you mind taking me home? I'm perfectly able to pour you another beer if you want one."

Nicolas put on a smile and stood. "Of course, I'll take you home if you don't mind riding in an old car."

"Oh, that sounds like fun."

The Steward residence surprised Jason. It broke with the tradition of maintaining buildings that reflected old values meant to show off the social status of their ancestors. Though the basic structure was old, the current Steward family had altered its appearance, adding a lot of glass and some annexes to have more room for a pool, a billiard room, and a bowling lane.

Herbert Steward, owner of the local bar *Steward's Heritage*, greeted him and Matthew with stern formality and invited them to have a seat in the salon. Mr. Steward's sons, Michael and Nathaniel, appeared more laid back, calling Matthew's tailored suit a *cool outfit*, and looking at Jason as if he wasn't the type of guy the FBI should hire.

Jason swallowed the unspoken insult and began the interrogation. The Stewards admitted consistently that they had regular contact with the Turners because the families had similar interests — the development and prosperity of Florence Town. None of the men knew anything about their guests or their whereabouts. They all seemed surprised at the information about three dead men, claiming they had never seen the FBI's broadcast or read about them in the paper. The elder Steward claimed he didn't like watching TV anyway, and that only his sons had TV sets in their rooms.

Once more, Jason was reminded of life in the sixties, when a TV was an expensive piece of technology that some people rejected as too modern.

When asked about Roker and Bronsteen and whether they ever visited his bar, Mr. Steward crossed his arms and nodded, grumpily.

"Yeah, they came in, but I threw them out after a drink. The haggard-looking guy there—"

"Milton Roker," Matthew said.

"Yes. He was a rabble-rouser, a troublemaker. You don't want such persons in a decent establishment."

"Did he quarrel with the guests?"

"He tried to . . . speak to the women in an intolerable way, if you get my meaning."

"With your wife, too?"

"I'm divorced, but my ex-wife would've eaten that guy for breakfast."

"You're saying Roker flirted with the female guests?"

Mr. Steward scoffed and shook his head. "That wasn't flirting, Agent Montagna, it was cheap pickup lines. He wanted to get under their skirts."

"Did his behavior cause him more trouble than being thrown out of your bar?"

"Who knows? It's possible."

Michael lowered his voice but couldn't keep out a hint of amusement. "He should've taken a whore, but couldn't afford one, I bet."

"Did you witness any arguments he had with any other woman or a man — a husband, maybe?"

Michael exchanged glances with his brother. "Listen, he might've tried his luck with every woman he met. Who knows what kind of trouble he got himself in? I don't. But I'm not in town much." He shrugged and smiled lopsidedly, then wiggled his brows when he said, "If I want to go to town, I choose a bigger one with more . . . entertainment."

The Stewards claimed they didn't know Gilbert Hanson or what happened to him.

The brothers explained, in detail, that they were interested in sports — a lot of sports. Michael mentioned that he ran eight miles every morning. Nathaniel claimed to be an excellent swimmer and liked bowling. Both neglected to mention that they were also excellent shots, a fact backed up by several medals, cups, and photographs on the mantel and along the walls.

"Oh, that . . ." Michael snorted when Matthew inspected each trophy. "Yeah, sometimes we shoot. At targets."

"Do you have a shooting range in or outside the house?" Matthew asked.

"Yeah, that, too." Nathaniel leaned back on a large chaise longue. "But we're always careful. There's a concrete wall behind the targets, and we only practice when there's no one around."

"There are rumors that you take your guns into the woods from time to time."

"We hunt, yes, in the proper season. Those are our woods.

They've belonged to our family for centuries. We can do what we want there." Nathaniel protruded his chin. "Or do you want to tell us otherwise?"

"No." Matthew shook his head and took down notes. "Where do you keep the weapons?"

"In a locked cupboard." After a scowl from his father, Nathaniel sat up straight and changed his tone to sound business-like. "We know the rules, Agent Montagna. After all, Sheriff Reese wouldn't have given us a license to carry guns if we weren't qualified." He stood. "Is there anything else you want to know?"

"We would like to see the weapons."

"Come on, seriously? What for?" Nathaniel looked from his brother to his father. "We didn't harm anyone."

"Two of the dead men were found with shotgun wounds. Both men had been in town prior to their homicide. It's our right during the investigation to inspect the weapons we find."

"You're implying my sons or I were involved in a homicide?" Mr. Steward shook his head. "That's absurd, agents. There are a lot more weapons in town than ours." He looked at his sons with a father's pride and a wink. "Sometimes their behavior isn't gentleman-like, but they wouldn't direct their guns at people. Do you have anything, any lead that connects my sons to the killings?"

Jason wasn't about to admit that the bullets had been removed from the bodies. "We're following many leads, Mr. Steward, and this is but one of them. If you don't mind, we would like to see your weapons now."

"That means you don't know what kind of weapon the men were shot with." Clearly annoyed, Mr. Steward rose from his chair. "Honestly, agents, you're overstretching your authority. As I see it, you're absolutely in the dark about the murders and the weapons used. Now you claim you've got the right to examine the weapons we possess. I'll tell that to your superior."

"You can do that, sir." Matthew flashed a friendly smile. "I'm sure you'll understand that your behavior implies you've got something to hide, and that might cause my partner and me to come back with a search warrant for your premises."

"Are you threatening me?"

"I'm describing the course of events, sir." Matthew didn't budge when Mr. Steward stepped closer. "I'm telling you this because I want you to know that my colleagues will knock on your door."

"Let them see the guns, Dad." Michael shrugged. "There's nothing to it."

"It's harassment." Mr. Steward's look said he wanted to throw out the agents or invite them to the shooting range as targets. "But to avoid further . . . visits from your agency, please, follow my sons. They'll show you what we've got."

Outside on their way to the car, Matthew lit a cigarette and stopped to look back. "You know, I hate people like the Stewards. They do whatever they want and think they're gonna get away with it. Did you see the photographs on the mantel? Michael's holding a *Remington 783*, an expensive piece, custom-made if I had to guess. I didn't see that in the cupboard. Did you?"

"No. Interesting." Jason slipped behind the wheel and waited for Matthew to join him. "It's not enough to arrest him right away, but it's a step forward."

Nicolas lay awake in his bed, staring at the ceiling, reflecting on the evening.

Joanne hadn't made her intention a secret. When he

crossed the threshold to her rooms, she had taken off her tailored jacket, lost her shoes on the way to the bar, and dropped her purse and gloves on a small table against the wall. She offered him another beer, and when he didn't follow her into the apartment, she stood, frowning. Then slowly, understanding that he wasn't about to spend the night with her crossed her face.

"You aren't coming, huh?" she asked as she pushed back a strand of hair behind her ear. "Afraid of a married woman? Afraid that my husband will show up and try to throw you out?" On the way back toward the door, she made a dismissive gesture. "Don't worry. After spending a day here, he's already on his way home — back to his normal life in Richmond, back to what he calls his *fulfillment in life*." She cocked her head. "I can't convince you to stay?"

"No, ma'am."

"Oh, it's back to *ma'am*? What a pity. I like *Jo* much more." She curled her lips to a smile. "A gentleman through and through, huh? Can't say that I'm surprised. But I'm still disappointed. I did have expectations for the night."

"You're too valuable for a one-night-stand, Jo. You're a wonderful woman and a good wife. You're also a good daughter-in-law, faithful to the old man. I'm not —"

Joanne put a finger on his lips. "Don't say you aren't worth sleeping with me, Nick, because that's BS. I made advances at you, not the other way around. I wanted you right here — or a little bit closer and with less clothes — and you knew that when you took the seat at my table."

He smiled and cast down his eyes. The same moment, she stood on tiptoes to kiss him tenderly. Surprised, and yet flattered, Nick returned the kiss, then stepped back and wished her a good night.

Samuel was sitting at the desk with a laptop organizing his schedule for the following week when Gabriel strutted into the living room.

"What about the last bomb?" Gabriel clenched the backrest of a chair and stared at his brother. "What happened? There was nothing in the news about it."

"Either it didn't explode, or the news reporters have their hands full with three and can't afford a reporter at the last one."

"Damn your fucking coolness! Those bastards will have us by the balls if we don't do what they say!"

"Lower your voice. Father's upstairs, and you know he hears the sinner's lament through the basement."

Gabriel looked up toward the stairs and lowered his voice. "Have you heard from Oscar? Anything?"

"Of course not." Samuel finished typing and closed the laptop. "The target's difficult to enter. Maybe he needs more time. Be that as it may," he interrupted his brother, "we can't change it anymore. Have faith."

Gabriel snorted and pushed off the chair. "That's all you have to say? Have faith? I was raised with the belief that we have all we need in abundance only to learn that Father's fool-hardy dream is eating up our savings. I know he wouldn't understand that our concern lies with his heritage. I know his horses are the last things he wants to give up." His tone turned mocking. "*All Turners are born benefactors*, as Father would say."

"You have to admit that parts of our enterprises are profitable."

"Oh, good grief, what're you talking about? We make more money with drugs and the sperm bank than Father does selling foals or yearlings! Not to mention that he throws out money for the hospital while the Stewards laugh behind his back." Gabriel waved a hand to stop Samuel's argument. "I know Gilead's clever in investing money, no doubt. But even he said we're at our limits. Damn, why did father throw Herb out, claiming that he was financing the hospital to make up for the criminal behavior of his sons? This was as stupid as it was stubborn."

"It's no less true. Michael's a loose cannon in the true sense of the meaning."

"Father must've known that the Stewards wouldn't see anything with more glee than the Turners losing their riches."

Samuel had seen the numbers on the various bank accounts and couldn't follow Gabriel's reasoning. "I can only repeat it—have faith."

Gabriel shook his head, chuckling bitterly. "You can say what you want. If we don't expand our business, we'll lose big time. And if this bomb doesn't blow up, we can pack up and immigrate to Asia."

"I don't like Asia."

When Nicolas woke, his muscles—especially his shoulders—still ached dully, but he forced himself out of bed and into his clothes. It was close to sunrise when he jogged across the premises toward the old stable. As he had expected, a man from the vigilante committee was on duty and barred the way. Nicolas convinced the man with a stretch of the truth about his new job, and that he had no idea about horses and needed to talk with Alexander.

"But you won't go in there alone," the guard insisted.

Nicolas thought about knocking the guard out. He rejected the idea when the guard followed him into the stable but stopped and let him go to the stall alone. Alexander was already up and standing at the bars.

If possible, the ATF agent was more worn out than before. His bearded face looked gaunt, and his movement was slow.

The hands around the bars trembled. His eyes, however, got livelier when he recognized Nicolas.

"Are you okay?" Alexander asked.

"Don't worry about me." Nicolas groaned at the sight of Alexander's dirty clothes and naked feet, still tethered with the heavy irons. "I'll get you out, Alex. I swear, I won't let you suffer any longer. Who's got the keys?"

"You can't change my position here. Get away and send the cavalry, if you've found out something that's worth it."

"Did you know that Roker and Bronsteen are dead? They were killed and found in the woods close to Madison in March. I suspect the Steward brothers. What do you think?"

Alexander exhaled in surprise. "Dead? So Roker built the bomb, and they killed him afterward? No, wait. Do you know how they died?"

"No, the FBI's on the case because it was suspected that the woods serve as a serial killer's burial ground. There was a third victim—Gilbert Hanson. He had an accident while driving for the Reese Company and talked about getting compensation. That's a cruel way to deal with unpleasant demands." Alexander lifted his hand. "Back to Roker. Roker tried to get at Charlene one night. I knocked him out, and he didn't try again. Jebediah, though, had an eye on her, too. Claimed that she was in love with him, even told that to her father. If Jeb learned of Roker's interest, and that he tried to force himself on her, he might've snapped. After all, Roker was living in the guesthouse, in reach of Jeb every day."

"All right. But would he kill Bronsteen, too?"

Alexander shook his head. "Jeb's a bruiser, a bully. I don't think he's cold-blooded enough to kill someone—unless on the spur of the moment. Do you remember Ty's remark about Jeb and a knife? No? Tyrone praised him for *what he did with a knife*, and Jebediah barked he didn't want to hear it anymore. He looked ... haunted." He renewed his grip around the bars. "No, Jeb's not a killer — not in the true sense of the meaning. Tyrone might, but only from a distance. He's not a fighter."

"I know." Nicolas smirked.

"Yeah, you knocked him out pretty fast. The Stewards would do it, I agree with you. They look like they're having fun every time they can hurt someone. Go. But don't talk with the sheriff. He might — "

"I got to know his son. That was bad enough." Nicolas looked at the adjacent stall and the cage. From one moment to the next, his heart was racing, and his breath turned ragged. Nausea rose in him, and he broke into a sweat. He had to look away to listen to Alexander's words.

"Tell Freeman what you found out so far. Don't worry about me. Honestly, don't risk your freedom for mine. I can stand being in lockup for another day." He forced a smile that made his haggard features even more prominent. "If they let me out, I'd first check what Jeb and his buddies have stored in that shed a quarter-mile away. There was a lot of activity with trucks coming and going. I wonder what kind of stuff they smuggle."

"Never giving up, huh?"

"Nope." Alexander stepped away from the bars when the guard and another man arrived. "Leave."

Nicolas turned away, but the second man called out to him before he took a step.

"Hey, new guy! What're you doin' here? Taffner sent me to look for you. Go and help him in the big stable. A horse was wounded, and they need a helping hand over there. Hurry!"

Nicolas exchanged glances with Alexander, then ran out of the old stable. He wanted to dodge the task, but another groom was already waiting for him when he crossed the yard. Nicolas sighed and bowed to the inevitable.

The explosion at the *Orthopedic Supply Company* in Hopewell, Virginia, ripped apart the basement storage near the garage. It destroyed stored goods and five cars parked close to the blast area. Firemen onsite complained about thick smoke emerging through the broken doors, which hampered their attempt at extinguishing the fire.

Freeman arrived at the crime scene three hours after the explosion. He was confronted with seasoned firefighters grinning like the Cheshire cat, and talking gibberish non-stop. Some sat on the pavement, water bottles in their hands and a hysterical laugh on their lips. Others shuffled aimlessly between the trucks and only stopped when the medics took their arms. None of them could answer questions seriously or coherently, so Freeman turned away from the wannabe-comedians to find the chief, hoping for clues.

"Is there anything wrong with your men, Chief Carson? Too many *Saturday Night Live* shows in a row?"

The officer-in-charge scratched his head, squinting against the large beams they had erected to cast more light on the site. "I wish! The company told us this is storage for medical products such as artificial limbs. We expected acid smoke from plastic, but the smoke resulted from burning marijuana."

Freeman stopped his laughter from erupting when Carson remained serious. "I understand."

"Half of my men are affected. I called in the second team and requested new equipment. We extinguished the fire, so the rest is up to you. I recommend breathing masks, or your men will also turn into Jim Carrey impersonators." Carson emptied a water bottle. He faced the crime scene and shook his head. "How the hell is it possible there were drugs being stored?"

"We'll figure that out later." Freeman turned to his men

and told them to find the source of the explosion and make sure to secure evidence of the explosives. "Is the basement stable?"

"Yes, the structural integrity is sound. The explosion destroyed the goods and set fire to the drugs. It blew the doors off the basement, but the building is safe."

Chief Carson turned away when Freeman's cell phone buzzed again.

"What's up, Derek?" He turned away from two stumbling firefighters in order to find a quieter space to listen.

The young trainee sounded excited. "Sir, I went through the traffic cam videos once more and found the same van at the bombing site in Gillanburg and later in Richmond. It must've driven there straight away."

Freeman nodded to himself. "Do you have the license plate?"

"Yes."

"Find the van's current position and report back to me."

"Yes, sir."

Though he sounded unsure, Derek didn't argue, leaving Freeman with the impression the trainee was able to follow orders—a necessary and cherished trait. He put his phone back in his pocket and geared up to help his team find the source of the explosion. He hoped he wouldn't have to collect his wits from the debris.

On the way back to Washington, DC, Jason developed a headache that quickly grew to a migraine. He allowed Matthew to take over driving and took his medication. When his cell phone worked again, he called Freeman to report the results of the investigation, but Freeman cut him short.

"First, we know the C-four used for the bombs is the same that Milton Roker had under his nails."

"That's good news."

"But it gets better. We've got the van the bombers used. It's parked outside a residential area in Post Oak. I'm on my way to alert my team and send them out to investigate."

"We're close." Jason quickly checked the map on the navigation system. "We can get there before they make a move."

"Be cautious. Keep them from running, but don't play hero." Freeman gave him the name and address.

After finishing the call, Jason turned to Matthew. "We're making a detour to Post Oak to collect a bomber." He fed the system the new address and sipped coffee before he dialed Sullivan's number to inform his boss about the investigation.

Matthew frowned. "All right. But do we have—"

Jason lifted a finger when Sullivan picked up the phone. Before Jason had a chance to explain the situation in Florence Town and ask for support for further interrogations, Sullivan interrupted him, complaining about Jason's late call and meager results.

Jason took the accusation lying down, refrained from further explanations, and swore he wouldn't call his superior ever again without being able to present the criminals in handcuffs.

Nicolas arrived in the stable to find Taffner and the vet trying to control a restless horse.

Taffner's face reddened as he turned to Nicolas. "Where the hell have you been? Jacob told me you'd be here, so where were you, damn it? Here, take over and hold her still!"

Nicolas took the lead rope and put his weight into holding the fidgeting horse as best as he could. The mare had a bleeding wound on her left front leg, and the vet was trying to apply a bandage while the horse tried to evade the treatment with all its strength. The mare's eyes were so wide that the white was showing, and she was huffing air through her large nostrils. All her muscles seemed as tense as a bowstring. Nicolas had known large dogs before, but a lively, trembling, fearful horse was new to him—and much, much bigger. All he could do was follow the vet's orders and keep the horse from rearing up. It was tough, strenuous work, and he and the vet were sweating profusely within minutes. The vet complained about the ill-bred horse, and Taffner grumbled about its sensitivity. It was all the same to Nicolas. He just wished the mare would calm down and endure the treatment so he could get on with his day.

Taffner wiped the sweat off his brow. "So you're a groom now, huh? You climbed up the ladder quick. I hope you're worth it, Nick. Wouldn't like to see you disappoint the old man. He claimed you'd make your way and learn fast."

"So he told you I'd be here?"

"Yes, he did." Taffner's expression was sly. "He knows his people. He's good when it comes to judging them right."

Nicolas countered another attempt the horse made to escape and wasn't sure that the old man was right.

"Interaction with the ATF and—as a bonus—a tangible clue to a possible bomber." Jason whistled through his teeth. "I hadn't thought this would happen in my lifetime."

"I hadn't thought that I'd ever be so happy to leave a peaceful town behind." Matthew continued humming along with another *R.E.M.* song. He took the highway exit and steered the car through the morning traffic.

Jason agreed with a curt nod, but his thoughts were with his boss's shattering behavior. Sullivan appeared to revel in the misery of his agents, as if their frustration fueled his life essence. Jason had made up the metaphor and relished its sound. He imagined their boss as an alien creature with long tentacles, slurping on the misfortunes of his human inferiors to live a satisfying life. The more he fantasized, the more Sullivan turned into an ugly creature with two heads and a large mouth full of teeth, which he sank into his victims after clutching them so they'd never escape again.

Matthew's voice snapped Jason from the images of monstrous tentacles about to wind around his throat.

"That's the address," Matthew said. "Let's see if Mr. Hank Parker is at home." He parked the car at the curb. "Are you all right?"

"I feel a little strangled." Jason put on his bulletproof vest and checked the magazine of his weapon.

"You can be sure it'll be a real feeling if you leave me high and dry."

"You don't—"

Matthew geared up and stowed two magazines in his belt. "No, I don't trust you to have my back, because you've given me no indication whatsoever that reassures me you'll do a proper job."

"Thanks a bunch."

"The van's in the parking lot left of the apartment building."

Matthew moved forward without waiting for him. Jason followed, cursing under his breath that he was forced to struggle with an ignorant *schmuck*. He drew his weapon when they reached the van. It was empty. Matthew made quick work of the lock and searched the interior. Jason called CSU to come and tow it in for a thorough investigation at HQ. They told him they were already on their way.

Matthew closed the back door when Jason spotted a young man entering the parking lot, matching the picture of the suspect Freeman had sent to his cell phone. The young man slowed his steps before he turned to vanish back into the building entrance.

"Hank Parker! Stop! FBI!" Matthew was already running when Jason opened his mouth to warn him.

Jason thought about tentacles and their use when he gave chase after the much faster escapee and Matthew, who was tall and seemed born to run. Jason felt like a sloth trying to keep up with a cheetah.

The door had nearly shut when he reached the handle and slipped through into a dark hallway with graffiti on the walls and little light from overhead bulbs. The hall—full of other things Jason refused to identify—had several junctions, and only the sounds of the men's footsteps gave him direction. How was he supposed to have his partner's back when the man ran away from him? Still, he did his best to catch up.

He spotted both men at the end of the hallway to the right. Matthew was gaining on the fugitive, but the young man sidestepped and avoided being overthrown. Matthew passed him and hit the opposite wall. He cried out, pushed off the wall, and rammed his elbow into the man's face.

Forced back, Parker glanced over his shoulder, turned to the right, and sprinted with doubled effort into the next hallway.

Matthew grunted but didn't appear to notice his bleeding nose as he hurried past Jason once more. They heard the fugitive run upstairs. Jason wondered why he didn't try reaching the street level and escaping through a back exit.

Parker's motivation became clear when he called for a companion named *Coby*. Jason took the stairs two steps at a time, but Matthew was still ahead of him, breathing heavily.

The first shot missed Jason by inches and put a hole in the plaster. The echo numbed his hearing and caused a ringing in his ears. More shots followed, so he couldn't follow the shouted conversation between the men, only their agitation.

Jason flattened against the wall, trying to determine whether there would be more shots, more enemies, and where he could find cover. Matthew flung himself forward, prone on the floor, and skidded to the other side so that he had the door in view. He shot twice through the slit, then got back on his feet, weapon trained, and advanced along the wall.

"Cover me!" Matthew ordered.

Jason swallowed his nervousness around the lump of fear in his throat. Three shots erupted from the apartment. Jason and Matthew returned fire and—simultaneously—approached the door. Matthew showed him two fingers and indicated he'd go in first. Jason refrained from commenting that they had a SWAT team for such operations. Though support would be helpful, it would take the team too long to get there. He nodded curtly, and if he wasn't mistaken by a trick of the light, Matthew grinned at him.

Alexander watched Jacob shuffle down the aisle, bent like a tree in a storm, and this time the patriarch looked his age. Upon reaching Alexander's stall, he straightened, sighing, and put his hands on his back. His demeanor resembled a sinner who comes before his judge and expects to be expelled from Heaven.

"Yesterday evening, I called my old friend, Carlton Loman, and while we talked, he confessed he had spoken with Charlene."

"Is she all right?" Alexander clung to the bars, bracing for the worst. "Is she safe?"

"Oh, yes. Yes, she is." Jacob inhaled sharply. "It slipped Carlton's mind that he had talked with her several days ago and that she told him she wouldn't return home but wait for her lover to come for her. When my friend told her that Jebediah was still here, she claimed that she was in love with you, Alex, and that Jebediah never had a chance." Jacob shook his head slowly.

"I told you I—"

"I had an argument with Carlton about that," Jacob continued, ignoring Alexander's outburst. "I accused him of withholding information, but he said he wished he'd never heard of *that damned outsider* and that his daughter should be with him . . . and with Jeb. I told him that you were held captive because of Charlene's sudden departure and the assumption of the crime behind that. He laughed and claimed that *all those miserable buggers don't deserve any better*." Jacob paused and lowered his gaze. "I'm sorry I misjudged you."

Alexander's fists tightened around the bars until his knuckles were white. He spoke through clenched teeth. "And you didn't consider it necessary to free me yesterday?"

"I do not share Carlton's opinion, but I was convinced there was a crime behind it when his daughter left so unexpected. I believed my grandson."

"Your grandson is—"

"My grandson is my problem, Alex."

Alexander didn't know what to say or where to put his anger. He rattled the bars. "Have you ever been in shackles, Jacob?"

The old man held his gaze. "No, never."

"They're heavy. They restrict your every movement and let you know your freedom is lost. You can't escape, and you know it. There's nothing you can do. They're stronger than you, relentless. Jebediah ordered that I wasn't allowed to go without them—even in here. They're around my ankles when I wake up and when I go to sleep."

"I understand that you're pleading for compensation, and I will—"

Alexander banged his hands against the bars. "This isn't about money, Jacob. Your grandson is a hardcore criminal.

He's in league with people who are sadistic and without morals. There's Tyrone, and there're Michael and Nathaniel Steward. Even Gordon Reese! He provided the cage Nick was kept in the other night. Are you truly so blind that you don't see what's going on in your own home?"

Jacob lowered his chin and murmured, "I'll pay you generously, and of course, you're free to leave. If you want to, take your accusations to the sheriff." He looked back down the aisle, where Taffner was closing in with long steps. "Is the mare okay?"

"She's fine. The vet just left."

"Thank the Lord for small mercies." Jacob stroked his beard while Taffner unlocked the stall and fumbled with the locks on the leg irons. He grimaced at seeing the chafed ankles. "We have to take care of Luanne. That's the new mare I bought."

"That's what you care about? Your horses?" Alexander panted. "You allowed me to be punished on your lands by your grandson? You looked away when you saw me in shackles like a hardcore criminal. How could you do that? How did you justify your action?"

Jacob looked at Alexander, and if there was anything in his gaze, it was pity. "I do have a hand for the mare and know how she thinks, but my strength is reeling, and my knees ache this morning. Would you do me one last favor before you leave?"

Alexander didn't know what to say. He was grateful to be free at last, but also immeasurably angry about his imprisonment and that Charlene's father had prolonged his suffering—willingly and knowingly. He was angry that Jacob hadn't believed him in the first place—that no one had believed his claim that Charlene was in love with him.

Taffner held his breath when Alexander slammed the stall door open vehemently, but he refrained from blocking his way after seeing Alexander's threatening glare.

"Here." Alexander pressed the shackles into Jacob's hands. "Take them. Use them on Jebediah. He deserves punishment, not me."

"I know, but—"

When Jacob looked him in the eye, Alexander swallowed all the accusations that came to his mind. Jacob wasn't the one to blame. "I must do one thing before I join you. And it'll be the last thing before I call the police."

"Hmm, very well. Unless Jebediah is involved. I don't want you to fight with him."

Alexander read the fear in the old man's eyes that he would lose his rebel grandson to his enemy's wrath.

"I wouldn't fight him, Jacob. I would knock him out and drag him to the police to have him arrested. He's a killer, and I think you know it."

Jacob flinched at Alexander's harsh tone, but he stepped aside, and Alexander ran out of the stable.

CHAPTER THIRTEEN

Jason followed Matthew as he kicked in the door and shot at the same time. A cry of pain erupted. Matthew was inside the apartment, gun aimed to the left while Jason turned his weapon to the right. Hank Parker sat hunched behind an armchair, panting so heavily Jason would've found him in the dark.

"FBI! Up with you! Show me your hands!" Jason approached cautiously when Parker followed the order and stood on wobbly legs.

The suspect's eyes were wide. "Don't shoot me, please!" He laced his fingers behind his head and made a step forward.

"Drop the weapon!" Matthew barked. "No, no! Drop it!" Matthew shot again and cursed at the same time. Coby howled with pain and thudded to the ground. "I told you to drop it! Fuck! We need an ambulance!"

Jason didn't waste a second to check the damage. The moment he lowered the gun to pull out the handcuffs, Parker lunged forward. Jason dropped the cuffs but was too slow to level his gun again. His back collided with a cupboard, driving all air out of his lungs. He was stunned for a second and lost his grip on his gun. He imagined Matthew rolling his eyes at his ineptitude and doubled his efforts to throw Parker off him. He evaded the uppercut aimed for his chin and drove his fist into Parker's stomach as hard as he could. The lanky man grunted and stepped back. Parker struck out for another assault, but Jason was faster and punched his face with the culminated frustration of a man provoked one time too many.

Parker fell backward against a chair and slumped to the ground. This time, Jason didn't take any chances, turned him on his belly, and handcuffed him. He picked up his gun, panting, and holstered it.

Matthew pulled a towel from a nearby chair and pressed it on Coby's shoulder wound. "An ambulance, damn it!"

Breathless and grumpy, Jason pulled his phone to dial nine-one-one and reported the shootout with one victim. Jason noticed the resemblance of the two men—both had dark brown hair, brown eyes, and a lanky frame. Hank appeared to be Coby's younger brother.

"Hank Parker, you're under arrest for attempted murder by a terroristic attack and resisting the FBI." Jason was tempted to kick the man while he was down.

Matthew glared at him. "You know he can't hear you?"

"I read him his rights. After attacking me, he forfeited his chance to hear them." Jason bent to take away Coby's handgun. "And you're bleeding."

Matthew sniffled and wiped his nose. "Feels like it's swelling."

Jason provided him with a handkerchief. "We've got a first aid kit in the car."

"Yeah, later."

Jason took over pressing the towel on Coby's shoulder wound so Matthew could sit back and tend to his nose.

"What about you?"

Jason couldn't hide his astonishment. "He bruised my back, but the vest took most of the impact."

"You punch pretty hard. He's still out cold."

Jason had a list of retorts come to mind but dismissed them. "I didn't want to leave all the fun to you."

"Yeah, fun." Matthew groaned and put back his head. "Fun is a cold beer and a good football game."

Jason thought it would also be fun watching Sullivan, the

Two-headed Monster, fly back to outer space.

Alexander made a short detour to his room, changed his clothes, and put on his boots. His cell phone was dead after ten days in his bag. He cursed but couldn't wait for it to recharge. Quickly, he collected his burglar tools and a knife.

His ankles and feet hurt like hell, but he tried to ignore the pain. He limped more than he ran across the large yard toward the shed. On the way, he looked for something he could use as a weapon, for he was sure to find a guard protecting whatever the Turners wanted hidden.

He was right. One man stood in the shade of the shed, smoking a cigarette, looking left and right, and bored to death. Nothing was going on, and the guy probably wondered why he had to stand guard with a rifle slung across his shoulder.

Alexander had no cover in this part of the yard, so there was no chance to enter the shed secretly. Instead, he decided to pick a fight if need be. The guard, a stout man of Mexican descent with a large mustache and tanned skin, blew out smoke as he narrowed his eyes. Alexander approached cautiously, watching the man's body language, and tried to assess his opponent's aggressiveness.

The guard grunted and stepped forward, raising a hand. His English bore a Spanish accent. "Hey, I don't know what you're looking for, but this is a closed area, okay? Go back to the stable or wherever you came from."

"I need to see what's in the shed."

"No, you don't. No one goes in there."

"Sure did. I saw a transport deliver something. Do you know what it was?"

"It doesn't concern you, sucker. Move on!"

Alexander reached the other man's position and was on

him so fast, the guard had no time to pull the rifle around. The man lifted his hands, and was strong enough to withstand Alexander's first attack, but he stood no chance against an agent's fighting skills, and his anger that finally found a vent.

Alexander panted loudly when he bent over the unconscious man. His lungs hurt, and his heart was beating so hard it was almost painful. He hadn't realized he'd lost so much of his physical condition in nine days of imprisonment.

He used the skeleton key to open the padlock at the door. Inside the shed, the light was dim, and it took a moment until his eyes adjusted to have a look around. Shelves were neatly stacked with more than two hundred packages wrapped in plastic sheets. Alexander scraped an edge and sniffed the contents.

"They're dealing with marijuana?" he mumbled, flabbergasted. "I'd never thought of that." He stuffed a small package in his pants as evidence. Then he continued inspecting the shed for any other useful hints of what the Turners were doing when they were not breeding horses or producing wheat and grain.

He stopped when he heard voices outside.

Nicolas ignored Taffner's barked order to muck out the stables and ran toward the parking lot to head for Belmont. He didn't pay attention to the crude jokes behind him, or Abner's comment that he was hurrying to slip into another woman's warm bed. He drove as fast as he dared to Belmont and stopped at the first gas station outside of town to call Freeman from a public phone.

"Sir, we're quite sure Jebediah Turner killed Milton Roker, and someone else murdered Bronsteen shortly after. We still don't know about the last guy, Gilbert Hanson. However, the Stewards are known for their gunplay, and Nathaniel almost confessed that he's the one who'd kill people if need be. We need an FBI team here. CSU and a forensic team, too. Alexander's been locked up by Jeb and his minions and looks terrible. I don't know if we can solidly book one of the suspects for murder, but your friend won't last much longer."

"I'll send my men to help you out. Where do we find —"

Out of the corner of his eye, Nicolas saw a tall man approach him. He swiveled around in time to dodge the stranger's hand reaching for his shoulder but had to drop the receiver. "What the —"

Nicolas's opponent was as tall and at least as broad as he was. He had seen the guy around, frequently, working as a vigilante for the Turners. The man's appearance did not pose a threat, but the cattle prod in his right hand was another matter. Nicolas managed to sidestep the first lunge, but quickly learned he couldn't disarm the guy in hand-to-hand combat. He turned to run for his car. At the same moment, a black van cut him off and stopped with its brakes screeching. Nicolas stumbled against the fender, evaded to the side to run on, but his advantage was gone, and the vigilante thrust him hard against the car, simultaneously shoving the prod against his right side. Nicolas cried out in pain. His knees buckled, and he had no strength to turn around and fight. The electric shocks sent him into spasms.

He collapsed beside the front wheel, breathing against the pain, and trying to stay conscious while his vision blurred. "Bastard."

"Shackle him!"

It was Tyrone's voice, and Nicolas made an effort to lift his gaze to glare at the man.

"Sucker, I knew you'd be trouble when I first saw you." Tyrone watched as the vigilante cuffed Nicolas's hands behind his back. "When Adam told me you'd visited Alex this morning, I knew something was wrong. Hell, and it *is* wrong." He walked back to the booth and hung up the phone. "Put him in the van, Darren, we don't have time."

Darren pulled him up so vehemently that Nicolas cried out. There was no hope that pedestrians would see him. It was too early, and the gas station was too far out of town to attract customers at this time of day. Nicolas was pushed hard into the back of the van.

"Secure him on the seat," Tyrone ordered as he slipped behind the wheel. "I don't want him to move around and make a fuss."

Darren happily obliged and fastened the seat belt. "Anything else, Ty?"

"Yes." Tyrone turned on the seat, smiling like Wile E. Coyote on his way to executing one successful plan. "I've got duct tape in the back. Use it."

"Very well." Darren went to open the trunk.

"You won't make it far," Nicolas said, still breathing raggedly. "You murdered Roker and Bronsteen, and I bet if the police look closer, they'll find more bodies."

"Nope, they won't. And the FBI was already here and left empty-handed." He shrugged. "See, we've got nothing to hide. We are a respectable family with a sitting mayor to lead this wonderful town. And you won't throw dirt at us. No, you won't."

Nicolas stowed the information that the FBI had already been to town. "Will you pull the trigger, or leave it to the Stewards because you're too gutless to do it yourself?"

"You don't know what I'm capable of." Tyrone huffed. "Others faint at the sight of blood or break down and bemoan their fate, though what they did was justified. I won't."

"So I'm right, and you killed both men."

Tyrone clicked his tongue. "Trying to push me to confess? Nick, I wonder who you are."

"I'm—" Nicolas tried to move away from Darren but had

no room. He was gagged with a strip of duct tape, and Darren got back into the van.

"Time to move on." Tyrone put the car in gear and turned it around.

Jason waited while Matthew received first aid for his bloody nose. Hank and Coby Parker were arrested, and a tow truck was pulling the gray van to the FBI's CSU station for closer examination. Freeman had some words to say about his and Matthew's boldness for going after the brothers alone, but Matthew responded, with a wink and a smile, that success overruled idiotic behavior every time.

Back at the office, Jason and Matthew spent an extensive amount of time in the cafeteria — partly to dodge Sullivan's inquiry — then returned to their desks to meet with Agent Miller from CSU.

Since the day Nicolas had gone on a covert operation, Miller had walked around the office like a man condemned to eternal damnation. He had no smile for anyone, reported his work results via email, and couldn't be cheered up by praise. Even his colleagues at the lab shook their heads and avoided working with him if they could.

Jason watched the lab technician shuffle through the aisle and offered an amiable smile. "Anything worth knowing?" he asked as he skipped through the file.

"I wanted to ask the same." Miller pushed a strand of hair out of his face. "Any news about . . . the investigation?"

"No. Not yet," Jason said.

Miller cleared his throat and stared at the papers on Jason's desk and the floor, sighing. "The van contained fibers from different clothes, hair, DNA traces on food boxes and plastic cutlery. The intensive search resulted in samples of C-four matching those already identified by ATF and our lab."

"Yes! That's good news." Jason's cheer was met with a skeptic frown. "Okay, what else?"

"You're searching for two more men, white, male, in their twenties. Both men smoke. Obviously, they drove a part of the way together and had the explosives with them. We've got a partial fingerprint on an old food container. Once we've finished comparing it with those from Hank and Coby Parker, we'll run it through the data banks. If I come up with any leads, I'll let you know."

Jason understood his look. "Yes, thank you. If I learn anything about Agent Hayes, I'll let you know."

Miller smiled briefly, but as if he had violated his own rule fell back to his brooding mood, excused himself and left.

Matthew raised his brows to his hairline. "He's truly, madly in love with your partner. Do you consider him a competitor?"

"Stick to the case, Matthew. I've got no time for this." He read the report and handed it across the desk. "Let's go back to Hank and squeeze him some more. We can accuse him of at least one bomb attack. Maybe he'll help us find his partners."

"You can't offer a deal without Sullivan's approval." Matthew leaned back in his chair and looked at Jason skeptically. "If you do, he'll have you by the balls."

"Not if we get the answers we need."

"We still don't know if Roker built the bombs."

"Yes, we do." Jason cleared his throat. "Freeman told me it's the same C-four as found under Milton Roker's fingernails. We can prove his connection to that bomb, at least."

"That's good news. Why not tell me right away?"

Jason pressed his lips tight and broke eye contact.

Matthew exhaled loudly. "Come on, *Agent Beckham*, I can tolerate some protectiveness, but not endlessly. We've got to work together, so don't exclude me at will."

"I'm not—"

"Hell, you just did it *again*! Damn it! This isn't a case you're solving with your buddy Hayes. You're working with *me*. That includes talking with me and tolerating me to be here."

Jason hit the keyboard, pretending to select another menu, but Matthew stared at him and waited until he couldn't evade anymore.

"You behave like a rooster afraid of losing its position. You can't be surprised, can you?" Matthew shook his head. "I've been an agent for sixteen years. Don't you think I'm aware of your protectiveness? *Nicolas's desk, Nicolas's computer, Nicolas's mug* . . . You make me feel as if I'm taking away everything that's dear to you. What's eating you, man?"

Jason made a gesture and thought about leaving the room. Matthew gave him the impression that a table between them wasn't enough protection if the conversation turned violent.

"I haven't worked with anyone else since I got here," he said defiantly. It cost him to remain seated and answer Matthew's inquiry. "Nicolas and I started working at this office together. I was recently divorced, more whipped than cream, and . . . intolerable. He was the overly motivated freshman with the tendency to try and improve everything done at the office."

Matthew stroked his short-cropped beard. "So you fit perfectly together."

Jason detected a sarcastic smile and looked away. "Yeah, right, make fun of me. That's how you're dealing with everything, huh?"

"I understand you've got a special relationship."

"Concerning our *work*." Jason couldn't contain his anger. "I'm not fond of working with any other agent, and yes, my worry for him is eating me up. So smack me for being protective. I'm like that."

"I'm not out to smack you, Jason. I'm just saying that . . ." Matthew lifted and dropped his hand. "We've got a triple murder case on our desks and eight people blown up by bombs. We need to solve the cases, or Sullivan will have our asses on a plate. I'm not here to dispute your relationship with Nicolas. As I told you before, I like the guy. He set my head straight when I needed it and—"

"You did?"

Matthew stabbed him with a glare. "So . . . We can connect Roker to the bomb, and we have two minions in custody, who might tell us about their placing and the reasons behind the attacks." He stood and put on his jacket. "Let's go. You wanted your balls on the anvil. Let's see whether Sullivan swings the hammer."

"You're going nowhere, Alex!" Jebediah shouted.

Alexander leveled the rifle, stupefied that someone knew of his presence already. He'd figured Chief Taffner had the misfortune to run into Jebediah on his way to the stable, or the vigilante had reported about Jacob's decision to let the *outsider* go. Still, Jebediah had responded much faster than Alexander had anticipated. He looked around, but the shed had only one exit.

"I'm armed, Jeb, and I'm willing to shoot my way out! You're going to jail for what you did!"

"Brave last words." Jebediah chuckled. "Either you give up, or we'll blast you to pieces inside the shed. Your decision. I'm here with four of my men."

"You won't shoot the stuff you're hoarding in here. I bet your customers wouldn't wanna see the weed go up in flames."

"Maybe. Let's face it, Alex, it's a standoff. We might not get in without you shooting one of us, but you can't get out if you want to live."

Alexander tried to get a glimpse of what was going on through a slit in the wall. Jebediah was telling the truth. He could see him and two men, armed with short-barreled guns that could be loaded with buckshot or bullets.

"Damn it!" Alexander checked the magazine, and his hopes vanished. The vigilante he had knocked out had forgotten to load the rifle. "This is just my luck," he mumbled.

Outside, the vigilantes took position. Jebediah stayed in the background and directed his minions with gestures. Alexander expected them to shoot from the rear side to force him out through the door, so Jebediah would have a clear shot at his chest.

He didn't want to be shot—not here, not now. He thought about Charlene and that his endeavor and his suffering were in vain if he died in the farthest corner of the Turner premises to be buried in a shallow grave. Maybe the cavalry would ride to the rescue, but even if Nicolas had informed Freeman about the imminent danger, the ATF needed two hours at least to arrive with sufficient forces.

A large SUV droned toward the shed, then the engine died, and two men got out. Alexander didn't need to see them to know that Nathaniel and Michael Steward had arrived to back up Jebediah.

Alexander cursed under his breath and hung his head, knowing he stood no chance against the combined firepower of six men. It was devastating to realize he had risked so much and gained so little. There was no hope someone would come to rescue him. Neither farmhands nor grooms would dare stand up against Jebediah, and if the men knew the Stewards, they would run for their lives.

Accepting his fate, no matter its color, Alexander put down the rifle and went to the door. "Don't shoot! I'm coming out!"

"Nice and slow," Nathaniel snarled, just like *Dirty Harry*.

"One move too many, and you'll bleed your life out in the dirt. You got that?"

"I got it. Just hold your fire!" Alexander opened the door and stepped out into the sunshine. He turned and lifted his hands.

Jebediah stood to the right, grinning like a fool. Michael waited on the left with the rifle butt pressed against his thigh like the old big-game hunters did after killing an elephant. Nathaniel held his rifle pointed at Alexander, ready to put a bullet in him if he tried to escape.

"For Harry and Lloyd, every day is a no-brainer." Alexander shook his head. "You two can't stay away when there's someone to kill, huh?" He knew his life was forfeit, and this was much harder to accept than he thought.

Jebediah wouldn't lock him up again. He knew too much now and was witness to a crime that couldn't be explained or glossed over. The Turners were dealing in drugs—it would be too much for anyone in town. It would break the family apart, sending more members behind bars than any other crime they committed. Alexander regretted that he wouldn't see Charlene again, the love of his life. He regretted that they had spent so little time with each other. His heart ached as he imagined how she would react when she learned he was dead.

"On your knees!" Nathaniel ordered.

"Oh, you're gonna shoot me right here?" Alexander looked left and right, seeking any possible chance to survive the day. "You have to bury me deep so that no one's gonna find me."

"Not so lucky." Michael handed his brother the rifle and used a zip tie to shackle Alexander's hands behind his back before he frisked him thoroughly. He found the tools and the knife and also the package. "You stole marijuana? Seriously? Did you want to get high on the way out? Get up and into the car."

"Fancy piece," Alexander said, referring to the large lights mounted on top of the cab. "For hunting at night?"

"We always catch our prey, yes." Michael's wide-open eyes glimmered with excitement.

Suddenly, Alexander understood what they were up to. It was too late. If he didn't die right away, he wouldn't last the day. Alexander was forced to lie down between the seats, and Michael tied his ankles.

Trust a few. Fear the rest.

CHAPTER FOURTEEN

Nicolas's mind whirled with thoughts of the cage that still stood in the stall in the old stable, and that he didn't want to spend another day in captivity, penned up like an animal. One night had been horrible, another one would break him. In his despair, he tried to press the release of the seat belt prior to the van reaching the Turner premises. Sweat stung in his eyes, and his right hip was still numb from the zap of the cattle prod. He grunted and yet tried to move inconspicuously.

When the van turned the corner to the driveway, Tyrone stopped and told Darren to get out and ask the vigilante standing nearby about Jebediah's whereabouts.

"He left with Mike and Nate," Darren said upon his return. "Do you want me to come with you?"

"No." Tyrone backed up and drove toward town. "I know exactly where they're going." He hit the gas and glanced at Nicolas in the rear mirror. "This is going to be fun, sucker. A lot of fun."

Jason scratched his head as he slumped in his chair and dialed Freeman's number. In an attempt to deliver a concise report of the case, Jason had his notes handy. He didn't get any further than saying his name when Freeman told him about the operation he had just launched to get Nicolas and Thomas out of Florence Town.

"Finally." Jason's heartbeat sped up. "Can we do anything? Do you need help?"

"My team's on its way, and, no, we've got enough men to contain the situation. Your CSU will be very helpful. I already spoke with Gerald, and he set the wheels in motion." Freeman offered a short summary of the plan, then asked, "Why did you call in the first place?"

"I guess it's not that important, but I wanted to inform you about the ongoing investigation. The Parker brothers were helpful, but not by much. They admitted they drove around and might've passed through Gillanburg and later through Richmond. They deny, of course, that they placed the bombs or had anything to do with the bombers, etcetera. We know they must've lived elsewhere, because the apartment was clean, much too tidy for these guys. I assume they were with the Turners, but I have to send pictures of them to the sheriff in Florence Town and hope someone recognizes them."

Freeman grunted. "Nothing that ties them to the crimes aside from the van?"

"CSU is still on it, and they're disassembling the van as we speak. If they find clues, I'll let you know."

Freeman paused, and Jason heard him talking with a woman in the background. When he back on the line, he sounded cheerful.

"Guess what we just found out? You will be surprised."

"You have my attention." Jason settled back in his chair and started playing with a pen.

Freeman laughed. "Okay, I'm glad to hear that. The *Natural Beauty Cosmetics Company* is a competitor to *Fine and Pure Cosmetics*, a company recently acknowledged at the stock exchange. The Turners have held shares from the beginning. *Fine and Pure* stock is gaining value due to the complete drop-out of *Natural Beauty.* Thus, the Turners are making money fast. And I mean, really fast."

"Now you've got me. Are you saying that the liquid fertilizer company is also noted at the stock exchange?"

"No. The management changed, and they now charge a third more than last year. I suppose the target was chosen to bomb them out of the market in reaction to their drastic increase in prices."

"The Turners had been a customer?"

"Yep. They're buying from a competitor who charges less. I compared the numbers." Freeman sounded pleased. "Now, ask me about the third bomb."

Jason had the whiteboard in view. He pursed his lips. "What about it?"

Freeman made a humming sound. "As my agent found out, the hospital in Florence Town is partly financed by profits from their affiliated *Florence Research Center*. The total dropout of the research center in Richmond increases their profits here, as well."

"That explains a lot." Jason made notes on his pad. "Okay, that leaves bomb number four, the burning marijuana."

"I've got no idea. Either they mixed up the targets or expected something else. The company, though, has got no ties to the Turners or their associated companies. There are no competitors in sight that might take advantage of the bombing, not to mention that more marijuana was destroyed than artificial body parts. I handed the case to the DEA."

"Is it possible the Turners have more skeletons in the closet than any of us imagines?"

"Be as it may," Freeman replied. "I have to go and head a rescue mission."

Lying on the floor, shoved between the seat of a bouncing SUV, was not a comfortable position. Alexander groaned as another bump in the road caused the restraints on his wrists and ankles to chafe more.

Jebediah kicked Alexander's legs. "Tell me, sucker, what

did you do that Jacob let you go?"

Alexander craned his neck to look up. "He found out the truth — that Charlene's in love with me. All of your shenanigans didn't work in the end." Though he didn't feel like it, Alexander bared his teeth in an evil grin. "She's mine, and even her father accepts that."

"No longer, you bastard."

Alexander could tell by the young goon's expression that his macho attitude was an act. He assumed Jebediah had accompanied the Stewards because staying behind would look cowardice and would've ruined his reputation.

"Killing me isn't as easy as it looks, huh?" Alexander sneered.

Jebediah looked away.

"This is going nowhere, Jeb. You won't get away with murder, even if you don't pull the trigger. What about Roker? Was that easier because he had tried to misuse Charlene?"

Jebediah clenched his fists and his teeth, obviously trying to contain his anger as well as his fear.

"And then Bronsteen had to be eliminated. Was he a threat, too, or just . . . a collateral damage?"

"If the shithead is bothering you, I'll gag him," Michael announced from the passenger seat and turned around. "I've got a few gags in the back to . . . Hey, are you getting queasy? Should we stop so you won't puke in the car? Hell, get your shit together, Jeb. Remember, you asked *us* to come and help you out."

"And we did," Nathaniel said with conviction. "Just don't lose your nerve now."

"I won't." Jebediah couldn't look at Alexander. "And, yes, gag him. He won't stop babbling."

Alexander huffed. "You're a coward, Jeb. You leave the dirty work to your minions and turn away."

"Shut up!" Jebediah yelled at the top of his lungs.

"Wow, hold on!" Nathaniel braked on the shoulder of the road.

Michael climbed out, opened the back, and rummaged around.

Alexander bumped Jebediah to force the guy to look at him. "You are a murderer, Jeb, and you're gonna pay for your crimes."

Jebediah swallowed hard and stared through the window while Michael gagged Alexander, cackling and wearing an evil grin the whole time.

Jason looked up when Matthew walked back into their work-space.

"Some hours to think things over can work miracles," Matthew announced, looking smug. "I thought Coby was the weaker one — injured and all — and I was right."

Jason turned to fill his coffee mug. He avoided looking at Matthew to not let him see his disapproval. "You returned to interrogate Coby Parker *alone*?"

"Well, I had some ideas and thought I'd ask him right away. So, yes."

Jason swallowed the comments jumping around his mind and sipped his coffee. "What did he tell you?"

"I accused him of placing at least one bomb." He put his coat on the backrest of his chair. "Told him the damage and human casualties he caused will result in a lifetime sentence, but if he cooperated, there might be a chance the judge will vote in his favor. Maybe. I didn't promise anything."

"You took him off the meds?" Jason lifted his gaze briefly.

The older agent had his way of dealing with a case, believing results came first.

Matthew stared at him, and his jaw dropped open.

"You . . . you think I left you out because I violated the suspect's rights? Are you out of your mind? Seriously, do you think I wouldn't do this by the book?"

Jason hesitated, searching furiously for a diplomatic way out. "Well, tell me that we got another lead."

"Yes." Matthew fetched a cup of coffee, responding in a neutral tone. "He told me the name of another partner — Oscar Henstridge. I got his address and informed local police in Fredericksburg to confirm he's home. The SWAT team is standing by. They're preparing for departure as we speak. We can join them."

Jason looked toward Sullivan's office, but the senior agent had left for an appointment with the chief of police and wouldn't show up for another hour. Quickly, he checked his emails and read Miller's report. "Coby told the truth. Miller confirms that Henstridge had been in the van. It's his hair they found." He looked up, mellowing for the sake of the investigation. He decided, however, to mention Matthew's behavior to Nicolas.

"Okay, so we're going to catch another bad guy." He switched off his computer and followed Matthew toward the garage. "If you do this again, I'll take it to the boss."

"My timing, or that I threatened the suspect with shooting his kneecap if he didn't cooperate?"

Samuel massaged his forehead with two fingers in a vain attempt to get rid of his headache. He was nauseated thinking of the work waiting for him and the threats his partners from the south had uttered during their last meeting. He wanted out of the deal, but the Mexicans had made it clear their arrangement couldn't be altered or terminated. Moreover, they were thinking about expanding their business in Virginia. If he had it right, the Mexicans referred to human trafficking and other ventures he considered repulsive. Though their leader had been pleased with the successful destruction of his competitor's marijuana, Samuel dreaded the next confrontation and further demands. If the Mexicans proposed sending kidnapped victims to the Turners, he wouldn't know how to turn them down.

Needled by the lasting pain, Samuel pondered involving Sheriff Reese and the vigilante committee to help the Turners with their Mexican problem, but he couldn't decide whether their participation would lead to closure. He didn't know the size of the Mexican gang, or whether he would endanger his family with the murder of the goons who transported the marijuana.

The problem was too complicated to solve alone. He stood a long time at the window overlooking the property, but no epiphany appeared.

To distract from his growing despair, Nicolas let his thoughts travel back memory lane. He imagined Jacklyn's contagious laughter, her happiness about the new home, her exuberance when it came to choosing carpets and furniture. They had sat on the couch discussing colors, and more than once, Nicolas had been surprised when she wanted to know his opinion. It wasn't an act. She truly wanted him to be her partner in every part of her life. It was astonishing.

Nicolas remembered one late evening when they had sat with a glass of wine, debating the pros and cons of white furniture. Out of the blue, she had laughed, set down their drinks, and pushed him back on the couch, calling him a *caveman* because he loved soft brown colors for their calming effect. The little argument had led to an amusing struggle on the couch, then on the carpet, and eventually on the bed. Somewhere in between the change of location, they had lost their clothes, and Nicolas had seduced his lover with his hands, his tongue and — much to her pleasure — with his rod. Jacklyn had permitted him to take her from behind, and he had relished the change of position. It was a true gift from her, a sign of trust that sent shivers down his spine. He had been careful, almost restrained in his approach, though the heat of the act took his breath away.

Even though a part of him knew he was being taken to his execution, the other part fought bitterly for hope that he would survive this day and return to Jacklyn to hold her in his arms again.

Tyrone looked at him in the rearview mirror. "I'm wondering — who are you working for? I no longer believe that you're some loser who needed a place to stay. You're too interested in our doings." He scoffed. "Maybe you were searching for something you could blackmail us with. Well, I can tell you, others tried and failed. We're a big family, and we protect each other."

Tyrone raised his brows as he steered the van through a large gate and along a graveled path past a huge manor with lots of glass that reflected the sunlight. "Did you know Alex prior to working here, or was he some kind of soulmate you met in the mud? I bet you had some things in common. When Alex got here, he was so . . . obliging I wanted to puke. He won the old man over in two days flat, and he hired him as a groom though everyone could see he had no idea about horses." Tyrone shook his head, chuckling. "Jeb said Alex was out to make the old man add him into his last will. Yes, that's not as stupid as it sounds. Our grandfather has strange ideas from time to time. And Alex knew how to play the role to make himself irreplaceable. Suddenly, he became a horse whisperer. Imagine that. This scumbag from nowhere turns out to have a hand for horses. And Jacob fell for him, asked for his opinion, let him have his way with the foals, talked to him about horses and breeding for hours and hours.

"While he pushed us away, Alex turned into the beloved son he never had." Tyrone's chuckle turned malevolent. "But then the wonderful replacement son made a mistake—he set eyes on Charlene Loman. And old man Loman didn't approve." He nodded toward the windshield. "That was the turning point. He had gone one step too far to be tolerable, and bang, Jebediah had him by the balls."

Close to a hunting lodge deep inside the woods, Tyrone stopped his van behind a large black SUV and got out. Nicolas put his thumb on the release for the seat belt and waited until Tyrone was around the hood. The seat belt came loose, and Nicolas turned to the right. When the door started to open, he kicked with all his strength to push it wide open. Tyrone cried out as he fell on his butt. In an ill attempt to stop his fall, he used his right hand and cried out again when it cracked. Nicolas wiggled free of the seat belt and was out of the van in no time.

While Tyrone tried to get back on his feet, Nicolas turned to the left and ran toward the forest.

"Fuck this!" Tyrone cursed. "Nate! Here's a runner!"

Nicolas headed for the small path behind the first line of trees, then turned east toward the road the van had taken. He needed to get back to the street and find help. Behind him, someone cocked a gun and shot. Birds flew up in panic. Nicolas hastened on.

"Stop and come out! Now!" Nathaniel shouted. "The next bullet won't miss! I know exactly where you are!"

Nicolas took it to be a ruse and ran as fast as his shackled hands allowed. He brushed against twigs left and right but made good progress.

A bullet hit the trunk in front of him, ripping off bark and leaving a fresh wound of light brown wood. Nicolas stopped, panting, thinking furiously for any way out. He couldn't imagine how Nathaniel knew which way he had taken, and yet he didn't dare to go on.

"I said come out! Now!"

The second bullet shattered the branch left of him and cut it in half. Shocked by such precision, Nicolas stared at the fallen branch and judged the bullet size—hit by one in the shoulder, he'd bleed to death within minutes.

"Last chance!"

Nicolas exhaled and closed his eyes for a moment. He could choose between being shot on the run right now or being executed at some remote location after digging his own grave.

He chose to live a few hours longer.

After Jason shared the news that the ATF was sending a rescue team to free Nicolas and his colleague from the Turners, he tried to judge Matthew's mood while *R.E.M.* sang a song about a man on the moon. He was sick of listening to just one band throughout the ride, but considering their strained relationship, he preferred to stay quiet and endure the music rather than fight about a radio station.

Oscar Henstridge had a list of criminal offenses longer than Jason's arm, including robbery, assault, and using explosives to blackmail bank employees to fork out money. Jason and Matthew assumed the guy had been the replacement blaster after Milton Roker's death. Jason put his hopes on Henstridge's confession, assuming he had no allegiances aside from himself.

R.E.M. started singing *Losing My Religion*, apparently one of Matthew's favorite songs. Jason had a hard time trying to not roll his eyes and moan with distress at Matthew, who was singing along too high and off-key. He suspected Matthew was trying to needle him, which was another reason why he preferred to go through the case details again instead of wreaking his anger on his partner.

Jason stopped the car a block away from the suspect's home, and they got out.

Henstridge lived in a suburb of Fredericksburg, in a small, run-down house that appeared close to collapsing in any kind of wind stronger than a whistle. The wooden fence was broken in many places, and empty cans, garbage bags, and remnants of plastic containers lay scattered on the untidy lawn. A broken chair leaned against the stairs leading to the main entrance. The wooden door was open while the screen door hung haphazardly on its hinges.

Jason listened as Al Warner, the stout SWAT team leader, explained in a gruff voice that his men would go in first. He assumed the suspect was home and maybe hiding behind a self-made barricade. Infrared cameras showed three possible targets roaming the three-bedroom house.

"And I think they've got a lot of firepower in there. Take it from me—such a guy won't surrender. We'll drag him out overwhelmed or dead."

Back at the car, Matthew put on his bulletproof vest.

"You don't want to storm the building with them, right?" Jason frowned. "That's why we've got the SWAT team—to avoid getting shot by those bastards."

"I'm aware of that." Matthew armed himself. "But I want answers, not a dead bomber. He won't help us bring down the Turners with two bullets in his head. Take it from me—I know how men like Warner work. It's their method to shoot first and ask questions later."

Jason turned away to take a deep breath. If Nicolas had proposed such a move, Jason would've followed. He felt the pressure weigh him down while he pondered joining Matthew or staying behind.

"You stay here," Matthew said with a lopsided smile. "I wouldn't want you to catch a bullet. Nicolas would deliver a beating I don't want to endure."

"Are you pampering me?"

"Oh, Jason, I didn't mean to ruffle your feathers." Matthew's tone was cheerful. "I love getting involved. You don't. That's okay."

"You consider me a coward."

"More probable is you've got more common sense than I do." He turned away to tell Warner he'd be with them and received a helmet and earphone.

Despite his nature, Jason was angry. Matthew had him out-maneuvered, and would surely use his reluctance against him, one way or the other. There was no way Jason could justify staying behind and watching his interim partner march into danger. Cursing his hesitation and Matthew's teasing, Jason geared up.

Nicolas was shocked at seeing Alexander close to the hunting lodge, bound to one of the pillars. He was gagged as well, so all they could do was exchange glances of mutual commiseration.

"Are you ready for your greatest performance?" Nathaniel asked as he slung his rifle across his shoulder. He was in such an exuberant mood his hips were swinging as he walked.

"Ready or not, we'll give you a head start of an hour." Michael freed both Alexander and Nicolas from the gags. "You'll enter an area of a hundred acres of woodland, in which you can do what you want. You can stay where we'll drop you or run in hope of finding a place to hide." He grinned. "There're a lot of places to hide, but be aware we know them all."

"And how long are you gonna chase us?" Alexander asked. "If you can come after us as long as you want, we stand no chance."

Nathaniel and Tyrone laughed out loud while Jebediah stood aside, chuckling but not looking pleased.

"You won't make it far, anyway," Michael said with conviction. "You can run or walk or try to slip inside a tree. No matter what you do, we'll find you sooner or later."

"It's not really fair, huh?" Nicolas said. "You've got high-end weaponry, and we've got nothing. If you wanted a competition and not a slaughter, you'd give us guns."

"Oh, now you think you can dictate the terms? No, suckers, you can't." Michael reached inside a bag and pulled out two hoods. "Jeb and Ty will lead you into the woods now, release you, and come back. We'll set the time."

"This is nothing but a delayed execution." Nicolas looked at Jebediah, desperately hoping for a turn of events to his benefit. "Are you okay with that? Do you enjoy the idea that they're gonna shoot us like fish in a barrel? Do you look forward to seeing us bleed to death? Maybe they'll call you to dig the graves—somewhere close to Madison? Or maybe this time they'll choose a place further away, so you have to drive our dead bodies through the county. How do you like that?"

Nathaniel laughed out loud and pointed a finger at Jebediah. "He got you! You're not the one burying them, huh? Would make your stomach flip. And, hey, Tyrone—you shouldn't laugh so hard. You claim you're quite a digger! Only that you lost interest after fifteen minutes!"

"Get over it!" Tyrone barked. He glanced at Jebediah, then turned back to Michael. "Do you want to hunt them now or talk them to death?"

Jebediah looked like he wanted to turn away and let his breakfast see the sunlight again.

"Oh, great words from someone who can't fight a man penned up in a stall!" Michael chided.

Tyrone pulled his weapon so fast he startled everyone but

Michael. "Let's do this, or I'll shoot them right here!"

"Wo-ho, gunslinger!" Michael lifted a hand. "You had your chance, but your buddy called us. You won't ruin my day."

"Yes, don't ruin his day, Ty," Alexander said mockingly. "You could kill us and make him dig the graves. How about that?"

"Shut up! All of you!" Nathaniel boomed. He pulled the hoods over Nicolas's and Alexander's heads. "Mike and I will take them to the starting point. You stay here and twiddle your thumbs if you want to." He pushed Nicolas toward the path leading into the woods. "Amateurs!"

Jason was no coward, but the shootout got on his nerves the longer it lasted. As Warner had predicted, Henstridge and his companions lived in a house built like a fort, a revelation that briefly shocked Jason and Matthew and forced them to alter their M.O.

The police officers were welcomed with machine-gun fire, making storming the house complicated. Jason heard Matthew's voice over the intercom saying he'd go left to try and circle one of the suspects. Even without a military background, Matthew blended in and knew his moves. Warner hadn't hesitated to accept his support, while he had looked at Jason with quiet reserve. In his anger, Jason almost forgot himself and felt an urge to go in first, if only to prove his value. His instinct of self-preservation won, so he stayed in the second line.

He had entered the living room when he heard a whistling sound as if someone had left a kettle on the stove.

"Out! Everybody out!" Warner shouted via intercom.

Jason turned on his heels and ran toward the exit, then flung himself down the stairs and onto the ground. A bear trap snapped up, so he rolled in the opposite direction, avoiding the jumping metal fangs. Behind him, an explosion rocked the property, shattering glass and wood. Shards burst across the patio and the lawn like confetti. Jason covered his head with his hands, fearful of sharp edges, and at the same time afraid to crawl away to where there might be more traps waiting.

When he dared to change position and looked back, one side of the house had a gaping hole of plaster, stones, and splinters. The roof was partly shattered but still holding. Two SWAT team members stumbled toward the street and collapsed, coughing and groaning. He heard Warner's muffled call for an ambulance and his order for each man to acknowledge their position and give a damage report.

Covered with concrete dust and debris, Jason got on his feet, swaying, ears ringing. The rational part of his mind ordered him to get away from the disaster site and take cover. The other part demanded he search for wounded team members and his partner, who'd been close to the destruction area.

He admired the SWAT team members who — apparently — didn't think about caution or self-protection when they entered the destroyed building as quickly as possible. They jumped across a broken window and shoved splintered wood to the side. He forced his body to follow the team in spite of the dust that hampered his breathing.

The intercom delivered fragmented reports about the location of injured comrades. Jason located and helped up a police officer and escorted him outside, keeping an eye out for the traps. Back inside, he anticipated the hoodlums were still around and carefully treaded his way toward the rear side of the house. He swallowed his heart back down his throat, and scooping up what courage he had left, proceeded with his search. He found a badly wounded officer by a fallen wall, and when he couldn't free him with his bare hands, called out to Warner for assistance. Out of the corner of his eye, he spotted movement and assumed it was probably Matthew.

When he turned to greet his partner, the man glanced in his direction, then turned away and fled through the backyard.

"I found Henstridge! Repeat, I found Henstridge!"

Freeman checked his watch for the umpteenth time. The helicopter pilot did what he could, but he couldn't cover the distance from Washington, DC, to Florence Town any faster. While in the air, Freeman demanded reports from his crew on the ground. Six vehicles were heading to Florence Town while one was headed for Belmont to check the situation at the gas station where Nicolas had placed the call.

"I can land in one of the corrals," the pilot announced, "but I'll most certainly scare away all the horses."

"I don't give a damn if they run. Put the bird down!"

The pilot nodded and landed the helicopter expertly and as close as he dared to one of the buildings. As expected, the horses shied and madly ran in the other direction, while people in working gear stopped what they were doing and looked up. Freeman jumped off the moment the skids touched ground.

"Can anyone tell me about the whereabouts of Alexander Leeland?" he shouted.

The men shook their heads in unison, and Freeman wondered whether they didn't know or weren't about to tell him. He was in a hurry and had no time for games.

"Once more—I need to know where Alex is. I'm also looking for Nick Murray!"

The farmhands exchanged glances, then one man said, "I saw Nick this morning, but he left in his car."

"And after that? Did he return? Did anyone see him later

on?"

"No, he didn't return." The farmhand looked around, but the others shook their heads. "No. No one has seen him since."

"Alex?"

"Ask the grooms. He's with them." The man pointed toward a large stable. "You should ask one of the Turners. They should know where they are."

Freeman deployed two of his men to go search the stable. "Fine. Where do I find them?"

The men pointed toward the manor far across the yard.

Freeman sighed and checked his watch again, then started jogging.

"He's heading toward Tenth Street north. I'm in pursuit," Jason panted over the intercom.

Warner's voice came through crackled and hardly understandable. "Support's on the way. Just keep him in sight, don't act!"

Jason would've laughed if he had any breath left. Henstridge had shouldered his *Mac-10* machine pistol, but there was no doubt he would use it if any police officer got close.

Jason wondered about the other thugs and their positions. He glanced over his shoulder and saw a man in a leather jacket with a pump shotgun trained on him. He cursed, jumped across a low fence, and ran straight on. If the gangster shot, there was nothing he could do about it anyway.

Henstridge was still heading down the street. He glanced back now and then, obviously angry he couldn't reach a safe distance. Jason expected the guy to stop and shoot at any moment, if only to force him to take cover.

Behind him, shots from two different guns were fired. Jason jerked, fearing the impact, but he remained unharmed.

Someone cried out in pain. More shots erupted, and a man with a dark voice shouted an order.

Jason had no time to glance behind him. Henstridge had reached the corner and a broad street with traffic. He brought the *Mac-10* around and trained it on the first car that didn't evade fast enough. Brakes screeched as a blue *Volvo* stopped abruptly. Other cars in the lane honked, some steered to the left, some braked and came to a skidding halt. A truck rushed by in the left lane, horn blaring.

"No, no, no!" Jason sped toward the intersection, took a stand, and fired.

Henstridge was rounding the bumper when the bullet's impact flung him to the pavement. Jason didn't take a chance and shot again. The gangster slumped near the front tire and didn't move. Cautiously, he approached the man, shotgun leveled, finger around the trigger. At this point, he didn't give a damn whether Henstridge was able to testify or spend his last breath on a suburban street in Fredericksburg. He did feel better when he disarmed the hoodlum and discovered the man had merely lost consciousness. A steady pulse told him Henstridge was alive, at least for now. He took no chances, though, and put the man in handcuffs.

"Suspect's wounded, unconscious at the corner of Tenth Street and Madison. Send an ambulance, please." He expected Matthew to chime in and mock him, but there was only Warner's levelheaded confirmation.

Exhausted, Jason stood with hands on his knees, congratulating himself when no one else would.

CHAPTER FIFTEEN

Nicolas panted badly. In spite of the head start, without weapons and in unknown terrain, both he and Alexander stood no chance of escaping. The Stewards knew these woods by heart and wouldn't break a sweat if they couldn't find them in the first hour. He stumbled across some roots and caught himself, only to ram his shoulder against a trunk.

Behind him, Michael laughed. "Oh, this'll be fun. Ever been in the woods, dudes? I bet not. You'll run around in circles like ants without a trail of scent to follow. We'll watch you, and then, bang, you won't see us coming."

Nicolas cleared his throat. "You've got a thermal scope mounted, right? That's how you found me so quickly."

"Best you can get," Nathaniel replied, obviously proud of his equipment. "While others go for a drink at the bar, I spend my money on sights and ammo. So don't worry that I'll just wound you. If my bullet hits you, you're dead."

"Refreshing."

"A grim sense of humor? That's good. I hope you'll both try and run. I've had—" He stopped talking and started laughing. "Oh, I shouldn't tell you too much."

"They won't outsmart us," Michael said.

"Stop. This is a good place." Nathaniel undid Nicolas's handcuffs. "Don't try anything fancy. You're free now, but stay where you are and leave the hoods on until we're gone. You hear me? My rifle's trained on you."

Nicolas heard the men retreat and stood still. If they were to have a chance, he wouldn't ruin it now.

Freeman wasn't a runner, and the distance between the landing site and the manor was greater than he had anticipated. He was out of breath when he reached the broad entrance stairs and felt as if he had been thrown back in time by at least two centuries. The butler, who looked at him cautiously, seemed to have lived at least that long. Freeman showed his ID and requested to see the Turners at once.

The butler had him wait in the entrance hall. Freeman looked through the window at the land surrounding the house. The property was so large, it would take at least a day to search at all buildings, basements, and sheds. CSU could send all their teams, and none of them would be bored.

Freeman turned around at the sound of approaching heels.

"I'm the first Turner our butler found," a lady said apologetically. "I'm Joanne Turner, daughter-in-law of Jacob Turner." She reached out for a handshake.

Freeman admired the lady for her equanimity when confronted with a senior agent in full gear and a helicopter in the back yard.

"Agent Freeman, ATF, ma'am. I'm looking for Alexander Leeland and Nick Murray. Both men are supposed to be in danger, and if you can tell me their current whereabouts—"

"In danger?" She made a sound of utter pity that didn't fit Freeman's expectation. "I—" She took a deep breath, paling. "My apologies, Agent Freeman, but this comes as a shock. I talked with Nick just a few hours ago, and I hoped to see him around this morning." She cleared her throat. "All right, what I can tell you is this. The Stewards came here earlier today with their monstrous SUV—a black one with four large lights mounted on top of the cab. They drove off like maniacs just fifteen minutes later." She ran a hand through her hair, ruining the perfect hairdo. "You must know they wouldn't show up out of the blue without a reason."

"Did you see Alex or Nick inside the SUV?"

"No, but I saw Jebediah in the back seat—he's one of Jacob's grandsons, and he looked angry. For a moment, he appeared to be speaking to someone in front of him—on the floor. Nathaniel Steward was driving, and his brother rode shotgun." She shook her head. "I don't like to admit it, but together they're known to cause mischief. I can't tell you exactly if Alexander or Nick was with them—I didn't see them through the window." She bit her lower lip, frowning. "How do you know that they're in danger?"

"Nick called me and asked for support and immediate extraction."

"Extraction? Excuse me, but what has the ATF to do with him?"

"He's working for me. Where on the Steward premises will they be? Do you know where exactly they would take him?"

"The Stewards live further north. It's a big compound with lots of woods around it. As far as I know, they've got a hunting lodge. A big building—fitting their ego. You can't miss it."

"Thank you for your help."

"Wait a moment! Please, let me know when you've found him."

"Will do." Freeman put aside all other questions he had and returned outside. He checked in with his men about the search for Alexander. They hadn't found him, but a farmhand had claimed he had seen him run toward the western fence. He hadn't been seen since, but there had been a large SUV and a lot of commotion. "I'm on my way!"

Jason was still catching his breath when an ambulance arrived on the scene. He consoled the driver of the *Volvo* and reassured her that the thug would no longer be a threat. He felt some pride in his accomplishment. He hadn't merely saved the lady — he'd prevented Henstridge from escaping. It was a good feeling, and he strutted back toward the criminal's house when another ambulance stopped in front of the building.

"Where's Matthew?" he asked Warner, who was directing his men to secure the house and help those injured. A bad feeling settled in his stomach.

Warner pointed over his shoulder. "He caught a bullet in his vest before my men could take down the second threat. Sorry to say, but your partner's on his way to the hospital."

Jason's high mood plummeted. "So he was the one right behind me."

"Yes, Agent Beckham. From what I learned, he was in pursuit and got in the way when the gangster wanted to stop you." Warner shook his head. "Tough bastards in their own league. I haven't seen such defenses for some time. CSU will have a ball securing evidence."

"I bet," Jason said absent-mindedly. "What about the third man?"

"Dead." Warner looked back toward the half-collapsed house. "Two dead, one alive for interrogation. And I hope they didn't clear the house of all the good stuff." He smirked. "Not a bad cut for the day."

Jason couldn't join Warner's cheerful mood, thinking of the wounded and dead police officers. "Tight security for Henstridge. I want him guarded twenty-four-seven, and I don't mind him handled roughly."

"Sure."

"I . . . I'll go see my partner."

"You do that." Warner's tone was commiserative. "I'll take it from here."

"Thanks . . . for your support."

"Well, you didn't do so bad yourself."

Jason heard doubt in the man's voice but had no room in his mind to bristle. He nodded curtly and left.

When Nicolas didn't hear the brothers anymore, he took off the hood. He was sweating profusely. Alexander stood left of him, looking worn out and hopeless. He wiped his face and looked around. The woods were dense, and they could hardly see sunlight through the thick ceiling of branches. Right in front of him, the land rose to a hillside with large boulders that looked like hunchback giants bowing toward the ground. A soft but chilly wind rustled the leaves.

"How are you?" Nicolas asked as he matched his pace to Alexander's.

"Nick, what does it matter?" Alexander took a deep breath, obviously trying but failing to hide his pain with every step. "Jacob released me after old man Loman told him the truth — finally. And I had nothing better to do than run straight into the next trap. They're buying and selling marijuana! Imagine that." He shook his head while they ascended the hill. "The Turners, the Stewards, and who knows what the Reese family is hiding? This town feels like an assembly of goons, each one protecting and supporting the other. If they kill us, they'll sweep everything under the rug . . . again."

"I called Freeman right before I was captured. He's on his way." Nicolas touched Alexander's shoulder. "Hey, we've got to stay ahead of them for an hour, maybe two. If they stick to their word —"

Alexander scoffed. "Seriously? I bet they're hiding somewhere close. Nick, these aren't honorable people. Have you thought about it? They hunt men for sport. We're today's entertainment for them, and they don't give a fuck whether they granted us an hour." He panted when they reached the hilltop and put his hands on his knees, groaning. "It'd be better if we split up. You're much faster without me."

"Forget it."

"No, I mean it. Look around. We have to go up and down and climb the rocks if we wanna keep the direction. Do you know where we're going?"

"Further west is a clearing, if my memory is correct. About two miles from here."

"You've got a map in your head?"

"Your boss made me memorize the surroundings of Florence Town in case I had to chase someone."

"He was thorough."

"Yes, he was. Come on."

"You expect Vernon to send a helicopter. Good." Alexander straightened and looked back the way they had come. "Honestly, I don't know how long I can keep up with you."

Nicolas had wondered the same. Alexander looked as if he'd collapse any moment. "Think of it, Alex . . . an hour. Even if the Stewards come, we can make it."

Alexander grinned. "Like in *First Blood. This time he's fighting for his life.*"

Jason pondered what to say to his partner when he found Matthew sitting on a gurney in one of the emergency rooms. A nurse was bandaging his ribs up to his shoulder. Judging by the way Matthew was clenching his teeth, the bullet had hurt him despite the bulletproof vest. Jason stepped into the room with his gaze cast to the floor, half expecting the older agent would cut him down to size.

"Hey, it's kind of you to drop by," Matthew said, his tone nonchalant. "I was wondering how I'd get back to the office."

Jason didn't buy his friendly smile. "Warner told me you —"

"What about Henstridge? Did you get him?"

"Henstridge was hospitalized with gunshot wounds to his

upper arm and thigh."

"Effective."

"Knock yourself out." Jason ran a hand through his hair, at odds with his behavior. He didn't know why he was angry. "He's in high security."

Matthew thanked the nurse and reached for his undershirt. "Not everything I say is meant to be sarcastic."

Jason bridged the distance and rolled up the shirt to help Matthew put it on. "I know."

"I told you to stay behind."

"Yeah, and I was at the wrong place at the wrong time. I get it." Jason sighed as he pulled the dress shirt over Matthew's shoulders to button it. "Just my luck."

"But you arrested Henstridge." Matthew got off the bed clumsily, suppressing a whimper. "That's your success."

"You caught a bullet meant for me. That's not what I consider a successful day."

Matthew chuckled while Jason held the jacket for him. "I had your back. That's how it should be. Thanks."

"You're welcome. What does the doc say?"

"Just two bruised ribs. It'll hurt for a few days. So don't make me laugh, and don't hustle me into chasing another bad guy, and I'll be fine."

They left the hospital, and Jason waited at the passenger door until Matthew had settled in the seat.

"No *R.E.M.* tape on the ride."

Matthew bit down hard when he burst out laughing. "Jason, you bastard, I told you!"

Jason got behind the wheel, grinning like the Cheshire cat.

Nicolas looked back the way they had come. "They're already behind us."

"I told you they wouldn't wait an hour," Alexander said

breathlessly when they heard rustling in the valley they had just left behind.

"They're bastards and don't even stick to their own rules." Nicolas reached out to help Alexander across the next boulder and into the relative safety of an assembly of rocks that shielded them against the thermal scope. They both had to catch their breaths. "We can't outrun them."

"And the rescue's not coming." Alexander squinted at the sky. "They won't find us if we don't get to that clearing."

"It's the ATF. Don't they have IR resolution on their helicopters?"

"Some of them." Alexander wiped his sweaty face. "I'm beat, Nick. I won't make it far." He reached out to touch Nicolas's arm. "Please, go. You don't have to die here."

"You sent me away this morning, and this is what came out of it. Maybe you should've left and not tried to play detective. Come on, I've got an idea. Up that hill over there."

"You're killing me."

"I'm trying to get us both saved." Nicolas grinned in spite of the gruesome situation. "Hey, show a little backbone."

"You're quoting *Indiana Jones* at me?"

"What?"

Jason helped Matthew take off his jacket and put it across a chair. "We might've identified Henstridge as one of the bombers, but he won't talk with us, let alone confess the crime or who was with him."

Matthew sat down, barely suppressing a groan. "He's a hardcore criminal, and even if we take him off the pain meds—which we can't do under the law—I'm convinced he wouldn't budge. He knows what's waiting for him if he gives in."

Jason handed him a cup of coffee.

"Thank you." Matthew pointed at the whiteboard Jason had plastered with notes and pictures of their investigation. "Summing up, we've got some leads, some evidence, three murdered men, and no murderer we can arrest."

"We know the connection between the killed blaster, his replacements, and the bombings." Jason sipped hot coffee as he stared at the notes. "We know the origin of the explosives and that the attacks were planned meticulously, considering that the purchase of the C-four was done in November."

"However, we haven't identified the buyers."

"Not yet. Freeman's on it. His men check all companies who've got a license to buy and sell the stuff. It's just a matter of time."

"Let's get back to the bombings. We arrested the Parker brothers and Henstridge, whose companions are dead. Four men were in the van that transported the bombs. The evidence in the house we raided today will help us shed light on this. In my opinion, that's enough to speak with a judge." Matthew grinned. "You should do it."

"I could, but what we've got so far would merely suffice to accuse the men of transporting the bombs and armed assault. Make no mistake. There's no hard proof they were at the targeted sites at the time of the explosions. Video surveillance inside the companies was sparse, and the men dodged it effectively. I'm not convinced, so why should a judge believe me?" He stared into his coffee cup, waiting for the one idea, the one clue that would solve the case.

"As soon as Nick and his ATF colleague are here, I'm sure we'll have everything we need."

Jason nodded but looked at his cell phone on the desk. Freeman had sounded as if both agents were in imminent danger.

Alexander's breath sounded like a badly-tuned whistle as he treaded his way uphill once more. He wanted to give up. He wanted to lie down and wait for the bullet that would end his life. The spark that kept him going was his partner's imperturbable belief that there was still a chance to survive, regardless of his condition. While Alexander doubted his body was up to the strain, Nicolas seemed convinced they could make it. His optimism was contagious, and Alexander knew that without the FBI agent he would be dead already.

He wanted to thank him, to tell him that one day he'd repay him somehow. He would think of something. When Nicolas turned to lend him a helping hand over yet another large boulder, a shot erupted from the valley below, and Alexander was flung forward against the stone. He cried out, but Nicolas grabbed him, then held him when his strength was reeling and he thought he'd lose his footing.

"Hold tight, Alex! Don't let go! I'll pull you up!"

Alexander felt his right hip going numb, along with his thigh and calf. He put his foot on the ledge to steady himself. One steep step up was all that was needed. Nicolas tightened his grip with this left arm and pulled with all he had. Alexander grunted with the strain as he tried to put weight on his right foot and make the step before the pain set in and he couldn't move anymore. Nicolas leaned back and pulled Alexander's weight with him, grimacing. Alexander found a hold for his left foot and pushed up until his upper body was over the top. Nicolas grabbed his belt when the second shot rang through the valley. Nicolas sat on his butt, and Alexander feared he would be shot as well.

"I'm okay." Nicolas crawled backward, allowing Alexander room to follow. "Here. Behind the rock. Stay here." He knelt in front of him, eyes wide, panting. "How bad is it?"

"Doesn't matter. What's your plan?" Alexander leaned against the stone, breathing raggedly. He saw more stars than leaves and tried to slow his breathing before he passed out. "Go! Do what you had in mind."

Nicolas faded from sight, and Alexander prayed he would see him again.

Freeman's pilot found the hunting lodge and circled the area. He saw the black SUV and a van parked behind it. No one was in sight, and the pilot shook his head when asked whether he could land. The woods around were dense, and the next clearing more than two miles away. Freeman ordered the pilot to head that way nevertheless and told his crew in the backup cars to split up and follow. They were fifteen minutes outside of Florence Town.

Samuel joined Gilead at the window overlooking the fields in the north. From where he stood, the workers looked like ants crawling around as they busily prepared the soil for planting.

Now that the helicopter was gone, everything seemed to go back to normal. At least, that was his hope. After the conversation with Joanne, Samuel was no longer certain the Turners would see the end of the day in freedom. He was thinking about packing and leaving when Gilead put his hands in his pants pockets and pulled up his shoulders.

"Your plan worked . . . whatever you did. I checked the numbers, and yes, we can breathe a little easier. Debts were paid and . . . well, the family's private accounts are recovering." Gilead twitched his brows. "Whereas your definition and mine might vary."

"Fine." Samuel sipped his iced tea and managed to smile. "You could book the income as planned?"

"Of course. The IRS won't find anything. Several stocks look promising these days." Gilead frowned and focused on the field again. Though they were alone, he lowered his voice. "Did you have anything to do with this?"

"I don't know what you're talking about. You invest the money the foundation gathers. That's not my business."

Gilead wiped sweat off his brow. His lips were a thin, bloodless line, making him look even more like a bank manager constantly under pressure. "You know what I mean. I read about a bomb attack at a cosmetics company in Richmond."

"So?"

"It was completely destroyed — nothing's left. One of our biggest competitors is off the market for good." Gilead shuffled his feet and swallowed audibly, then glanced at Samuel and hesitated with his next sentence. "You can't tell me this is a coincidence."

"It's a coincidence."

Gilead didn't look convinced. "Innocent people were killed. This is nothing you should take lightly." He cleared his throat. "I saw a truck arrive two days ago."

"Just another delivery that doesn't concern you." Samuel made eye contact. "They deposit their goods and move on as soon as possible. We take the money just for storing their goods for a certain amount of time."

Gilead's face relaxed briefly. "It's an expensive rent."

"Yes, it is." Samuel put a hand on Gilead's shoulder and forced a smile on his face that had nothing to do with joy. "Don't burden yourself with thoughts that lead to nothing. Enjoy the numbers and be assured you'll watch them grow."

Nicolas lay prone to peer over the boulder. He spotted Nathaniel and Michael, armed with hunting rifles, talking with each other, obviously having a great time. They zigzagged through the valley but didn't look up. They had apparently heard Alexander's scream and expected to find their prey bleeding up the next hill.

Quietly, Nicolas retreated, grabbed a long, broken branch and pressed it under a large rock close to the ledge. The stone was loose, but it was heavy. He had hoped to have Alexander's help when he tried to move it, but he was lucky his partner was still alive. While putting his weight on the branch as a lever, he remembered Nathaniel saying he could kill his target with one bullet. Had he missed Alexander on purpose? Did he intend to slow them down but not kill them right away? Did the brothers enjoy the hunt so much they didn't want it to end so quickly?

Enraged, Nicolas pushed harder to move the stone closer to the ledge. Once more, he checked their enemies' position. They had crossed the valley, secured the rifles across their shoulders, and were climbing up. Like Alexander and Nicolas, they had to keep focused on where they could find a hold. The boulders were slippery with moss, and some had cracks that would break a man's hand, but Michael, who came first, was an excellent climber.

Nicolas waited until both men were in line with each other. Then he gave the stone the final push.

Nathaniel looked up when he heard the sudden rumble. "Mike! Watch out!"

The stone was more than twice as large as a football, and it didn't bounce. It fell straight at Michael, who let go of his hold with one hand and swung to the side, but he couldn't evade the impact completely. Nicolas saw the stone hit his left shoulder before it tumbled to the right and therefore missed Nathaniel. Michael screamed in pain, still holding to an edge with one hand.

"I've got you!" Nathaniel shouted as he kept his brother from falling. Michael was still howling in pain when Nathaniel steadied his body and helped him five feet down the slope so he could sit down. "I'm coming for you, bastards!" Nathaniel shook his fist in Nicolas's direction.

Nicolas immediately rushed back to Alexander. "Hey, one's down, the other will get here any minute. Up with you!"

Alexander groaned and lifted his bloody hand off his hip. "Not like this."

"Nathaniel knows we're up here, and he's pissed that I hurt his brother. He won't wait for me to give you first aid. Come on!" Nicolas grabbed Alexander under his right arm, pulled him to his feet, and steadied him when his knees buckled. "We can make it. We'll find another place to hide, and then I'll knock down Nate, too."

"Nick, please . . ." He groaned loudly.

"Keep going, Alex! I don't think I can carry you!"

"I thought—"

"Shut up and run!"

Alexander felt like he'd been thrown into an absurd end times movie in which he was one of the last men on earth trying to save mankind while machines were taking over. It took him a second, and another stumble, to realize his mind was stuck on the plot of *Terminator*. If he'd had any breath left, he would've laughed. He even imagined helicopters closing in with their searchlights and their large guns directed at the poor soul on the ground. He held tight to Nicolas's shoulder and limped as fast as he could.

Blood oozed from the wound at his hip, and his right leg was numb and almost useless. He did his best to ignore the pain that was increasing slowly but steadily. His heart thudded heavily in his chest, and he was losing strength fast. He slipped from Nicolas's grip as soon as they reached the next line of trees, collapsing to the ground.

"No! Get up again!" Nicolas crouched and gripped him under the armpits.

"I can't."

"You can." Nicolas clenched his teeth, and sweat trickled down his face, which was contorted with worry.

For the sake of the younger man, Alexander gathered his strength and held tight onto Nicolas's shoulder once more. His right leg throbbed with pain and couldn't carry his weight, but he leaned against Nicolas and trudged on.

In front of them, the noise of rotor blades grew louder. Alexander waited for the off-screen speaker to recap the development of the machines and how the *terminators* had diminished mankind in the war until only a few rebels remained. His perception was blurred by exhaustion. Behind them, he heard shouts to surrender, followed by gunfire.

Beside him, Nicolas gasped and doubled his efforts to take them out of harm's way. "Come on, it's not far now!"

Alexander hung his head and used his dwindling energy to put one foot in front of the other, hoping the automatic part of his body would take over and help him survive. Through the mist of pain, he heard steps in front of them and shouts echoing without meaning. He barely felt Nicolas's shoulder under his grip and was slightly aware that Nicolas held tight to his waistband in order to keep him upright.

"We made it!"

It was a shout of joy and relief, and Alexander tried to lift his head. Disoriented and at the end of his rope, he couldn't make out more than silhouettes and didn't know whether there were friends or foes approaching. He tried to form a sentence, but the darkness around him deepened, and he lost his grip on Nicolas's shoulder.

Nicolas went down with Alexander and worried when he

couldn't wake him up. He turned around to find Nathaniel fifteen yards behind him, the hunting rifle trained on him. "Fuck!"

"I told you I'm gonna get you!"

Nicolas stared into the black muzzle. At this distance, a shooter would never miss. Panting, Nicolas waited for the impact of the bullet, thinking nothing was worse than being shot when help had already arrived.

Nathaniel took another step forward, clearly relishing the pleasure of killing his prey. The smile on his face died when three men came running through the underbrush, arriving from the clearing where the helicopter had landed. Quickly, Nathaniel swiveled around and ran into the woods.

"Get him!" Freeman shouted over the clamor of the rotor blades, and two men in full gear took up the pursuit.

Nicolas lifted his gaze to Agent Freeman, who crouched beside Alexander and checked his vitals.

"That was a fucking close call," Nicolas grumbled.

"These are fucking big woods."

CHAPTER SIXTEEN

Nicolas sat in the back of the ATF van, legs dangling through the side door, enjoying a bottle of cold water. A medic was taking care of Alexander, and another one had bandaged a bleeding wound on Nicolas's right arm he hadn't noticed during the hunt. The past hour seemed like a nightmare, their escape a miracle, and the arrest of Nathaniel and Michael Steward a well-deserved reward for the ordeal he and Alexander had suffered.

Nicolas had given his statement in an abbreviated version. He would write the full report at the office. Looking back, Nicolas considered what he had lived through in the past six weeks. His relief that it was over had no bounds, and his exhaustion spread through his whole body. He wanted to lie down and yet felt the urge to tell Freeman everything he and Alexander had found out on the mission.

"Hey, you need a rest." Freeman approached, putting a hand on his shoulder. "You look dead on your feet. I'll have both of you taken to the hospital."

He forced a smile. "I'm okay. It's just a scratch."

Freeman raised his brows while he lowered his chin. "For this mission, Agent Hayes, I'm your boss, and your boss is telling you to stay a day at the hospital. If the doc says you're okay, I'll believe it."

"What about the Turners?"

"Their place is being raided as we speak. I brought search warrants for all three premises, and I'm looking forward to what CSU and the teams will turn up."

Samuel stood at the window overlooking the premises. He gaped at what was happening, and his mouth was dry. "The ATF is raiding our place! This is unbelievable!" A part of him wanted to run, while the other part accepted that it was too late. His hands trembled.

Jacob turned on his chair. "You can't believe it, or you don't understand that your decisions are backfiring? Whatever you ordered, you're facing the consequences now." He poured another glass of iced tea. "What kind of shenanigans did you pull off? Are you in trouble because of the . . . stuff you stored?"

Samuel swiveled around. "You know?"

"I told you before, I know a lot. It's a pity that so much good that was done here will drown because you and your brothers are too greedy."

Samuel jerked at the officers storming across the porch. "You would've given away the entire fortune for horses and the stupid villagers, who don't even say thank you."

"What's so bad about that?" His father squinted, obviously unruffled by the continual shouts that rang through the house. "The people are happy here. That's all that counts."

"Happy? You want them happy? I can't believe it. Didn't you ever think about us?"

"You and yours? You're a greedy bunch of scalawags, who live off the money our ancestors collected." Jacob sat up straight. He narrowed his eyes as he added a cutting edge to his words. "If ever one of you needed to start without a penny in your pocket, could you do it? I doubt it."

"That's not the point. You were throwing away money as if you had no family!"

"Maybe that would've been for the better."

Samuel swallowed against the throb in his throat again. Armored vehicles had delivered men in black uniforms who were roaming the yard and gathering the farmhands and the grooms for interrogation. "They're searching the whole compound." He didn't see Jebediah anywhere and hoped his son was far away.

"How much of this mess can be traced back to you?" Jacob turned his head a fraction. "What about Roker and Snakey? Will anyone talk about who killed them?" The look on the old man's face clearly said he had known about his sons' criminal activities all along.

"Talk?" Samuel couldn't cope with his father's sudden revelations. "No—I mean, I don't know." Samuel's heart beat hard against his ribs as his father glared at him. "Roker . . . he tried to rape Charlene. He . . . he stumbled into Jeb that day and—" He broke off, seeing Jacob's stunned expression.

The old man gathered his wits quickly. "But you knew you had to get rid of him. And you also knew it was time to dispose of Snakey, I suppose, after he asked too many questions." He lifted his chin. "Though I suspect you had someone doing it for you, huh? You don't have the guts to take a man's life."

Samuel paled and broke into a sweat. His voice was a hoarse whisper. "You know?"

"By the love of God, when will you realize that nothing happens on this estate without me knowing about it? Jebediah used to brag about his . . . *abilities* . . . if there are any. He's a show-off of the worst kind." He stopped Samuel with a move of his hand. "I know you and your brothers reached out to those damned dealers from Mexico. I know you made an arrangement to use this place as a reloading site. I suppose the money was too good to pass up. How did you contact them, anyway?"

"Jebediah . . . he somehow arranged this . . . deal."

"Ah. Well, I'd assumed that much. Probably with Tyrone's help." Father watched the forces on the ground interrogate the farmhands and a few vigilantes while more men surrounded the manor. "Was it worth *that* result? Did you intend to boast about your transactions with those faceless dealers?" Jacob narrowed his eyes. "Was it the plan to wait for my death and then rob the town? Undo everything I invested, and let the people suffer?" He shook his head and interrupted Samuel's effort to explain again. "You and your brothers have degraded into pitiful criminals, greedy for money and even more money. What are you hiding in the basement of the guesthouse? More drugs?"

Samuel was too upset for a blank face, but by pressing his lips tightly together he managed to keep relief out of his face. He couldn't believe his luck that his father hadn't taken a look while Roker was still there. Still, his heart beat fast and painfully against his ribs. "No, father, no drugs."

Jacob huffed, clasping his hands behind his back again and watching the police forces. "Then what about the strangers who moved in and out like ants stealing sugar? Was Roker mad, or did he build a bomb down there?"

"A bomb? What're you talking about?"

Father glared at him, and Samuel realized his breathless response had given him away.

"The occasion that your lies convince me has yet to arrive. I heard the strange folk you invited talk about ingredients and targets. You know I don't sleep well, and I don't need eight hours to wake up refreshed. Some nights, I roam the house like a spirit, and I wander around the yard to contemplate. In those nights, I hear a lot — voices, engines, boxes being pushed onto trucks." He cocked his head. "The means of your enterprise are various. Now tell me. How much of your crimes can be traced back to you? I need to know, because there's little time left until these officers outside will knock on the door and demand answers. I don't want to be arrested because of your misdeeds."

Samuel stared at the black uniforms and feverishly thought of a way out, but his mind was numb.

"I thought so." Jacob scoffed. "Oh, the irony of it! Murder, deceit, and reloading site for illegal goods. What will you do now?" When Samuel didn't reply, Jacob took a deep breath. "I think I'll not only talk with my lawyer about the accusations at hand, but also about a serious change to my last will."

Samuel shuddered and wished he could escape his father's vitriol.

Jason picked up the phone. From the moment Freeman had told him about the rescue mission, he had worried more than a teenager prior to his first date. "Beckham."

"It's Freeman. Just wanted to let you know that Thomas and Nicolas made it out of the woods — quite literally. They're on their way to DC as we speak. ETA in two hours."

"Are they . . . okay? Injured?"

"Thomas was nicked by a bullet. Nicolas is okay, more exhausted than wounded. I ordered both men taken to George Washington Hospital."

"I'll be there." Jason ran a hand through his hair. A thousand thoughts ran amok through his head. Most of them had to do with gratitude, and that he needed to call Jacklyn. "What about the Turners? Did you arrest them?"

"My men surrounded the compound and didn't let anyone out. Evidence was delivered to the judge in charge of the district, and we're raiding the place." He paused, asked a question that was muffled, and when he got back on, he sounded stressed. "Looks like we've got some runners we have to take care of. I've got to go."

Jason put down the receiver and let go of the breath he

hadn't known he was holding. "They're free. They're on their way here."

"What happened?" Matthew asked.

"I can't tell. They escaped." He dialed Jacky's number. "That's all that counts, at least for me."

Jacklyn had seen Nicolas in a hospital bed before. Back then, he'd suffered burn marks on his throat and a long gash on his calf while in captivity. He still carried the scars as a reminder of the dangers of his job. He could be injured every day while investigating, and she couldn't do anything to prevent it.

She would've loved to see him change professions. Seeing him wounded and exhausted only underscored her opinion. An office job was a much safer alternative. However, he considered the prospect of spending his work time at a desk boring, even intolerable. In one of their long conversations, Nicolas had pointed out he wouldn't give up his job even if he suffered injuries and injustice. In the same breath, he had granted Jacklyn the decision about how their love life would evolve. After a moment of stunned surprise, she had accepted his grand offer. The memory of the hour that followed their deal made her smile.

As quietly as she could, she pulled up a chair and sat down to watch Nicolas's relaxed face. She longed to touch him and assure herself he was no illusion. For now, she had him back, but it wouldn't keep the nightmares from returning. Sighing, she leaned back on the uncomfortable chair and had just drifted into a daydream when out of the corner of her eye she spotted Agent Freeman standing at the door.

He beckoned her to follow him into the corridor.

Jacklyn was relieved to see him. "From what the doctor told me, Nicolas suffered a minor gunshot wound on his right arm and some bruises from several brawls, I assume. The doc said I can take him home when he's through with his examinations." She cleared her throat and suppressed the urge to weep. "Jason told me you sent a rescue team?"

"Nick called and asked me to pull them out. Thomas wouldn't have lasted many more days. He was the captive of one of the Turner sons and treated badly. The way he looks, it was about time I brought him home."

Jacklyn broke eye contact and took a deep breath to quash her fear that the entire mission could've gone south. "Were they successful, at least?"

Agent Freeman hesitated, hands propped on his hips. "Let's say we haven't evaluated all of the evidence. We'll know more in a few days. Several people are under arrest as murder suspects, and a lot of marijuana was found. The Turners have a lot of explaining to do. Charges are being written as we speak." Agent Freeman looked through the open door. "I just came here to see how Tagline's faring."

"Nick's job's done, I suppose? I couldn't stand to see him working the next few days."

Freeman lifted his eyebrows. "I never want to push my agents to the point of breaking. Yeah, take your friend home, cuddle up with him, and celebrate for a week if you want. I just need his report on every detail." With a sad smile, he concentrated on Thomas again. "He'll be a happy camper the moment he's released. It'll be a hard quarrel to keep him in this bed once he's awake."

Jacklyn almost slipped and shared her knowledge of methods to keep someone from running, but she restrained herself, smiled, and went to fetch coffee for both of them.

Vernon pressed his palms on the foot of the bed. The doctor had said Thomas suffered a minor shot wound on the hip. An inch to the left, and the bullet would've shattered the hip bone. The doctor was worried about Thomas's general health. He was malnourished and had lost too much weight. His feet and ankles were raw with abrasions and would require special care for days, if not weeks. He'd be in pain for several days, and a scar would probably remain on the hip, but in the end, he'd heal completely. If nothing out of the ordinary happened, Thomas would be released in three days. Vernon hadn't objected. He knew Thomas well enough to predict his first words.

Thomas's eyes fluttered open, and he looked around, assessing his surroundings. He wiped his mouth and took a few deep breaths.

"Welcome back, Tom."

Thomas licked his lips. His voice was hoarse. "Okay, when did I pass out?"

"I can't tell you that, but what I will tell you I'm happy the man who was hunting you was a bad shot."

"I doubt that," Thomas whispered. He looked around. "Where's Charlene?"

Vernon nodded once. His hunch turned to reality. "At my house, waiting for you."

"Is she all right?"

"Yes, and happy to have you back. Don't kill me over not bringing her here today. She caught a cold and decided to stay home. Okay?"

"Okay."

Freeman couldn't believe his friend was so obliging. He hadn't expected Thomas to accept his little white lie without question. "I admit I'm happy she stayed home. I'm still convinced there's a mole at the ATF. We're getting closer, but—"

"No need to tell me. Still, I can't wait to see her. I miss her so much." Thomas looked at the IV drip on the back of his left hand, then further to the adjacent bed where Nicolas was sleeping peacefully. "Is he okay?"

"Totally exhausted, but, yes."

"Good. Help me get the bed adjusted. My hands are trembling too much."

Vernon lifted the head of the bed and held a cup of tea for Thomas to drink. He didn't see his friend's hand shaking, but from experience, Vernon knew his friend had to be weak as a kitten.

"Thanks." Thomas tilted his chin and spoke quietly. "Who's the lady at his side?"

"His girlfriend." Vernon twitched his lips almost to a smile. "Judging by that look on your face, you hadn't expected a woman like her."

"She doesn't look like she's playing in his league."

Vernon glanced at Jacklyn. She wore a classy gray two-piece suit and a white blouse. Her carefully powdered face and stylish hairdo gave the impression of a wealthy business-woman. "I can tell you she's a strong-willed woman, and very sophisticated, if you ask me."

Thomas glanced at her, but when she lifted her gaze, he turned back to Vernon. "Tell me, what happened in the woods?"

"We got the tip that you'd been taken away in an SUV that belonged to the Stewards. That's why I ordered the helicopter to fly over the area. I'm happy we arrived in time."

"Thanks. What about the Turners?"

Vernon set down Thomas's cup, pulled up a chair and sat down, crossing his arms on the backrest. "The raid was a success. Several Turner family members were arrested and taken to the ATF HQ for interrogation. I requested support from the FBI, and they sent their CSU to investigate. Nicolas made a crucial statement, and together with yours, this case will be airtight." Vernon nodded toward the FBI agent. "He was dog-tired but insisted on telling me everything he could remember."

"What about Jebediah Turner? Did you arrest him and his weasel cousin, Tyrone?"

Vernon would've given a lot to dodge the question, even more so when Thomas repeated it insistently. "No, we couldn't arrest Jebediah and Tyrone. Some other men are on the run, too. We don't know how they slipped our forces, but the arrest warrants were sent to every police station. The men will be caught, don't worry."

The heart monitor showed Thomas's agitation, and it didn't take long for a nurse to show up and ask Freeman to leave.

"I'll be back."

Thomas smiled, but sadly. "I know you've wanted to say that for a long time."

Vernon tapped his forehead in a mock salute. "Yep, that's true. Rest, my friend, I'll drop by tomorrow."

Nicolas opened his eyes to the vision of Jacklyn's beautiful face, a sight he had missed for so long. He was speechless when she bent to kiss him gently. He exhaled in pure bliss and growled when she dared to move away from him.

With a smile, she kissed him again, then whispered, "We aren't alone, my hero, and we are being watched."

"I don't care." He made room so she could sit on the bed. "How are you?"

"What shall a woman say when her lover returns after a successful mission? I'm overwhelmed, Nick, and very, very happy you're still in one piece." She caressed his face. "I heard all about your bravery and how you saved your partner and the day, so to speak."

"I was lucky." He broke eye contact to glance at Thomas, but the agent didn't look in his direction. "It was a close call."

"I don't think I can stand all the gruesome details. I spoke with the doctor, and he'll release you tomorrow morning. I made arrangements so I can be here and will stay with you at home for at least two days."

"Pampering me?" He waited for her to kiss him again. "Oh, yes, that'll speed my recovery, *ma Cherie*."

Jacklyn gave him a lopsided smile. "I do have some other things in mind, but you'll see that when we get home."

Joy surged through him like never before. "Home with you . . . sounds great."

"Oh, yes, it is."

Jason twitched his brows. "Almost done here, huh? The doc is letting you go today?"

"Yeah. Jacky will be here in a moment." Nicolas sat on the edge of the bed and put on his shirt. "Any news on the investigation? Did CSU find anything useful?"

"Anything useful?" Jason didn't know whether he should snort or laugh. "Nicolas, the evidence Miller and his team found is a-fucking-mazing! Maybe the gangsters tried to clean up the basement after they had built the bombs, but they failed big time. Miller's preliminary report contains fingerprints of Roker, Bronsteen, Henstridge, and two others, probably those killed in the shootout with the SWAT team. There were also remnants of C-four explosives, and they got the results of the comparative shots they took with the hunting guns found on the Stewards premises. Michael had hidden the gun, but not deep enough, and the residues found in the wounds connects them with the ammo Michael used. Additionally, he had confessed his crime to you, in a way."

"Why hadn't he thrown the weapon away?"

"Matthew recognized it on a photo—the young man won trophies with that gun. Maybe it had sentimental value."

Nicolas scoffed and shook his head. "That means Michael

shot both Bronsteen and Hanson?"

"Yes, the first one by order of Jebediah Turner. Hanson had to die because Sheriff Reese considered the driver a threat to his wife's enterprise, whereas she claims she would've paid Hanson more money. The judge will have to decide whether she'll be accused of complicity in murder. The Stewards hid the cars in the woods — covered with branches and leaves. No one would've found them without explicitly looking for them. The area is huge." Jason handed his friend a pair of socks. "The sheriff's not talking, but — " When he saw Nicolas struggle with the socks, he crouched in front of him and helped him get dressed.

"What about Jebediah and Tyrone? Thomas told me they haven't been found yet. Is that true?"

Jason sat on the bedside again. "Unfortunately, yes. They escaped. If they're clever, they'll run away as far as they can." Jason shrugged. "If we have the numbers right, four men are on the run. Local police stations are on high alert. The more important information concerns the Turner companies. At first we couldn't find a reason for the bombing targets, but then, piece by piece, it became clear. The *Florence Research Center* took advantage of the total loss of the center in Richmond, and the same goes for the cosmetic Company in Richmond. The fertilizer company was a target meant to distract from the other two, even though the Turners might've been angered because the company raised prices last year."

"So this was about money the whole time?" Nicolas bent to tie his shoelaces. "Nothing else? It's pathetic, huh? What about the marijuana? Where did it come from?"

Jason wagged his head. "That's a question more difficult to answer. ATF knows the drugs originated from Central America, but without testimony, the dealers can't be found. The ATF analyzed data they got from traffic cameras, but so far, they couldn't determine any trucks or vans heading for the estate. Concerning the burnt stuff at the fourth explosion, I think it was done because the marijuana belonged to a competing cartel. But that's a job for the DEA. Jacob Turner isn't saying a word. He pointed out that he wants to talk to his lawyer, and he claims that the actions on his premises were done without him. After all, he's an old man, and I don't see him accused of complicity. He wanted the best for the Florence Town inhabitants. You will be interrogated, too, once you're able to do so."

"I already got the invite to the D.A.'s office." Nicolas stood and took a deep breath. His head swam with dizziness, and he steadied himself at the foot of the bed.

"That was fast." Jason turned when Thomas entered the room on crutches. He used the moment to introduce himself. "Thanks to you, a whole bunch of criminals could be arrested. I'm convinced the murderers will be sentenced to a long life in prison."

"I hope so. Packing up?" Thomas asked Nicolas.

"Yes. I hope the doc will let you go soon, too."

Thomas sat down on the bed and thanked the nurse for her help. "It's not on me. I feel fine, but . . ." He shrugged. "Vernon might've told the doc I'd be on the hunt for Jeb the moment I leave the hospital. And, yes, that's quite true."

"He and his companions won't get far," Jason said. He omitted the fact that Thomas looked as though he wouldn't be doing anything but shuffling from his bed to the bathroom for the next few days, let alone hunting escapees. To Jason, Thomas looked like victims found in containers after being locked up for weeks.

"That's what Vernon keeps telling me, but in my opinion, you're underestimating the man's abilities. He was clever enough to lead a criminal enterprise and avoid detection. He's involved in the drug dealing, and I know he's ruthless if he thinks he can get away with it. Tyrone, on the other hand, won't hesitate to kill a man to get his car or his weapon." He lay down carefully, grimacing with pain. "If you think any police officer can arrest them, you're mistaken."

Jason held his tongue. He knew both Thomas and Nicolas had lived through experiences he couldn't comprehend. Obviously, Jebediah Turner was a hardcore criminal rather than the disobedient offspring of a hard-working family. "Anyway, rest assured that everything will be done to catch them."

Thomas's gaze told him he couldn't be more mistaken.

CHAPTER SEVENTEEN

Nicolas followed Jacklyn on a tour through their new house. She pretended she was a real estate dealer, highlighting all details for a potential buyer. Nicolas played along, although his anticipation rose with every passing minute. She urged him to sit down in the kitchen for a snack, then she insisted on showing him the garden when he was done.

Smiling exuberantly, she turned to kiss him on the porch. "Do you like it?"

"I'm impressed, Jacky, and I mean it. I saw the pictures you took on your first visit. It's outstanding what you've accomplished." He embraced her and kissed her brow. Her joy was contagious, and he was the happiest man on earth. "My wonderful lover. You outdid yourself. Though . . . there's one thing. Is there no bedroom in this big house?"

"I wanted to save that for last."

"Well, then . . ." He swallowed, searching for words to tell her what had been on his mind since they left the hospital, and yet he couldn't find a way to start.

"Let's sit down." Jacklyn pulled him toward the couch in the large living room. "I can see something's bothering you." She sat, but he chose the place on the carpet in front of her. "You don't want to—"

"I'm right where I want to be." Nicolas caressed her calves and kissed her knees. Lowering his head, he exhaled. "I thought this would be easier."

"If you're trying to tell me you're gonna leave me for a younger woman, I swear I won't rip your head off. Or . . . just a little bit."

He cherished her attempt at making light of the situation, and finally looked up at her. "The brothers caught me on the highway from Belmont, handcuffed me, and took me to an old barn. I thought they were doing this to kill me where no one would ever find me, but . . ." He stopped seeing the worry in her eyes grow. "I want to tell you, but I don't know whether you can stand it."

"I can stand everything, Nicolas. I'm here for you."

He took a deep breath, and when she didn't waver, he went on. "They were not out to kill me. They wanted to make me talk, and Jebediah came up with the idea of putting me in a dog cage overnight. I put up a fight, but I lost, and they pushed me in there and locked the door. It was so narrow . . . so narrow I could hardly move. I tried to break out. I kept try- ing the whole night, but I couldn't free myself and had to wait until I was released. And when I saw it again two days later, I thought I'd turn and run. I was so afraid to be put back in there I couldn't breathe." He assumed the confession shocked her, but she kept her face blank and nodded for him to carry on. "It was . . . horrifying. Nothing like that has ever hap- pened to me—that I'm afraid of a *thing*." He pressed his fore- head against her knees, exhausted and yet satisfied that he had unburdened his mind.

She caressed the back of his head. "I saw the marks of cuffs around your wrists, and I already decided to skip playing our game for a while. So that you can recover and . . ."

Nicolas lifted his gaze, eyes wide. "No, don't do that to me."

"But—"

"We've been through this before. I needed to tell you to help you understand why I might . . . hesitate or simply reject one of your ideas. I wanted you to know that it has nothing to do with you. I didn't mean to put an end to our games."

She cupped his cheeks and kissed him lightly on the lips. "I love you for your honesty. I love you for so many things. Are you sure you want to play, even though you were treated so badly? I wish for nothing more than to see you happy, and if that means leaving the shackles in the cupboard, that's fine with me."

He kissed her palm. "When I was locked up, I thought about us — about you. How much I love you and how I missed being with you. And that means I missed what we're doing in our games. Will you do me a favor?"

"Certainly."

"Keep in mind what I just told you — maybe leave out the gags for a while, too — but pick up from where we left off when we talked about the bedroom. Can you do that for me?"

Smiling mischievously, she kissed the tip of his nose, but her voice sank to a growl. "Be aware, beast, what I can do with you." She took his hand and led him to the bathroom. "First things first. Lose your clothes. I've got work to do."

Nicolas dropped a trail of clothes and many bitter memories.

Jacklyn scrutinized his appearance. "You've been away for six very long weeks. Now I need a machete to get through this bush."

"That sounds a tad exaggerated. Be careful with what you find in the bushes."

"I'll do my very best."

He loved the sound of her words, the seductive French accent, and the flippancy. He would've kissed her if he hadn't been tied to the bathroom wall. The new and improved holding rings above the shower stall were one of a kind, and Nicolas couldn't wait to see the bedroom. He understood why she had left out the details concerning their role-play. Being left in the dark increased his interest and kept him on tenter-hooks.

Jacklyn grabbed some shaving cream and a straight razor. He wouldn't have trusted anyone else with a sharp object close to his genitals. His lover, however, knew more about shaving a man than he did, more so when it came to his butt cheeks. He enjoyed her ongoing attention as a reward of being away for too long. He was aroused by every touch and couldn't hold back expressing his pleasure.

Jacklyn slapped his now hairless butt. "Over my dead body, beast, no moaning! You'll keep quiet, or I'll quiet you."

"Nicely put." Nicolas craned his neck to see Jacklyn's face. Her eagerness was one of a kind and another character trait he loved. Done shaving, she released him, and he couldn't help but run his hands across the sensitive skin. It felt right to have lost his pubic hair to his mistress's eager hands. "Thorough."

"Necessary." Jacklyn cleaned the razor and splashed water over his lower body.

"It could be warm, at least!"

"No, not today. I want you fresh and eager after the long time I was deprived of your perfect body." She put the razor away and stood on tiptoe to kiss him. "You're still sure you want me to play with you?"

He met her halfway for a tender kiss. "I'd have told you if I changed my mind."

"Yep, the most honest man I've ever met." Jacklyn rubbed him down with a towel. "I'm so freakin' excited I don't know where to start."

"I'd know some places . . ." He hinted toward the bed-room. "I haven't seen the furniture."

"And you won't . . . not yet." Jacklyn presented him with a blindfold.

"That's mean, you know." Nicolas pretended annoyance,

but her stare made him comply. He couldn't have hoped for a more pleasant development for the afternoon.

"I'm the severe mistress, and you're the poor little sub who's got to endure everything I dish out. Sounds fair, right?"

She had his half-erect penis in her hand, and he hastened to follow her out of the bathroom. "Fair, of course," he responded in a mock submissive tone.

She laughed. "Oh, my beast, you'll suffer so much tonight, you'll cry uncle sooner than later."

"Would it be wrong to say that you'll have to make an effort to reach that goal?"

"Very wrong." She pressed her thumbnail into the sensitive flesh she held firmly. "You don't challenge your mistress. Period."

"Ouch! I get it." He sensed his surroundings change. "Bedroom?"

"The playtime version of something ordinary, yes. Nowadays, and in our context, it's the room where you scream, and I laugh in your face." Jacklyn pushed him onto the bed. "And you can scream as loud as you want." She was close to his face, and her words caressed him as much as her lips. "But no one will hear you. Intimidating, hmm?"

"Very."

Jacklyn slapped his face. "You aren't taking me seriously. That'll change."

He sensed her beside him on the bed but didn't know what she was up to until the fur-lined cuffs locked around his wrists and ankles. Within seconds, Nicolas was so hyped up he could hardly breathe. He couldn't recall having ever been so excited and full of anticipation.

"Jeez, living without my treatment was getting to you, huh?"

"You can't imagine." Knowing how much she loved his struggle, Nicolas tested the cuffs.

Jacklyn kissed his dry lips. Her voice grew suddenly husky with excitement. "Welcome back to my dungeon, beast."

Thomas ignored Vernon's attempt at small talk on the ride to his house. His heartbeat sped up the moment he entered the hallway of his friend's home.

Charlene appeared on top of the stairs like a young goddess, dressed in a white and red summer skirt and matching blouse. All words of welcome were blown from Thomas's mind. His throat constricted, and he was deaf to Vernon's comments and Teresa's greeting. He grabbed the handrail, or he would've fallen. He stared at Charlene, his mouth slack and his strength reeling. As if she understood his struggle, Charlene rushed down the stairs, taking two steps at a time.

She whooped with joy. "You're home! Oh, that's wonderful—you're here! You're finally here!" She put her arms around his neck, kissed his bearded cheeks and his lips, and whispered in his ear, "I missed you so much."

Thomas held her tight and buried his face at her shoulder, too relieved for words. He was only half aware when Vernon patted his upper arm and said something to his wife before they left for the kitchen.

"I thought I'd go mad waiting for you." She held him tighter.

His heart was overflowing with joy, eliminating the bitter feeling of how much time they had lost. "I'm so happy . . . I . . . I don't know . . ." Reluctantly, he released her, trembling. He'd thought about losing her for too long. His imagination of a life without her had darkened his days more effectively than the absence of any light.

Charlene smiled at him with the exuberance of a young girl. She had lost weight, and there were lines around her eyes that hadn't been there upon their parting. He detected worry in her eyes as she looked him up and down, but for a moment, he couldn't form words.

She read his expression. "Yes, I'm here. And I'm well. Everything's fine now." She kissed him again. "I couldn't believe when I heard about what happened in the woods. But you made it. That's all that matters."

He wiped a tear off her cheek. His voice quivered. "I didn't dare hope to see you again."

"I know." Charlene caressed his face with her hands. "When I saw Jebediah at the bus station, I thought . . ." She shook her head.

He calmed her with a kiss. "No one's gonna part us now." Thomas leaned his forehead against hers. He had forced his body to its limits and was close to collapsing. "There's so much I want to tell you, and yet, I'm so tired."

"Teresa and I prepared the guest room for us. Can you make it upstairs if I help you?"

He nodded but stumbled more than he wanted when they climbed the stairs.

Charlene helped him as best she could. "You should've stayed in the hospital for another day."

"It was hard enough to . . ." Thomas sat on the bed, exhausted. "I mean, waiting for you for another day . . . I'm glad Vernon convinced the doc to let me go."

Charlene helped him take off shoes and clothes and lifted his legs so that he was reclining on the pillow. His hip was on fire with pain, and he barely suppressed a whimper.

He gazed into her beautiful eyes. "I love you, Charlene, with all I am."

She bent to kiss him, and despite his injury, he pulled her across his belly so that she rested beside him. She was the most beautiful woman he'd ever met. He'd yearned for a reunion for so long, yet a part of him still couldn't believe that

Charlene would stay with him now. There were no boundaries between them, no angry father trying to pry them apart. He was so touched by the idea of staying with her, he was close to tears.

She pulled the cover over their bodies and snuggled close to him. "No tears, Alex, I'm with you. And I'm staying with you, no matter what'll happen."

"By the way, my name's not Alexander."

"I know, but I like it. You'll always be Alex for me."

A week later, Vernon reclined on his chair at the small Italian restaurant overlooking the Potomac. He lifted his beer in a salute toward Thomas, Jason, and Nicolas.

"Here's to you, gentlemen, for solving the case and not getting shot during the investigation. Well, almost not," he said to Thomas. "That's a success on its own." They clanked bottles. "The file is as thick as *War and Peace,* and Gerald agrees we've got enough to accuse the Turner family of drug dealing and Jebediah of killing Milton Roker. We also have proof for the Stewards' involvement in the death of Gilbert Hanson and Harvey Bronsteen. Additionally, they hired Roker and later Henstridge and his crew to build bombs on the premises, which resulted in four bomb attacks. I wish it would've been easier for you. Judging by your reports, you went to a lot of trouble and made difficult decisions in order to bring justice to the people. I bow to you."

"Thank you, Vernon." Thomas smiled broadly. "Well, I don't know about you guys, but I received the best reward a man can get for his endeavor. Charlene's with me, and we move into a house in the suburbs in two weeks."

"Wow! Great news!" Nicolas nodded his approval. "Well, my lovely lady finished remodeling our new house and the move without my help. But from what I heard, she knew who to call and ask for support." He pointed a finger at Jason. "Many thanks to you, my friend, for sending her the handymen she needed. Your support is appreciated."

"You're welcome." Jason folded his hands on his protruding belly, looking smug. "I wonder why she didn't ask for helping hands for the move, though I bet she didn't do it alone." When Nicolas looked taken aback, he quickly teased with mock panic and waved his hands. "Forget what I just said! Hell, I don't want you to run home and question her!"

Vernon laughed and put down his empty bottle. He signaled the waitress. "We were wondering, Nick, how a guy like you snagged such a class-A woman from upper-crust DC. Would you mind telling us?"

Nicolas frowned. "Upper-crust DC? What makes you think so? She's a physiotherapist, not a millionaire's daughter."

Vernon chuckled when Thomas gaped at Nicolas.

"Well, she looks the millionaire's part." Thomas shook his head. "I thought . . ." He lifted a hand. "Never mind. I was wrong."

Nicolas cocked his head. "You saying a guy like me doesn't deserve a hot chick like her? Oh, yes, I do. She made the right choice with me."

Jason lifted his bottle. "Amen to that." When the laughter subsided, he asked, "What's the next step? Is the attorney accusing every member of the Turner family? What about the vigilantes who supported them? Will there be charges against them?"

Vernon placed the order for beer and lunch for four. When the waitress left, he turned to Jason. "Every lead and every piece of evidence was evaluated, and CSU is still examining the families' computers. The case is strong, though. There's no excuse for the murders, and certainly not for terroristic attacks on the companies. Homeland Security will make sure those responsible will be sentenced. As far as I know, Jacob can't be connected to the crimes."

Vernon shrugged. "As much as we want to, there's no hard proof he was aware of the bombs or that he ordered the men killed. Even if we assume he knew about it, no judge will sentence him for the murders without evidence. The testimonies will make a difference." Vernon squinted against the setting sun. "As for the vigilantes? They'll probably claim they were doing their duty for security. If they're sentenced, it'll be for minor offenses." He frowned as he turned his attention to Thomas. "I hope Charlene will testify, too."

"I'll support her as best as I can."

"Jebediah and Tyrone are still on the run?" Jason asked.

Vernon shook his head. "A man matching Jebediah's description was arrested in Emporia while shoplifting in a grocery store."

"He acted alone?"

"Two more men were on the run and pursued, but the police report came in right before I got here, so I don't know any details. I'll keep you posted, though, once I'm back at my office."

Thomas set his bottle on the table with more force than necessary. "If the police arrested Jeb, Tyrone's not far away. He was never far away. He's like a dog on a leash. And the vigilantes are probably with him. Police have to watch out for Ty and the others. They'll try and free Jeb. It's just a question of hours."

"Jeb's the born leader," Nicolas muttered. "Without him, the others won't stand a chance. They'll make mistakes. We've seen that before."

Jason helped the waitress distribute the beer bottles. "I'll drink to that, and hope that the case will be closed soon and the prison doors locked." He lifted his bottle. "Nicolas, don't put me through this kind of ordeal again, okay? My poor heart can't take the stress. Thomas, thank you for watching over my friend's sorry ass."

"It was more the other way around, but . . . okay."

Jason ignored him. "Vernon, if we ever have the fortune to work together again, please, be more cooperative from the first moment on. Though I admit, the restaurant is a blast. So maybe, it was worth it."

Vernon leaned back, looked at Thomas, and pretended to have a cigar between his lips. *"I love it when a plan comes together."*

"Are you sure you don't want to play poker with us?" Vernon frowned. "I understand you want to spend time with Charlene, but poker is essential for your health."

"As is my lady." Thomas chuckled at Vernon's exaggerated sigh. "Come on, I went out for dinner with you and left her home. The rest of the night—"

Vernon lifted a hand. "Spare me the details." He opened the door, kissed Teresa, and flexed his fingers. "Okay, then, hug the lady, and I'll run Ted and Willy into the ground."

Teresa gave him a doubtful look. "As if you'd ever do that."

"It's my night." He turned to Thomas. "Play it nice up there. I don't want to call the cops because of your nocturnal activities."

Thomas burst out laughing. "As if you would!" He walked upstairs to where Charlene was waiting. "Hello, Miss Wonderful, how was your evening so far?"

Her kiss was full of emotion as she caressed the back of his head with both hands. "Dreadful."

"That bad, hmm? I think I'd better make up for the hours I was away."

"You should hold me tight." Charlene played her fingers along the curve of his ear. "Every hour you're away is one too many." She sighed, rolled her eyes, and laughed helplessly.

"I'm getting better, but it's still hard to let you go." She kissed him again and pressed her body against his. "I need you beside me, warm, naked. Let me touch your body, and I'll give you *all my loving.*"

Thomas swallowed. "I've never been asked more nicely."

"And you never will be by anyone else but me." She took his hand and led him toward their room.

Thomas woke to an irritating sound, much different from the usual ones in the house. He disentangled from Charlene's embrace and got up to put on pajama bottoms and fetch his gun.

The hallway lay quiet, the guests were long gone, and Vernon and Teresa had retreated to their bedroom. Thomas went toward the stairs. The moment he made out the beam of a penlight in the kitchen, Vernon appeared in the doorway of his bedroom. He mouthed *what's up*, and Thomas pointed downstairs. Without a word, Vernon reached for his gun and released the safety.

Thomas went downstairs first, cautious of the creaks of the steps. The rush of adrenalin accompanying the stress of fear made him wide awake, so he could hear and see everything clearly.

The soft sound of rubber footsteps came from the kitchen, and Thomas could make out the silhouettes of two intruders close to the counter. They were sneaking around, using a flashlight for orientation. Both men were of average height and slender, dressed in black clothes. Judging by the way they moved, they had done such break-ins before.

Thomas lifted two fingers and pointed toward the kitchen. Vernon made a small sound in his throat. It might've been disagreement, but Thomas stepped through the hall without hesitation. When he reached for the light switch, the first man saw him and retreated, gasping and spluttering a curse.

A shot disrupted the silence.

Thomas flung himself to the left and landed hard on his side. "That came from the living room!" He aimed at the patio door and shot without seeing a target. Glass shattered, and shards rained on the floor. He heard something tumble and fall with a heavy thud. A hefty curse in a high-pitched, whining voice followed.

Still on the stairs, Vernon flattened against the wall, but within Thomas's view. Vernon shot twice when the burglars got closer. One of them cried out and dropped to the tiles. He didn't move anymore.

Thomas got to his feet again, gestured where he was headed, then swiveled around the corner toward the kitchen. He shot the shadow behind the counter and crouched for cover when the fire was returned. Despite the ringing in his ears from the gunshots, he heard the men shout at each other. Three more shots boomed through the room.

Behind him, Vernon stumbled and cried out.

Thomas let go of his breath and forced back his fear, then moved out of cover for a clear shot. The burglar trained his weapon on Vernon, and Thomas saw the muzzle flash. He pulled the trigger and watched as the intruder fell against the cabinet and slumped on the floor, motionless. "Vernon, are you okay?"

"Yes! One's on the run!" Vernon shouted from the living room.

Thomas grabbed the burglar's weapon, checked for a pulse, and made sure the second man was unconscious, too, then ran into the living room. Vernon switched on the lights. The large window toward the patio was ruined, the glass door open. A large floor lamp had been knocked over and broken a small table. The carpet shimmered as if embroidered with diamonds.

"They knew what they were doing," Vernon said as he

showed Thomas the broken lock. "Who the hell are they?"

"The other one's gone?"

"I shot but missed. Whoever was out there is on the run. Are you okay?"

"Yep. Let's check who we've got in the kitchen."

They pulled off the burglars' hoods.

Thomas whistled through his teeth. "I know him. He's one of the vigilantes that Jebediah trusted to guard me. Why didn't he run? Who's the other one?"

"You tell me."

Thomas rounded the corner, and his frown turned to shock. "That's Jebediah Turner! He broke in to . . ." He put his hands on his knees, fighting to breathe.

"Sit down before you collapse." Vernon pushed a chair in his direction. "I bet he didn't come here to make amends, huh?"

"I can't believe they did this. That's too much." Thomas's hands trembled as he stared at his unconscious enemy. "They came to kill us."

"That's a fair assumption." Vernon turned to the stairs. Sirens wailed in the distance. "I bet my super-clever wife already called the cops." He patted Thomas's shoulder. "It's a night to celebrate. You arrested the most-wanted Turner family member. Congratulations."

Jebediah stirred and opened his eyes. Thomas stared at him, rigid in his rising hatred. The weapon in his hand had a life of its own and pointed at Jebediah's heart.

"Who told you where to find us?"

Jebediah tried to move, but stopped, grimacing. The shot wound below his collarbone was bleeding freely. "I should've shot you when I had the chance."

Thomas pressed his hand on the wound. "Tell me! Who did you call? Who helped you?"

Jebediah screamed.

"Spit it out!" Thomas insisted. "Or I swear you'll suffer more than this!"

"Fer . . . Ferguson!"

Thomas looked back at Vernon. "Our captain? Is that possible?"

"Yes. He's on my list."

"Damn it!"

Jebediah's chuckle turned to a cough. "You're fucked up! The whole time he's been playing you for a sucker, and you didn't know!"

"I'll call the deputy director right away." Vernon ran a hand across his head. "I can't believe it!"

Thomas was too angry to think clearly. "Where's Tyrone? I bet he was the one who fled across the porch." He shook Jebediah, but to no avail. The man had passed out.

"Police will catch him. He won't get far." Vernon's brows twitched. "Not without his brainy friend."

Thomas stared at Jebediah's slack features. His inner voice strongly urged him to kill the bastard and save everyone the trouble of a long trial. He couldn't fathom how dreadful it would be to meet him in court.

Finally, Thomas got up and headed back upstairs to hold Charlene in his arms.

As he passed the open front door, two police cars stopped, and four officers came running toward the entrance.

Four days later, Jason got up from his chair to welcome Vernon in his office. "Agent Freeman, how nice of you to drop by."

"Funny." Vernon pulled a chair and sat down, exhaling. "I was told you arrested that bastard, Ferguson. I want the key to his cell and five minutes alone with him. No cameras."

Jason cleared his throat, pretending to be shocked. "Wait.

The FBI is capable of interrogating a suspect. Your help — though appreciated — isn't needed. We've got enough bullies for the job." He smiled at Vernon's grimace. "Do you want a coffee?"

"I prefer tea, and it wouldn't help with my fury, anyway. Tell me, Agent Beckham, will he stand trial?"

Jason sat down and gazed at the file on his desk. "Of course he will. What we didn't know before was that Ferguson's stepdaughter is Samuel Turner's wife. Not the same surname, so we couldn't have connected those two in the first place. The captain stayed in contact with Samuel over the last several years. They called each other and exchanged emails. Most of them could be recovered. As it turns out, the Turners, the Reese family, and the Stewards all knew the district judge, Emerson Field. They formed a kind of brotherhood to protect their interests. That included exclusive information from Ferguson."

Jason shrugged. "So far, my colleagues and I haven't been able to determine whether their collaboration included illegal actions. But it's obvious they gave each other information about ongoing ATF investigations, trials in the district, and local police activities, including car searches."

Vernon nodded. "That's why we couldn't find drugs in the trucks driving toward the compound."

"We're still classifying the incoming evidence. Judge Field called his lawyer immediately and asked for support from fellow judges and the Supreme Court. To me, the evidence against Captain Ferguson is the strongest. There's no way he can deny slipping information to the Turners and thus interfering with the ongoing investigation."

Vernon folded his arms. "So my decision to keep Tagline's involvement a secret, even to our superiors, was the right one."

"How did you explain your agent's absence?"

"I told Ferguson I'd sent Thomas on an assignment, but I didn't mention the Turners."

"That saved Thomas's life. You're smart."

"Oh, you're trying to flatter me so I might invite you for lunch?" Vernon laughed and stood, pointing at Jason. "Okay, you win."

Jason grabbed his jacket. "It wasn't my intention, but if you insist . . . I won't refuse your humble request."

Vernon was still laughing when they left the office.

The End

YOU MAY ALSO ENJOY THE FOLLOWING FROM EXTASY BOOKS:

A Bodyguard's Vacation
Ann Raina

Excerpt

"Hey, my princess, enjoying the view?" Ethan sat down and put an arm around her shoulders. "It's our first real vacation aside from that weekend trip with your parents. Which was, if you agree, not the kind of vacation we had in mind."

Jazmin giggled and turned to lean against his chest. Their idea of having some private moments in the cabin—or even outside—had not been on her mother's list. "Don't tell me my mom's attempts at stuffing us with all the good things from the kitchen weren't appealing?"

"Nah, I won't say that. I just felt so . . . close to bursting like never before in my life. Not to forget all the wonderful stories of your extraordinary childhood."

"Oh, come on, that was so damn embarrassing."

"Not all of them. I liked the story about your mother teaching you first aid when you were about five. I think she still wonders why you didn't yearn to become a nurse."

"To have more than one subject at the dinner table, maybe?"

Chuckling, he kissed her hair. "Are you all right?"

"Weather's hot, boat runs fine, Ryan will kill us if we let him stand there alone the whole time. So, yes, I'm fairly all right."

"Do you think it was a bad idea asking Ryan and Cheryl to come with us?"

"No." She caressed his cheek and the dimple in his chin, smiling about his concerned expression. "I know that you paid half of Ryan's bill."

His brown eyes were suddenly full of worry. "You do? How?"

"Because he thanked me for our generosity."

"That boy never keeps his mouth shut." Ethan flinched. "I owe him big time, and it's a way to—"

She sealed his lips with a kiss. "It's all right. You just did it first."

"You agree with me?"

"Whole-heartedly. He was as happy as a kid when we did the booking."

They both looked toward the steering wheel. Ryan had switched on the radio and was dancing and singing, both with more enthusiasm than talent. He wouldn't be changing professions to go to Vegas.

"He is a kid."

She got up. "And I'll give him company. By the way—what was that at the breakfast table? There was nothing wrong with the question."

He looked up to her, reluctant to answer. "I did what I did, and maybe if I hadn't been headhunted, I'd still be with the army. I don't know that. It's wrong to assume, though, that I liked everything I learned. I don't have to be out to shoot a deer and gut it just because I can. Fishing is the same. I was never fond of . . . doing it."

Jazmin understood the insinuation and knew it was time to drop the subject. "Okay. Just don't bark at the kid too often. You know he's sensitive."

"He? Sensitive? He can be a ram when it comes to feelings. Ask Walter. I don't know how he survived three weeks with him in the wilderness. He avoided him the next six weeks, I think, just to recover."

"Ryan said he had fun." She winked at Ethan and walked up the three steps to Ryan, who stood at the steering wheel wearing a baseball cap and sunglasses. "Where're we going?"

"Lover's Beach, one of the beaches on Eleuthera's northern side. It's about sixty miles to go." He grinned. "It's a nice way to have a look at the open ocean. And I just thought it to be fitting." His expression turned regretful. "Imagine that."

"I'm sure it'll be great." She slipped onto the chair behind him, enjoying the wind in her hair. With Ethan and Ryan around, the memories faded away and she was at ease again. "Just some swimming and sunbathing on the beach?"

"We could throw anchor close by and go diving, too. All these places around here are great for diving."

"Thanks a lot. Not my cup of tea."

"Hey, it's the Caribbean Islands. It's all about diving, snorkeling, and watching the fish swim."

"It's all about having fun together."

He made the sound of a dolphin. "Like that?"

"Where did you learn to swim and dive like that? You're amazing."

"Oh, just for the few stunts in the water? Come on, Jaz, gimme some credit, okay? I need to impress Cheryl with something though—thinking this through, I assume that swimming is not the right thing for her."

"Not at all?"

"She likes sunbathing. I think." He pondered, then shook his head. "I haven't seen her in the water at all. She liked the idea of a vacation here, but I don't know if she can't swim or if she's not so fond of ruining her hairdo and makeup. We haven't spent that much time together, you know."

Jazmin kept the idea that Cheryl didn't join the boat trip on purpose to herself. "I'm sure when she sees you swim she'll change her mind. Well, I had fun yesterday. So, tell me."

Ryan dipped his sunglasses to look at her, then at Ethan, sitting at the stern and enjoying the view. "You didn't just come to give me company, did you?"

"I like to be with you."

"How can you be so at ease knowing how jealous he is?"

"Only when he's got a reason." She leaned back, inhaling deeply. "Right now I'm fine where I am. We don't need each other's oxygen to be happy."

"You had fun last night?"

"Your story about swimming and diving?"

Ryan stomped the ground and almost whined. "I'm so curious, and you're so non-revealing."

She laughed and playfully pulled down his board shorts a fraction.

He wiggled his brows. "Hey, I might like this."

"Is one woman not enough for you?"

"That's a question for a guy who's so proud of his assets! Jazmin, you've got no idea how hard it is to refuse all the offers I get."

"Well, being in a relationship is the best that could happen to you. Finally you know where you belong."

"And sometimes it's just so damn hard." He sighed and reduced speed when a larger yacht crossed their way. He watched it pass, waved to the children at the railing and got back on course. "Cheryl is a fine woman. Really, I love being with her. But that's the damn difficulty—she's away so often it's almost impossible to get this relationship going from step one to step two." He sighed again. "I want her to be around. I want to spend more time with her, do all the little things together, but since her bosses own an international corporation, she's constantly traveling around the world. A week in Tokyo, two days in Hong Kong and so on. I haven't seen her the last three weeks and now she was late for this trip. I know she can't influence the planes, but she told me before that she had changed to a later flight because of some . . . I didn't get it. And that's what happened. I had such high hopes that we could . . . catch up a bit. Spend time, have fun, learn about each other. Tell me, Jazmin, what shall I do?"

"If your love's strong enough, you manage the distance. You've done so for a year so far, which is pretty amazing given what you just told me. What makes you wonder whether you can keep it going any longer?"

Ryan focused on steering the Joyous Ride for a minute. The motor stuttered, then sprang to life again, and the boat gained speed. He frowned, listening, but when the motor ran smoothly he shrugged.

"I had hoped she'd be so happy with me that she'd try to find another job—one that wouldn't take her away every week. I didn't press the subject, but I made insinuations. You know, that she'd soon be sick of traveling so much that we didn't see each other for weeks. But I was wrong—and I still am—because she likes her job. She likes being the one calling the shots and being around the world in a month. Not to mention that she earns a lot of money, more than I do anyway. And she spends it, of course. Did you see her two-piece? And she drives a Jaguar. Everything else, she said, is below her standard." He shrugged, glancing over his shoulder. "She's not the type for giving something up just for a guy like me."

"Sorry to say, and maybe I'm wrong, but that sounds as if you feel used by her."

Ryan hung his head, and when he turned his expression was full of sorrow. Jazmin stood at his side and put a hand on his bare back. "Hey, talk to me."

Ryan pointed with his chin at Ethan. "Don't want him to know."

"He'll stay out of this. And I won't tell, no matter what you share with me."

He flinched. "Jazmin, that's not a subject that comes around easily."

"I'm listening, not judging. Only if you want advice will I give it to you."

His look was raw with suppressed emotions. Jazmin realized Ryan carried around many questions. "Do you know how much your friendship means to me? I don't want to burden you with—"

"It seems you want to talk with me. Now's the time. I guess we've still got some miles to cross, right?"

"Yes. Yes, we have." Ryan lowered his chin and glanced at her. "I'm trying to understand her, y'know? Though she does a lot for the company, she's not the boss. She never has the last word, and she's deeply disappointed when anything goes wonky because one of the three men crosses her proposal. Without her—and I'm sure they know—the company wouldn't run so successfully. Still, she has to obey their rules. Sometimes they stick square in her throat and she's angry and bitching." He shrugged, avoiding her look. "But she can't show that to them."

"And when she's with you . . ."

This time it took Ryan even longer to answer. He played with the wheel and checked the radar. His answer was hardly audible. "I'm under her command."

Jazmin kept her face neutral. The revelation wasn't that surprising. She had heard insinuations in some of Ryan's references the last months, but had never doubted his love for Cheryl or the other way around. As was his way, he had made a joke out of everything. She worded her question carefully. "Do you like it to be like that?"

"Up to a certain degree—yes. I'm tolerant when it comes to sex."

"Again that sounds as if she exceeds your tolerance to a degree that's no longer okay."

Ryan closed his eyes and kept his hands on the steering wheel so hard his knuckles showed white. His voice held pain and disappointment. "I've always thought that sex should be fulfilling for both sides. I've learned that there are differences."

Now Jazmin was alarmed. "What did she do? Did she

leave you hanging?"

"It's just . . ." He shook his head, inhaling deeply. "That hit close to home, Jaz." He pounded the steering wheel once, looking at her with pain-filled eyes. "See, last night—we got into our room. She took off her clothes and went to shower, leaving me with the order to unpack her stuff. No loving embrace, no invitation to shower with her, which would've been nice." He shrugged. "It's not that I wouldn't like to do it for her—her being tired and all—but she didn't say it like a plea, a request. It was as if she considered me her secretary, who has to do as she . . . orders."

"She was bone-tired, Ryan. Stressed. There was no room for an affectionate night." She gently stroked the side of his head with her fingertips. "Don't be too gloomy about it. She needed sleep. Don't think that I'm always up and shining."

"But you wouldn't order Ethan around, would you?"

"No," she had to admit. "No matter what, I'd either ask him or just do it later."

"See?" Ryan swallowed. "And even if I understand that— and I've been trying to read her for the longest time—it's only one example. She demands . . . things of me that . . ." He broke off, grimacing.

"Ryan, if you don't like the way she treats you, you have to talk with her. She assumes that you like it. That you love her the way it is right now. If you're unhappy, she needs to know. She can't mind-read. No one can."

Ryan looked at her and stuttered, "I don't want to lose her. Please, Jaz, understand, I do love that woman."

"That makes it even more important that you talk with her to get things straight. It takes two to dance."

Ryan nodded, his lips pressed tight. Jazmin couldn't help but pull him close for a chaste kiss on his forehead. "You'll work it out. And if you need help I'm here."

"This means a lot to me, Jaz. Really. Thank you." He straightened and appeared to take a mental step back. "Want a beer? I could use one now."

"Sure. The cool box?"

"Under deck." Jazmin went to fetch three bottles, brought Ryan one and handed the other to Ethan.

"What was that?" he asked quietly, his gaze carefully guarded. "You and your hand in his hair? You embracing and kissing my best friend?"

"Do you trust me?"

Ethan looked up, frowning. "You know I do."

"Then don't ask."

About the Author

Ann Raina lives and works in Germany with cats and a horse (which has its own home). Riding and writing are her favorite hobbies without putting one above the other. Her latest series, starting with Twisted Mind, deals with FBI Agent Nicolas Hayes, his cases of capital crimes, and his demanding and commanding lover, Jacklyn Hollander.

In all her books she combines romance, suspense, and humorous elements, for no thrilling story can stand without a comic relief.

www.ingramcontent.com/pod-product-compliance
Lightning Source LLC
Chambersburg PA
CBHW071257170626
46809CB00001B/258